AF499101

If You *Loved* Me

Brianna Remus

Also by Brianna Remus

Falling for You Trilogy

Dare to Fall

Dare to Need

Dare to Love

Pebble Brook Falls Series

If I Asked You to Stay

If You Loved Me

Author Note

This book contains material that is not suitable for people under the age of eighteen. Adult themes include explicit sexual material, descriptions of physical touching without consent, violence, and difficult relationships.

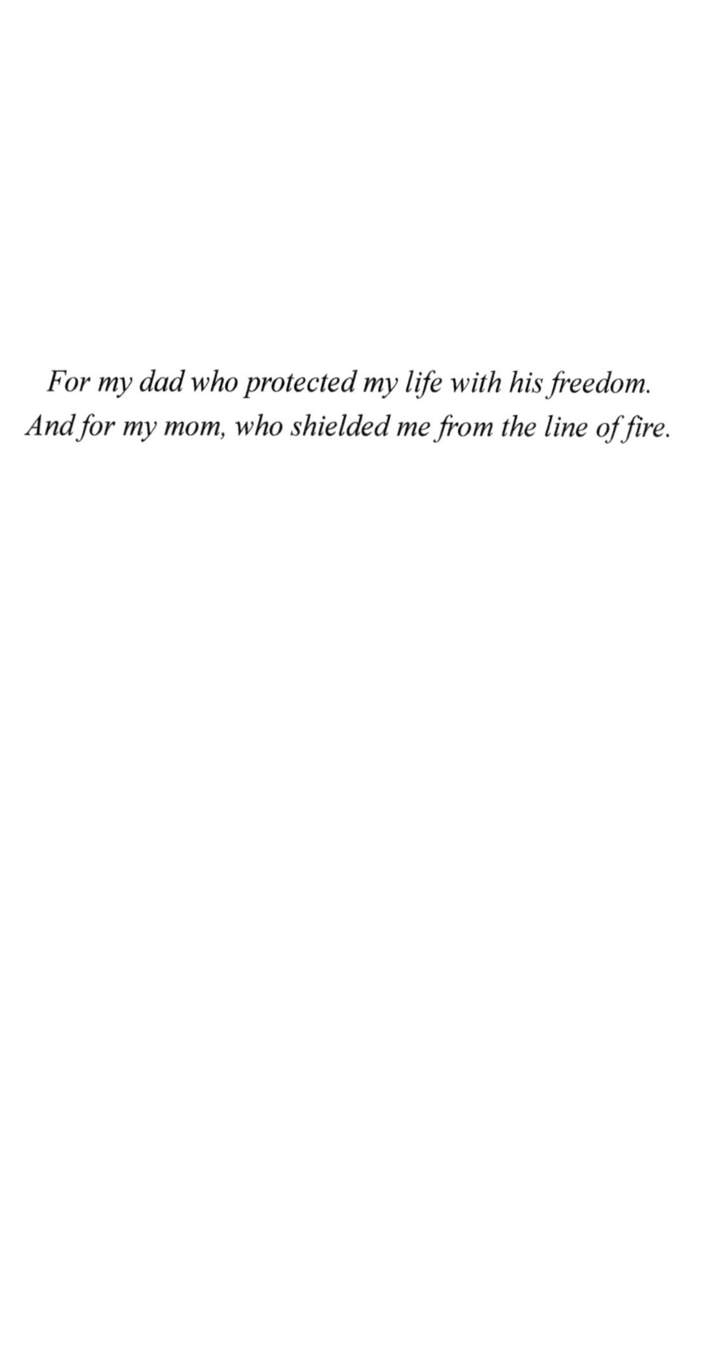

For my dad who protected my life with his freedom.
And for my mom, who shielded me from the line of fire.

Chapter 1

Sarah

"I'm a thirty-year-old virgin. My best friend is getting married in less than four months. All I do is work. And I'm going to end up like one of those cat ladies, except instead of being surrounded by cats, I'm going to be surrounded by dogs because I'm allergic to cats." I slammed the fridge door closed after pulling out the piping bags of icing.

"I'm doomed, Deacon."

His throaty chuckle sounded across the phone line. This was the third call I'd made to him since my best friend, Willow, and her fiancé, Johnny, got engaged this past summer. Somehow, it had taken a really long time for me to realize just how alone I was.

Sure, I had Willow, Deacon, and our friend group. But when Willow called to share the news of her engagement, I was struck with the startling reminder that I hadn't had a boyfriend since I was in high school.

High school. I was almost thirty years old. Which meant

that over twelve years had passed since the last time I had a boyfriend.

I groaned into my phone and Deacon finally responded, "You're not even thirty yet, Sarah. You still have a couple of weeks to figure this out before you make that very very sad benchmark."

"You are *not* helping!" I squealed, which only made him laugh harder.

"Okay, okay. I'm sorry. That was a low blow, I admit. Honestly, I don't think it's that big of a deal. You've been focused on making your business work for the past decade and there's a lot to be said for a person who goes after what they want like that. It takes focus and grit. I can see how it would have been hard for you to date, much less have a significant other in your life during that time.

"But it seems like your business is thriving, so maybe now is the perfect time to shift your focus a little bit to find someone who would add value to your life."

I mulled over his words. It was true. My life had been so consumed by turning my dream into a reality that I never stopped to think about what else I might want out of life.

It wasn't easy. Building what had now become *Sarah's Bakery*. I started by baking in my home kitchen and selling orders online until I could save enough money to buy a storefront.

That was a huge adjustment as well. The townsfolk of Pebble Brook Falls were amazingly supportive…until someone told them not to be. And that someone just so happened to be my mother.

Both my parents had expectations for me and becoming a baker was not one of them. When they started to notice how my bakery was taking off, my mother went out of her way to tell her friends that they should go somewhere closer to the city for their more important orders.

Two summers ago, she stole the wind from my sails after I landed my biggest order yet. An elaborate birthday party for little Tommy Jackson needed an amazing cake with cookies and other sweet treats to go with it because children's birthdays weren't just a celebration for the kiddos in the South. It was an opportunity for the wealthy to show off just how much money they had to spend.

I always thought it was ridiculous seeing parents blow thousands of dollars on children's birthday parties when they wouldn't even remember it a few years later. Not to mention that most children would be happy with a sprinkler and a slip 'n slide as entertainment.

I headed through the kitchen door and to the front counter to take a quick inventory of what was in the glass display case from yesterday.

"But who the hell is going to want to be with a thirty-year-old virgin, Deacon? Men my age want someone who at least knows what they're—"

I skittered to a stop when I noticed an abnormally large guy standing on the opposite side of my checkout counter. My cheeks immediately grew hot under his gaze and given the smirk that played on his lips, I knew he heard everything I'd just said to Deacon.

"Sarah?" I heard Deacon's voice through my cell phone

but it came across muffled like he was underwater. That was because my entire body was shutting down under the embarrassment that had me feeling like I was being consumed by the sun.

How the hell did Ranger fucking Adams get into my store? I wasn't supposed to be open for another hour.

Ranger must have seen me glance at the door because he shrugged his shoulders and said, "The door was unlocked and your lights were on, so I figured you were open."

"Sarah!" Deacon's voice boomed louder and clearer this time down the line.

"I have to go," I hissed into my cell phone before tapping my finger on the screen to end the call.

Sliding my phone into my back pocket, I ignored its vibrating as I tried to collect myself.

"Um, yeah. I must have forgotten to lock it when I came in this morning. We don't open for another hour."

Idiot. I was a damn idiot.

Ranger Adams was the most beautiful man I'd ever seen and I was telling him to get out of my bakery. With piercing blue eyes and jet-black hair that curled slightly, ending just above his shoulders, he had a dangerous look about him. Dangerous in the way that had my heart skipping a beat because I knew if he ever got ahold of me, I wouldn't be able to let him go.

That was exactly why I never told the man I'd been infatuated with him since I saw him picking up his younger sister in school. Not that I would have ever had the nerve to tell anyone that I was drawing hearts around our initials in my notebook as a freshman.

In fact, I was fairly certain I hadn't told a soul about my crush on Ranger. I knew part of the reason I didn't was that my parents would have thrown a fucking tantrum if they'd found out that their child had the potential to be tainted by the town's notorious bad boy. God. I could see my mother's face right now with her pursed lips and crimson cheeks stained from anger.

No. I kept that little factoid to myself—even hiding it from my best friend.

But I was doing a crap job of hiding it right now when the man was two feet away from me.

I shook my head, finally finding my words. "What I meant to say is that I wasn't expecting anyone. But I have plenty of options in the container from yesterday if you don't mind having something that isn't fresh from the oven."

Why am I sweating? Beads of perspiration gathered under my arms. I tried to play it cool as I clamped my biceps against my ribcage, hoping the sweat wouldn't show under my black long-sleeve shirt.

Ranger slid his gaze toward the glass display case, giving me a moment to really take him in. I'd only seen him up this close at Deacon's summer bonfire over a year ago. There were a few times when I'd seen him around town with his sister and each time I tried not to act like a total stalker by staring at him.

Just like I was doing right now.

But I couldn't help it. With his black cowboy hat, thick

eyebrows that matched his inky locks, and wide shoulders with sculpted muscles that were barely hidden beneath his black flannel…he looked like Rip from fucking *Yellowstone.* My mouth watered with thoughts of what it would be like to sit in *his* saddle. What his calloused hands might feel like against my sensitive nipples as he palmed my breasts.

"…twelve of these."

Shit.

"What?" I blurted out. I hadn't heard the first part of his sentence because I was too wrapped up in fantasies that would never happen. "I'm sorry. I just didn't catch the first part of what you said."

He trained those dark eyes on me and I swear he leaned closer. Or maybe it was just my imagination. My desire to be closer to him made my brain think he wanted the same thing.

His lips split into a lopsided smile that gave me the tingles right between my thighs. "Your blueberry muffins. I'll take a dozen of them."

"Blueberry muffins," I repeated as I gawked at him.

"Yup," he replied, his smile growing wider which made the edges of his eyes crinkle in the most endearing way.

I felt myself nodding as I moved to grab a box from the shelf behind me and somehow my feet got so twisted over one another that I ended up stubbing my toe against the brick wall.

"Fuck," I hissed, drawing my leg upward and bouncing around on my other foot.

"Are you okay?" Ranger came around the counter, arms extended like he was going to catch me.

"Yup!" I shoved my hands toward him to ward him off, feeling completely flushed at the thought of his arms wrapping around me.

"I got it. I'm good." I sucked in a lungful of air before I tested my right foot on the ground. My big toe was a little sensitive from the hit it just took, but otherwise, I was good to stand on it.

"Okay," he chuckled.

"Let me get you those muffins." I avoided looking at him as he slowly made his way to the patron side of the counter again.

When I was hidden behind the glass case I quietly chastised myself. Since when had I become this groveling woman who couldn't keep her wits about her in the presence of a handsome man? I was a business owner. A badass baker. I had a lot going for me. So what if I hadn't felt a guy's lips pressed against mine since I was in my late teens? I'd been focused on building something for myself. Breaking out of the mold my parents squeezed me into.

Taking a deep breath, I started placing the blueberry muffins into the box.

I popped my head over the case and asked, "Would you like me to keep one out for you to take on the road?"

His answer was immediate. "That would be great." The shadow of his cowboy hat slid over his eyes, making them even darker. So much life danced in those irises and I felt myself being pulled to start asking him all the questions I heard the townsfolk murmuring about when he was released last year.

I wasn't one to watch the news, but when his trial went live the entire town was up in arms about it. I guess that's what happened when one of the town's richest families had a son who got his face beat in by the guy from the wrong side of the tracks.

Some even said that Ranger should have moved away. That he and his sister were rotten.

Looking at him now, I knew that wasn't true. Behind the mysterious allure, there was kindness. And I knew there was more to the story than him just beating up LeRoy Cummings. Ranger didn't seem like the kind of guy who would put his hands on someone else unless they deserved it.

Or maybe I was a fool trapped in his charms.

I grabbed the final muffin from the case and slid the glass door shut. Careful not to touch him for fear of going up in flames from the heat I felt, I slid the lone muffin across the counter before folding the box lid closed and sealing it with one of my logo stickers.

"That'll be—" Holy mother of Moses. Ranger's lips moved over the top of the muffin as he took a bite. I'd never been into watching other people eat food. Honestly, it kind of grossed me out.

But seeing Ranger devour my blueberry muffin was downright sinful with the way he licked the small crumbs from his bottom lip. Seeing his tongue run along the edge of his mouth had me squirming with naughty thoughts of that tongue licking something else entirely.

When I snapped out of my debauchery, I realized

Ranger's eyebrows were lifted like he was waiting for me to finish my statement.

"Um." I swallowed the hard knot in my throat. "That'll be twenty-four ninety-nine."

I watched his torso shift as he reached for his wallet in the back pocket of his jeans which happened to be so damn tight I could see the outline of his large thigh muscles.

This man was the epitome of sex on legs and here I was, falling head over heels for it.

Trying to lessen the shake in my hand, I flexed the small muscles of my forearm and fingers as I reached across the counter and took his card. Once again, careful not to let our fingertips touch. There was no telling what I might say or do if I actually felt his skin against my own and I'd already made a total mess of myself.

"Thank you," I croaked out as I slid his card into the machine to read the chip.

I handed him back his card and with the tip of his hat he said in a gravelly tone, "Thank you, Sarah."

Melting. My insides were melting—turning into a giant pile of goo hearing my name on his lips.

I didn't have the wits to say anything back so I just nodded before he grabbed the box of muffins and headed out the door.

I stared after him, wondering how such a large man could have a smooth swagger as he walked.

Then my phone rang and I nearly jumped out of my skin.

It was Deacon.

I slid my finger across the screen. "Hey, sorry about that."

"You okay?" He sounded worried. Honestly, given the lust-driven stupor I was in, he probably should be worried about me.

I cleared my throat. "Yeah. I'm fine. Just had a customer come in when I was technically closed."

"Gotcha. Well, I wanted to tell you that I don't think you should worry about the virgin thing. When the right guy comes along, he won't care if you're experienced or not."

I walked back to the kitchen and threw open the fridge door. Leaning far into it, I welcomed the blast of cool air along my flushed skin.

"Thanks, Deacon. I appreciate you saying that. I was actually going to ask you to do the honors and teach me some skills, but I think you might be right."

Deacon must have choked on his coffee because all I heard was a pained gurgling noise.

"No. There's no way in hell I'd touch you with a ten-foot pole."

"Thanks for that." I scowled, even though he couldn't see me.

"Just being honest. That would be like having sex with my sister. Just…no."

That had me chuckling. "Well, I appreciate you lending an ear. But I have to get back to work now."

"Any time. Talk soon."

I tucked my phone into my apron pocket and stepped away from the open fridge.

I hoped Deacon was right. That the guy I finally gave myself to would understand why I'd waited so long and that he would be okay with my lack of experience.

As I finished piping the last cupcakes and heard the kitchen door squeak open with Stephanie's entrance, I realized that I'd spent the last hour daydreaming about a man with long dark hair whose eyes pierced right through me.

Chapter 2

Ranger

Long chestnut hair, rich espresso eyes, and rosebud lips haunted me from the time I left *Sarah's Bakery* to this very moment as I walked up the steps to the main house. Maybe it was my prolonged stint in prison that had me fawning over her like a fucking puppy. Nearly ten years without contact with a woman did something to men like me.

I'd never been a player. The girls I hooked up with always knew exactly what they were getting with me. I made sure there was no mystery to the situation. Brutal honesty was a trait my father passed down to me.

I could still remember all the moments we shared together. The first time he had me break in one of the new horses, I'd hit my ass on the dirt too many times to count and my father just stood behind the barrier of the training ring giving it to me straight. Telling me how I was messing up and what I needed to do to fix it.

He never sugarcoated what he said and I always appreciated that about him because I knew exactly what I was getting. There was never a question in my mind about what he meant or what his intentions were in various situations.

So, I'd brought that quality into myself—worked on establishing my own truth and communicating openly about it. Especially when it came to women. Because I'd never been with a woman who I wanted to spend more than one night with. There were plenty of great ones who shared my bed. Smart, witty, adventurous. But none of them drew my attention the way Sarah Williams had this morning.

Which I found odd given I was six years her senior and barely had any contact with her other than seeing her around when I would pick up my sister from school. But two summers ago when I saw her at Deacon's summer bonfire, I felt like a shadow that had found its muse. I couldn't seem to stay away from her that night. Watching the reflection of the flames in her dark eyes as she tilted her head back and laughed at something her friend, Willow had said. The gentle curves of her body had my hands aching with the need to run them all over her. To pull her into my lap as I buried my face in her neck.

Fuck.

I pulled at my jeans, trying to loosen the crotch area where my dick was annoyingly erect. Not exactly the look I wanted to have as I brought my sister and Miles muffins for breakfast.

Taking a quick pause in front of the door, I adjusted myself so I wasn't showing before I cleared my head of any remaining thoughts of Sarah.

Most ranchers ate breakfast before they started work for the day, but it had always been tradition for my sister, Callie Rose, and me to eat breakfast together and despite all my years of trying to get that girl out of bed before the sun rose, I'd failed. So, I learned to accept my fate and celebrated the fact that I was even able to have these mornings with my sister again.

Ten years without them was hard. Even though it made the ranch work feel more difficult some days not getting a head start in the mornings, I cherished this time with my sister knowing how quickly someone else could take it away from us.

Stepping through the door, I called out, "I have breakfast!"

There was rustling and the sound of stools scraping against the hardwood. I rolled my eyes, remembering I needed to add some furniture pads to the kitchen stools before they wore holes into the floor. Callie had done a great job of keeping up with the place while I was away, but there were still a ton of things I needed to do to keep everything up to par.

Miles, my best friend since kindergarten, rounded the corner from the kitchen first. "Oh, man! You got stuff from *Sarah's Bakery*? She has the best cupcakes I've ever had."

When Miles grabbed the box of muffins from me I asked, "When have you gone to her bakery?"

A strange pull tugged in the center of my chest when I thought about Miles hanging around Sarah. We were similar in our approach of being honest with the women we slept with and I'd never been a jealous man. If a woman wanted someone else that just meant she wasn't the woman for me.

But this reaction I was having about Sarah was foreign to me. And I couldn't help but think about the comment she made to Deacon over the phone.

"But who the hell is going to want to be with a thirty-year-old virgin, Deacon?"

How a woman like that had gone her entire life without being shown the passion of sex was beyond me. Or maybe she was one of those who chose to save themselves for marriage. Not that there was anything wrong with that approach, it just wasn't the kind of ideology I subscribed to.

"I go there all the time, man," Miles said before stuffing his face with one of the muffins. "Like I said, best cupcakes around, and when the sweet tooth starts barking at me she's got the best fix in town."

I tried to hide the sneer from my face but when I looked over to my sister, she stopped her hand mid-grab and looked at me, her eyebrows raising in question. I shook my head, silently telling her to let it go. She shrugged and finished her reach for one of the muffins.

"So, what's the plan for the calves?" Miles asked.

I swallowed a bite and chased it down with the coffee Callie Rose had waiting for me on the counter. "I figured we could grab the calves on the front pasture and tag them first while we slowly transition the ones on the back pastures forward. I think we can have them all wrapped up by the end of the week with just the two of us working."

"Speaking of just the two of us, have you thought any more about hiring another hand?"

It was truly wild to see just how far the ranch had come in such a short period of time. While Miles and Callie Rose had kept things going while I was away, they barely broke even most months for the past decade. It wasn't for a lack of their efforts though. Ranch life was hard work and if you didn't have the gift of choosing the right cows and building relationships with wholesalers, you'd likely fail. My father never had the passion for it which was why he went into the military.

But every man who owned this land in our family before him had been gifted the ability to ranch well and that was passed on to me. So, when I got released I immediately got to work and within a year, I had the place turned around so that we started making a decent profit. Now, that profit was growing more and more which also meant the ranch was expanding and we'd need to hire some additional hands.

I just didn't like the idea of having strange men around my sister. Miles had always been around and we'd established one rule since our friendship began. My sister was completely off-limits. He'd respected that rule, but I wasn't sure if I could trust other men to do the same.

"Let's get through the rest of this year and we will re-evaluate in the new year. I think we can manage just the two of us until then."

"Yeah, that sounds like a plan." Miles scarfed down his third muffin and grabbed his cowboy hat from the counter. "I'm going to get a head start. I'll see you out there."

When he was through the door, Callie Rose lowered her coffee mug from her lips and said, "So, are you going to tell me what that horrible look on your face was about or should I start making guesses?"

She was always the one catching me off guard with her annoyingly good observation skills. I tried to play it off. "It's nothing. I was just thinking about all the work we have to do to get the calves tagged in time."

"Bullshit."

I heaved a long sigh. "I don't want to do this with you right now."

Ever since I'd gone away, I'd developed a habit of keeping my cards close to my chest. Prison was every bit as bad as people made it out to be and to protect yourself, you either aligned with the right people or you kept your head down and stayed out of sight. Not wanting to affiliate with any assholes and have expectations follow me on the outside, I chose the latter route and it definitely had a lasting impact.

Before being convicted, I told Callie Rose everything. She wasn't just my little sister, but my best friend. When our dad died in the war and our mom left us shortly after, we were all the other had to depend on.

Ten years was a long time, though. Even though she was still my best friend, the thought of being vulnerable and sharing what I was feeling had my skin crawling with tension. Vulnerability made you a target on the inside and even a year after my release, I was still adjusting to life on the outside.

She leaned forward on the island, her elbows propped on

the table before giving me a look that told me this conversation was nowhere near over.

But she gave me some respite when she said, “Okay. I’ll give you some space. But I’m here if you want to talk about it.”

“Thanks,” I murmured over the rim of my mug.

We stood in comfortable silence while each of us munched on the blueberry muffins and sipped on our coffees. Mornings like this were what I missed most when I went away. The freedom to just be. To enjoy the simple moments without having someone else telling me that it was time to go back to my cell.

When I looked at my sister, I wanted to say those things. I wanted to tell her how much this time with her meant to me. But I kept my mouth shut. That fear of vulnerability proving stronger than my own will at this moment.

Thankfully, she broke the silence before my thoughts dragged me back to a place I didn’t want to go.

“Do you think you could help me with some of the wiring for the grape vines? They’re really starting to take off and I want to get the wiring complete before I’m in over my head.”

“Yeah. How about tomorrow? I can take the second half of the day to help you with that.”

“Perfect. I was planning on taking today to focus on pruning and getting them ready for the first frost of fall.”

Callie Rose had always helped around with the ranch, but right after I went away, she left for college while Miles maintained what little cattle we had. She got her degree in agriculture business. She wasn't allowed to bring her paper degree into the visiting area of the prison when she graduated, but I could see the pride on her face. She was a first-generation college student and now she was using that knowledge to make our family ranch even more successful than I could imagine.

Even though our town was small and tucked away in the foothills of the Blue Ridge Mountains, there was a lot the townsfolk had to offer. From artisan coffee shops, countless festivals, and Sarah's divine desserts there was plenty to keep everyone satisfied. But the one thing Pebble Brook Falls didn't have was a winery. Knowing how much the town's wealthy would eat up the possibility of having fine wine made in their hometown, my sister had capitalized on an opportunity and I'd do everything in my power to help her succeed.

Eventually, she had plans to build a large seating venue at the south end of the property, next to the vineyard for people to come for tastings. More recently, I heard her talking to Miles about using it as a wedding venue sometimes too. She had a lot of grand plans and the first step was making sure the vines did well.

I watched as she drained the rest of her coffee and grabbed her small coat off the hook in the hall.

"See you out there," she said before turning for the door.

"Cal?" I called after her.

She stopped and looked over her shoulder at me. "I'm proud of you."

The smile that hit her face reminded me of how she

smiled as a young girl. Bright and full of life. In that moment, I felt overwhelmingly thankful that I had my sister. Even if I wasn't ready to open up fully, I could tell her how much she amazed me.

"Thanks, Ranger." As I watched her bound toward the front door, a little piece of my wall came crumbling down.

Chapter 3

Sarah

The bakery was filled to the brim with patrons. I wasn't sure what caused the uptick today, but I was thankful for it despite running around like a chicken with my head cut off. I nearly burnt an entire batch of chocolate chip cookies earlier because the line was so long and I couldn't break away from the cash register.

It also didn't help that I'd been completely distracted by thoughts of a certain man's lips and wondering how the hell someone could look so sexy while eating a muffin.

Thankfully, my cousin, Stephanie, came to my rescue and made it just in time for me to pull them out of the oven.

"Holy shit, Sarah. You've really made something of this place." The sound of my brother's voice cut through the ding of the oven timer that had been going off for a minute straight.

"Theo!" I tossed the cookie sheet onto the metal counter of the island and dashed for him. His chest rumbled against mine as he laughed a full belly laugh. The sound only made me squeeze him harder.

"Easy there, tiger. You're going to take me out if you squeeze on my ribs any harder."

"Oops," I giggled, pulling back to take a good look at my big brother. "Wait,"—I narrowed my eyes at him—"what's wrong with your ribs?"

He rolled his eyes. "Not much. Just a few broken ones."

"Theo! What the hell?" I pushed against his chest and he winced.

"Sorry," I mumbled, drawing my cheeks back in a grimace. "But seriously. What the hell?"

He shrugged like having broken ribs was just part of his job. Which, I guess it was now that he was a bronco rider and all. It was fairly normal for bull and bronco riders to walk away with a ton of injuries—if they walked away at all.

Though I was happy for my brother that he finally stopped living under our parents' thumbs, I wasn't exactly thrilled with the profession he chose after he dropped out of law school. I didn't like the idea of my brother becoming broken beyond repair, especially when he had so much life to live. But it wasn't my choice to make and I promised myself that no matter what he decided to do, I was going to support him in it.

He'd already sacrificed years of his life doing what our parents wanted him to do so that I could open my bakery without my mother bringing down a literal hammer on me. I was the biggest disappointment of her entire life, but my brother's success and willingness to pursue law helped to ease the burden of shame I brought to our family.

I didn't know how things would look now that he had dropped out and was home. Honestly, I didn't want to know.

"Mom's going to be pissed when she finds out about your ribs."

"Mmm, maybe this is a secret we should keep from her."

I huffed out a breath. "That's probably a good idea. That woman doesn't need any more ammunition than she already has."

"Sometimes, I think she manifests it out of thin air," he grumbled.

I could feel the weight of it. Our mother's ambitions. The goals she set for us to maintain her high society image. Every time I thought about it for too long, it felt like someone strapped a backpack filled with rocks onto my shoulders.

My dad wasn't any help either. Most of the time he was absent and the rest of the time he spent supporting my mom in whatever verbal lashing she decided to give me.

My brother and I stood in silence for a few moments. The realization of what his coming home would truly mean for us as a family was starting to settle in and I hated the feeling of the tightness taking hold in my chest.

So, I straightened my apron and rolled my shoulders back. "When do you start at the Carnelle's ranch?"

"Tomorrow."

"And you're going to work with broken ribs?" I arched a brow at him and he shot me a lopsided grin.

"It's all part of the job, little sis."

“Just promise me you’ll be careful.”

He pulled me in for a side hug and I tried not to squeeze him too hard this time. “I promise.”

“You know…” I drew out the words as I leaned back to look him in the eyes. “At that ranch, there’s a lot more to look out for than just the bucking broncos. I’ve heard Melody Carnelle likes to have her way with all the new riders who come through her family’s ranch.”

His face twisted into a scowl as he groaned. “That woman has always been a viper in the grass, hasn’t she?”

“Yup.”

“Honestly, if there was anywhere else I could train in Pebble Brook Falls, I’d choose it over the Carnelle’s ranch. But this was the only option for me to train and be close to home. Sometimes you have to take the good with the bad.”

I crossed my arms over my chest. “Unfortunately, when it comes to that family, I think all of it is bad. But, I get it. You’re trying to make multiple things work by pursuing your dream and being home. I’d just steer clear of her if I were you.”

“That’s the plan.” He moved around me and swiped one of the chocolate chip cookies off the tray on the counter.

“Hey!” I chastised, pointing at his chest. “I expect you to pay for that on your way out.”

He laughed around the ginormous bite he took. As his long blonde hair fell over his eyes, I saw the young, carefree version of him that had been stowed away for years. Theo was always the sweet one. Making sure the people around him were happy, even if that meant sacrificing his own joy.

Guilt had my heart clenching as I thought of the sacrifices he made for me. Mostly because I was selfish and allowed him to take the brunt of our parents' expectations as a burden to carry on his own. I let him do it, knowing that each passing year he spent doing something he hated, his bright blue eyes dulled each time I saw him. The only thing I was focused on was freeing myself.

Now that he was back home and I was witness to the joy that same freedom brought him, I made a silent promise to myself that I wouldn't shy away from our parents' shaming and disappointment at his expense. It was Theo's turn to live free.

"So, what's this I hear about Willow turning the Baxley estate into a new orphanage?" Theo's words cut through my thoughts like a knife slicing through buttercream frosting.

While I tried to keep Theo updated while he was in law school, it was hard to cover all the events of the past year over the phone. "You missed a lot while you were gone."

"Care to fill me in?" he asked, leaning against the counter right before he stole another cookie off the sheet.

I smacked at his hand, but he was much taller than me and evaded my attack before shoving the entire cookie into his mouth.

"You're diabolical. Do you know that?"

He smiled widely at me, revealing his mouth full of chocolate chip cookie.

I snorted and rolled my eyes.

"One of these days I'm going to kick your ass for being a pain in mine."

He smiled wider. "You love me too much to kick my ass. Plus, you're nowhere near fast enough to catch me to do it."

In a flash, I snapped my hand out and pinched him on his right nipple.

"Agh!" He reared back, covering the spread of his chest with his forearms. "Did you seriously just give me a titty twister?"

I smiled maniacally at him. "What?" I shrugged. "You challenged how quick I was. So, I had to prove you wrong. You might be my big brother, but I'm a hell of a lot meaner than you are."

He rubbed at his right peck while clutching his ribs and glared at me, sending me into a fit of giggles.

"Are you going to update me on everything I missed or are you just going to torture me some more?"

"Yeah." I grabbed the sheet of cookies on the counter. "Let me run these out to the case first and then we'll talk."

"Okay."

The crowd of patrons from the late morning rush had slowed a bit, but all the tables were still full as I quickly placed the cookies into the glass display case.

"You doing okay, Steph?" I asked as she counted change for Mrs. Bailey, one of the town's most notorious biddies. Ever since her husband died a few months back, she'd found herself titled as a hellacious flirt and a vicious gossip. I shot her a quick smile as she took the change from Stephanie and she just stopped, looked me up and down like I was a diseased rat, then sauntered off as fast as her hip replacements could take her.

Stephanie giggled. "I'm doing much better than you are. Knowing Mrs. Bailey, she probably has the rumor mill churning given that look she just gave you. What did you do to the poor woman?"

I shook my head. "I have no idea, but as long as she keeps having her biddie meetings at my bakery and spending her money on my cupcakes, I don't care."

"Good point."

"I'm going to head back to hang out with Theo for a bit. Are you okay to stay up here for a while longer without me?"

"Of course!"

"Thank you! You're a lifesaver."

I headed back through the kitchen door. "Okay, Stephanie's good, so I can chat a bit longer before I need to start the next round of cupcakes."

Theo was leaning against the counter with his arms crossed over his chest. "Where were we?" I asked.

"You were going to update me on the town's juicy gossip."

My heart shot through my stomach as I recalled the events of this past summer. There certainly was a lot of juicy gossip. The town had seen more in the span of a few months than it had in an entire decade.

"I guess the best place to start is that Willow finally got what was owed to her by her grandmother. We still aren't completely sure what led Madeline Baxley to give over her estate to the one person she tried to keep out of her family. The only thing we can think of is that Madeline wanted the estate to stay in her bloodline, even if the only surviving family member had tainted blood." I spat out the last words because the idea that my best friend wasn't considered pure due to her biological father being poor was such an archaic thought process. Cut us open and we all bled the same color and experienced the same pain. Money didn't change any of that, no matter how much some people wanted it to.

"I never liked the woman. Even when she smiled, it looked like she was frowning." Theo's face twisted in disgust.

Closing my eyes, I shook off the memories from last summer because I never wanted to see my best friend in that much turmoil ever again. "I'm just glad to see Willow putting all that money to good use. Honestly, I'm not sure if I would have the willpower to give up that gorgeous estate. But she seems perfectly happy living with Johnny in his house."

He nodded. "It takes a special person to be that selfless. I know she didn't have the best time growing up and it sounds like she wants to give to the future generation of kids who were just like her."

"Yeah, she's pretty amazing." I smiled.

"So are you, sis. Just because you weren't given an opportunity to give back in that way doesn't mean you wouldn't. I know you say it would be hard for you to give up something as grand as the Baxley estate, but I don't buy that for one minute. You've always been generous, kind, and thoughtful. I know you would give back in whatever way you could."

I blushed. "Thanks, Theo." He always saw the best in people. Even when we couldn't see it ourselves.

His big palm splayed over my bicep and he gave it a gentle squeeze. "I also wanted to say I'm sorry I wasn't here for everything that happened last year. I know you probably didn't get much support from mom and dad."

I snorted. "I hardly saw them all summer. Mom even robbed me of my largest account in some screwed-up attempt to teach me a lesson. She thought that by showing me that she was the one who actually controlled the citizens of Pebble Brook Falls I would fall in line and do something more worthy of my time than be a bakery owner."

Conflict danced in Theo's eyes. The anger that swelled from being pressed under our mother's thumb for too long was warring with the love he still had for her. I could see it because it was the same conflict that I felt swirling in my soul all the time. I didn't hate my parents for what they wanted for me. They were simply products of their upbringing and the pressures that society put on them. I just wanted them to be the ones to break the cycle. To realize how much their actions were tearing our family apart. That it didn't matter what Theo and I did for a living, as long as we were happy.

But, I'd grown to understand that hell was more likely to freeze over than my parents realizing the error of their ways.

"Let me talk to her, I can—"

"No," I cut my brother off. "No. You've already done enough to protect me. It's my turn to take the brunt of things for a while. Give you some space to live your own life."

Just as he opened his mouth to give me a retort, my phone pinged in my apron pocket. Not even a second later, Theo was fishing his phone out of his jeans pocket after his dinged as well.

"Speaking of the she-devil." He showed me the screen of his phone where our mom had sent a group text to both of us.

I reached into my apron and tried to stall the reflexive reaction of my heart plummeting through my stomach every time I saw my mom's name flash across the small screen. But there was no stopping it as I swiped my thumb across the screen and opened the message.

Mom

It's been a while since we have had a family dinner. I fully expect both of you to be home this Sunday evening by six o'clock sharp.

I groaned. "I thought we were done with family dinners."

Theo's sigh was a mirror for the internal upset I felt strangling my gut. "At least we'll be together?" he offered.

"Yeah. At least we'll be there together."

We stood in silence for several long minutes. Feeling the heaviness of what was to come from that family dinner put me right back into the countless times when my mother told me I wasn't good enough. All the moments I saw a disapproving look from my father. The moment I learned that my own mother had robbed me of my largest baking account two summers ago when she told little Tommy's mom to choose another bakery for his elaborate birthday party.

But as I looked at my big brother and saw the same worries etched on his face, I knew I had to be stronger this time. It was my turn to jump into the line of fire so that he could finally have his moment of peace.

Chapter 4

Sarah

Yesterday kicked my butt. Between meeting with Theo and learning that our mother decided to revamp the old family tradition of having Sunday dinner together and the huge crowd the bakery had throughout the day yesterday, I was dragging this morning.

Normally, I woke up with enough enthusiasm and energy to run an entire city, but today felt different. It felt like those years in high school and the first few after graduation when I could hardly get myself out of bed in the morning. Putting a smile on for everyone around me because I felt like there was no other choice. And I didn't want my sadness to negatively impact the people I loved.

It scared me.

Having those feelings of sadness creep in again. Having them latch into my mind like a ball and chain that felt much too heavy to carry. It was a constant battle for so many years of my life. Having parents who didn't understand me—who *chose* to not understand me—took a bigger toll than I was willing to admit to myself.

But when Theo left for law school, my parents found a way to shift their focus from me to their perfect son. The one who was doing everything right. Most people would probably think that I'd be envious of Theo. That I'd be angry he was getting all the positive attention.

But I loved it.

Selfishly, I loved it.

The more attention he got, the less time my mother spent trying to make me second-guess my life choices.

Now, things would be different. There was already a shift in me where all my focus was being pulled to tomorrow night and what brutal battle would be fought over the dinner table.

The bell over the front door of the bakery saved me from my torturous thoughts and for the first time all morning, a genuine smile graced my lips as I saw Mrs. Sheehan step through the front door, her large wagon dragging behind her.

"Hi, Mrs. Sheehan! How're you doing this morning?"

"I'm doin' just fine, dear. But I'll be doin' even better once I have my hands on those famous chocolate chip cookies of yours. I can never keep my ice cream sandwiches in stock when I use your cookies, you know."

Always striving to help others, Mrs. Sheehan had started purchasing my chocolate chip cookies a few years ago for her ice cream sandwiches instead of getting them cheaper from the store. Her support came during a time when I thought I was going to have to shut down the bakery and I was forever grateful.

"I can't let my cookies take all the credit for that. Your ice cream is the best in the state."

She waved her hand at me as crimson blossomed on her cheeks. "Oh shush. You're making this old woman blush."

"It's true! And everyone in this town is thankful for it."

"Hm," she huffed. "I just wish I would have been smart like you and decided on something people wanted year-round. The first chill of fall has barely made its way through and people are already starting to shy away from the parlor."

I started loading the boxes of cookies into her wagon as she dished her credit card from her wallet and continued, "Business is always great during the spring and summer months, but these mountain folk don't want a thing to do with ice cream when late fall and winter rolls around. Thankfully, the summer months help me squeeze by."

"Well, I know everyone is going to love having your ice cream sandwiches at the grand opening today. It will be the last hurrah before the cold settles in."

With the final box of cookies in her wagon, I straightened just as she said, "I am so proud of our sweet Willow Mae. Using all the money she has to do something good in the world. It takes a strong person to go through the trials of life and come out the other side still willing to give more."

"She's pretty wonderful," I agreed. "I'm really lucky to call her my best friend."

"And she's lucky to have you as well, Sarah. I remember a time when Willow was the odd one out and you chose to befriend her. To give her a safe place amongst a pack of wild wolves. It takes a brave person to go against the grain and extend a hand to others, knowing that it will likely make you the odd one out too."

I reached for her hand, feeling a swarm of emotions clog my throat. "Thank you for saying that, Mrs. Sheehan."

The twinkle in her eye told me she understood just how much her kind words impacted me. It wasn't a secret that my parents were disappointed in me. Especially since they made their opinion known every chance they got.

"I just call it as I see it." She gave my hand a quick squeeze before letting go and grabbing the long handle of her wagon.

"I'll be seeing you at the opening. I need to get a head start on these sandwiches so they have time to harden before I transfer them to the coolers."

"See you there." I waved goodbye to her as she made her way through the door and got back to work on the cupcakes I was bringing.

As I piped the last ring of icing, I was still feeling thankful for Mrs. Sheehan's kind words and how they'd come at just the right time.

The entire town had come to watch the grand opening of the *Hope for All Orphanage's* new home. In a stroke of cosmic luck, my best friend had been given her grandmother's estate after she passed away. I knew it was difficult for Willow to have her entire life change for the better at the hands of a woman she hated. But she was working her way through it and I was beyond proud to see all the good she was doing despite the circumstances.

The crowd was gathered on the front lawn of the expansive mansion with beautiful towering columns made of white marble that shot upward. The small wooden rocking chairs that lined the front porch—if you could even call it that—seemed out of place amongst the grand stature of the house.

It was similar to the one I grew up in, though I would have much preferred a smaller space like the home I had now. Sometimes the grandeur of a house took away from the natural beauty of everything else around it.

A large, bright red ribbon hung between the two columns that lined the entryway and in front of it Willow stood next to her fiancé, Johnny. Seeing the way he looked at her brought overwhelming joy to my heart. Two of my favorite people had faced all the odds against them and were still able to find a love I knew would stand the test of time and whatever future trials came their way.

But that same happiness I felt for them was coated with envy and I hated that. I wished I could just be excited for them and not feel the grip of jealousy when I was forced to face the fact that I was very *very* alone.

I could hardly recall the last time a man even kissed me and I knew for a fact I'd never been in love. The only thing that held my attention these days was chasing the success of my business. I'd blamed my loneliness on that chase for a long time, but if I was honest with myself I was afraid. Terrified really. That if I let anyone close enough to love me they'd see all the things I tried so hard to hide and run away from.

I wondered what Ranger would think if he knew how judgmental my parents were. If he was the kind of man who would look past that and see that I was different—or that I at least tried really hard to be different.

"Thank you all so much for being here," Willow started, drawing my thoughts back to the present.

"I have to say, I thought I would be surprised by the turnout today, but the truth is that this town and the people in it have always shown up for the greater good. Having grown up in the *Hope for All Orphanage* myself, I can say with certainty that it is because of the generosity of the people in Pebble Brook Falls that I was able to have clothes on my back, school supplies, and a few toys to open on Christmas. Today, I have the wonderful opportunity to give back to the next generation because of all your support."

Willow found me in the crowd with her gaze and I gave her a wide smile and a subtle nod. She returned my smile with one of her own before continuing, "Without further ado, it is my greatest honor and pleasure to introduce everyone to the new home of the *Hope for All Orphanage* at the Baxley Estate!"

Celebratory applause erupted from the crowd as Willow grabbed the giant pair of scissors from Johnny and cut the red ribbon. The final step to giving the forgotten children of our town a home—so grand—that it would surely make them feel like they had a place in the world, even when all hope of fitting in had left them.

I stood in place, clapping my hands vigorously as the crowd shifted around me. Only a select few had ever gotten to see the inside of the Baxley Estate when Willow's grandmother was still alive, so pure curiosity had everyone edging toward the front door for the tour.

Just before I took a step forward to find Willow and Johnny, the hairs on my arms stood on end. A presence I'd felt only a handful of times before had found me again. A spark that seemed to always find me, even if it had been gone for a long long while. It was the same fire that ignited in my belly a few days ago when I'd seen him in my bakery.

If I turned around, I knew I would find deep blue eyes that reflected the same depth of emotion as the ocean churning beneath a storm. The same stunning eyes I'd always admired from afar, hoping they'd land on me with more than gentle curiosity and kindness.

The sensation of his nearness lingered, taunting me to turn around and say *something*. Anything that would be worthy of his attention.

I can do this. I can talk to him and everything will go smoothly. I won't stumble over my words at all.

At the end of my short-lived pep-talk, I found the courage to turn around and say hi to Ranger just as Willow called my name. My gaze flicked upward to where she was striding toward me.

The feel of Ranger at my back slowly dissipated and I

tried not to look completely deflated at my lost opportunity. There had been plenty of chances for me to say hi to him—like at Deacon's bonfire two summers ago. But I let every chance I had of talking to my childhood crush slip between my fingers like warm butter. The biggest problem was that Ranger Adams was—by far—the most beautiful man I'd ever seen. With inky black hair that peeked out from the rim of his cowboy hat, sapphire blue eyes, towering height that dwarfed me, a beard that I'd daydreamed on more than one occasion of sitting on, and …yeah. Okay. Maybe I was a little obsessed with Ranger Adams.

But what girl didn't want a tall, dark, and brutally handsome cowboy? He was the one and only man that had crossed my mind in all the years I'd spent chasing my dream. And that somehow made him completely unobtainable.

"What did you think of the speech?" Willow asked, warding away my thoughts of unfilled fantasies. "I didn't want it to be too long or too short. But, I don't know. Maybe I should have included more about my own upbringing. Or thanking the townsfolk more. Or—"

"Willow, stop." I braced my hands in front of her. "You shouldn't want to change a thing about your speech because it was absolutely perfect." I smiled widely at her.

"Really?" she crooned as silver lined her eyes. "You really think so?"

"I do! You know I would tell you if I thought otherwise, but it was perfect. And I am so dang proud of you." Taking her into my arms, I squeezed her tightly, just like I used to do when we were kids.

"Thank you."

We pulled apart and she reached down, grabbing my hand. "Come on. I want to show you the finished renovations."

"Okay," I said a little too quickly as I stole a glance over my shoulder, scanning the scattered crowd for any sign of Ranger.

"Looking for someone?" Willow's brows were pinched.

"Nope!" I replied because the truth was that even if I did see Ranger, I was too much of a coward to actually do anything about it. And even if I did find my bravery and say something to him, I knew it could never go anywhere. There were expectations for girls like me and if I thought about bringing a guy like Ranger Adams home to meet my family, there would be hell to pay and I didn't want to put him through that kind of torture.

So, I let the thought of seeing him go and let myself fall away to the excitement my best friend had as she showed me all the amazing renovations she did to the Baxley Estate to ensure the orphanage's children would feel right at home.

Chapter 5

Ranger

With my left hand braced against the shower wall, I ran my right hand up and down my shaft. Squeezing harder as I got to the base and softer as my calloused palm edged closer to the head of my cock with each stroke.

Long dark hair and espresso-colored eyes flooded my mind as I imagined Sarah kneeling before me, taking my length in her small hands and stroking me up and down until she finally stopped teasing me and pulled me past those delicious pink lips and into her mouth where her warm tongue swirled over my tip.

Holy fuck.

Curling my fingertips against the tiled wall, my balls tightened against me as I shot a load all over the floor of the shower. Hot cum coated my hand for a few moments before the water washed it all away.

My breaths were quick and even though I finished in an embarrassingly short amount of time, the conjured image of

Sarah still played out in my mind. But this time, instead of her kneeling before me, we were back in her bakery and I watched her bend over as she placed muffin after muffin in the pink box she balanced with one hand. Her tight little ass poked out in her skin-tight jeans and I wondered what kind of exercise she did to keep that perfect peach.

Then I quietly chastised myself for letting my thoughts stray way too far because this woman was far beyond my reach. Hell, she probably stuttered over her words because she was afraid of me. All alone in her bakery before the townsfolk were even out of bed sipping on their first cup of coffee. The one guy she probably didn't want to be alone with had bombarded her.

Not that I blamed her.

LeRoy's lawyer made me look like a fucking douchebag who enjoyed being violent. Even though I'd served my time, I was sure there was still some hesitation in people's ability to trust that I wasn't actually the bad guy. I hoped Sarah didn't see me that way.

When I saw her yesterday at the grand re-opening of the *Hope for All Orphanage* I had an urgency to pull her aside and talk to her. To tell her that the rumors about me weren't true. They'd been orchestrated by a family with a lot more power and money than I'd probably ever have.

I was so close yesterday to reaching out and touching her arm to grab her attention before Willow got ahold of her first.

It was probably for the best because Sarah had her entire life ahead of her. She didn't need to be bogged down with a guy like me who had a rap sheet for a violent offense. Being with me would only bring chaos into her life.

As I finished my shower, I told myself I would leave Sarah Williams alone. That no matter how difficult it might be to stay away from her, it wasn't right for me to interfere with her life knowing how it would likely cause the town another uproar.

"Geez. I thought you were going to use up all the hot water on the ranch for how long you were in the shower," Callie Rose said to me as I made my way down the stairs and into the kitchen where she was leaning against the counter, a plate full of eggs in her hand.

"What the hell were you..." Her eyes grew big as she realized the answer to her unfinished question. "Nope!" she yelled. "Never mind. I do *not* want to know."

"Are you sure?" I snickered. "Because it sounds like you were interested in how I wrapped my hand aro—"

"Nope!" Callie Rose cut me off. "I'm perfectly happy not knowing what my brother does in his spare time. Even if he does use up all the hot water. Just keep those little tidbits to yourself, thank you very much."

I chuckled while she maintained a look of pure horror and disgust on her face. "Where's Miles?" I asked.

"I already made him breakfast. He wanted to get a head

start on tagging the calves since you'll be missing this afternoon to help me with the orchard."

"Mmm. Good call."

She reached behind her and grabbed the extra plate of eggs and sausage and handed it to me. The savory notes hit my nose and my stomach immediately clenched from hunger pains. "Thank you for making breakfast." The words came out garbled as I talked around the big bite of food I'd taken.

"No problem."

Just like most mornings, we stood together in comfortable silence. When I finished, I washed off my plate and put it on the drying rack next to the sink before turning back to my sister and noticing she had a faraway look on her face.

"What's going on?"

She blinked out of her daze and looked at me. "I was just thinking about how it'll be fifteen years since we lost dad this month. And fourteen since we lost mom."

I didn't like to think about it. All that we had lost because of the war. Dad was my best friend and even though he didn't want the ranch life for himself, he taught me everything he knew from his father because he could see how much I loved it. Riding over the green hills under the big open sky, herding the cattle and caring for them. Showing the animals the respect they deserved for the nourishment they would bring to our bodies. I'd always loved it and no matter the differences we had, my father had always supported me and my dream of taking over the ranch one day.

And I'd loved listening to his stories of traveling the world during his deployments. He always had a way of finding something in common with people, even if they were wildly different. That was what I missed most about him. The lessons he taught Callie Rose and me. All the family talks we would have under the stars surrounding the fire pit.

When we lost him I was devastated. It felt like the world was crumbling around me and I was floating through life with no clear direction. But I saw the way his death impacted mom and I knew I needed to take care of Callie Rose. She was so young and still needed a lot of attention—as all children do. Mom wasn't able to give it to her. The depression had kicked in…settled too deep. Until one day, Callie Rose and I made our way downstairs for breakfast to find a note on the counter saying she was sorry but she had to go.

I guessed being here was too much of a reminder of the love she lost. I had just turned eighteen and Callie Rose was only twelve. It wasn't the most ideal situation, but we made it work.

"Yeah," I sighed. "September is always a hard month, isn't it?"

She nodded slowly. "Do you think he would be happy about the orchard?" Her voice caught with emotion, pulling on my own heart.

I strode over to her and took her in a side hug, giving her shoulders a gentle squeeze toward my chest.

"He would have loved it. This land has been in our family for five generations. Knowing you were making it your own—using it for something that brings you joy—would make him damn proud."

"Really?" She rubbed the back of her hand under her nose and sniffed.

I gave her another squeeze. "Really."

She laid her head on my chest. "I don't know why I'm so emotional about this today. It usually doesn't hit me this hard."

"It's been a rough few years, Callie Rose. Sometimes the pain of loss hits harder when other shit happens."

"Yeah, you're probably right."

"I mean, I'm hardly ever wrong." That got me a quick elbow jab to the ribs, but I took the shot with grace because the smile on my little sister's face lifted the painful tug in my chest.

"Whatever, douche-canoe."

"Douche-canoe?! That's a new one."

She smiled at me like a feral Cheshire cat. "Yup. And I think it fits you perfectly."

I rolled my eyes. "Alright, enough of your shenanigans. Let's get to work. I'll meet you at the orchard around one."

"See you then," she waved me off as she headed toward the door.

The work Callie Rose had accomplished on the orchard was incredible. All the vines were neatly pruned, ready for the chill of fall and winter. Every plant was perfectly aligned with the next, which made my afternoon job a hell of a lot easier as we ran wires from post to post so the vines had something to grab onto as they matured.

Taking off my gloves, I found a spot on the ground and settled in just as Callie Rose came down the row with my glass of sweet tea. The year before I was released, Miles and she refurbished the old cabin on the property and made it all her own. She'd told me that as much as she loved having her big brother back, she didn't want to share living quarters in case I needed to 'sow my wild oats' after being behind bars for ten years.

While I hadn't been with anyone since my release, I appreciated having the ranch house to myself in the evenings. I needed the quiet to settle my mind these days.

"Here you go." She handed me the tall glass and settled in a dirt patch next to me. Her black wavy hair was tied back with a red handkerchief and it fell over her left shoulder that was covered with a tanktop and overalls strap. She looked every bit the farmer I knew she loved to be.

"This is pretty incredible, Cal. The vines are coming along nicely. I think you might even be able to start harvesting next fall."

She took a long swig of her tea and looked around at the surrounding vines. "Thanks. I have big plans for this place and it's been pretty awesome seeing them start to come to fruition. I've been enjoying taking the small harvest from the garden to the farmer's market every two weeks too."

"I have to admit, I was a little surprised at how well the

garden's been doing. Not sure who you got your green thumb from but it's definitely panning out."

She huffed out a breath. "Yeah, the few memories I have of mom include all the dead crispy plants she kept around the house."

"And every year, dad still bought her another orchid," I laughed.

"Maybe I was adopted and y'all just decided to keep it a secret." She shot me a playful glare.

"Nah. With those blue eyes? You're definitely an Adams."

She smiled and linked her arm with mine. "I'm so glad you're home."

Her words struck my heart like a baseball shattering through a window. I swallowed against the knot in my throat trying to keep the emotions at bay.

Ranch life was hard, but it was the epitome of freedom. So, being on the inside, locked away in a cage that wasn't truly meant to be mine was beyond anything I'd experienced. When our dad died, I'd stepped up. Became the man of the house and took over the ranch and all the other responsibilities of running the family and taking care of Callie Rose. It was hard, but I welcomed the challenge. I wanted to be the best person I could for my little sister, especially when our mom decided she couldn't handle it anymore and left us in the middle of the night.

But those ten years being locked away because of some bastard narking on me was an offense I will never forget.

"I need to tell you something," Callie Rose whispered as she lifted her head from my arm.

"What's that?"

She started eyeing the dirt in front of us like it was the most interesting thing in the world. My sister had always been a deep thinker. Sometimes to the point of having to pull her back from her mind so she could be present in the moment.

This time it didn't take her too long to say, "LeRoy Cummings is back in town."

"You saw him?" My heart rate immediately shot through the roof.

Her eyes were sad as she finally looked up at me. "I saw him last weekend at the farmer's market. I thought maybe he was just visiting his family, but I heard through the grapevine that he's moving back to town."

"Why didn't you tell me sooner?"

"I didn't want to get you worked up over something when I wasn't sure if he was back for good. I just got confirmation last night that he was buying a house."

Hot anger had my blood simmering beneath my skin. I wanted so badly to punch something, but seeing as how that's what got me put away in the first place I kept my clenched fists firmly in my lap.

So many years of my life were gone. Countless memories I could have shared with my little sister and best friend. Being forced to leave them to tend to the ranch when it was *my* dream, not theirs.

LeRoy Cummings had fucked up my life beyond imagination and to hear that the smug asshole was back in town knowing that I would never leave had smoke damn near shooting from my ears.

"Are you going to be okay?" I could hear the concern in her voice as she placed a gentle palm on my forearm.

I felt my nostrils flare as I closed my eyes and sucked in a deep breath. When I opened my eyes, I patted her hand. "Yeah. I'll be fine. It's just the initial shock of the news. That's all."

"Okay." She rubbed her hand back and forth over my arm. I hated the tears that lined her eyes as she said, "He's already taken so much from you, Ranger. Don't give him anything else."

Callie Rose was right. LeRoy would always be a douchebag looking for the next person to screw over for his benefit, especially if that meant someone else could be his fall guy.

Shifting my gaze ahead, I took in the endless rows of grape vines my sister had planted with her bare hands and the acres of hills beyond where our cattle grazed. I'd spent ten years of my life fighting to get back to this. To not succumb to the mindfuck of being locked in a cage for someone else's mistake.

No matter what he did, I couldn't let him rob me of more time. Because no matter how much money the ranch was starting to make, time was the one thing money couldn't buy.

Chapter 6

Sarah

I'm going to be late. It was the only thought running through my mind as I handed over the box full of pastries to Mrs. Gronemyer. She had to watch her grandchildren unexpectedly this afternoon, so she was running behind in picking up her order.

I should have just told her that she would need to pick it up tomorrow morning, but she sounded so frazzled over the phone and I didn't want to make her feel worse. But that small act of grace was going to cost me big time because it was Sunday, which meant that I was going to be late for our first family dinner in years.

My mother was going to blow a gasket.

As soon as Mrs. Gronemyer was through the door, I threw my apron over my head, grabbed my purse, and ran for my car. Thankfully, it was Sunday and most people were home with their families preparing for the work week ahead so the roads were fairly empty.

When I finally pulled into my parents' driveway, I glanced at the clock on my dashboard and noted the time was seventeen minutes past six.

"Gah!" I groaned to myself. When my mother said six o'clock sharp, she meant it. I didn't even want to pull out my phone that was snug in my purse because I knew I probably had dozens of text messages from her.

I threw my car into park and jogged up the stone steps to their front door. While my parents had less property than the Baxley estate, their house was very similar in its grandeur. When I was younger, I never paid much attention to what having such a pillar of a home meant. How it was a representation of what my family would expect from me. That I would need to find my way of accomplishing enough to have my own grand home. Or that I would need to find a man who could provide it for me while I ran the household.

As I gripped the long door handle that had beautiful spirals on each end, I felt the weight of the door like it was the weight I'd been bearing on my shoulders for years. Before I stepped through the entryway, I took a deep breath in, smelling the delicious aroma of fresh herbs and spices mixed with the savory notes of meat. I let my shoulders fall and I told myself that tonight would be okay. I was an adult. No longer forced to fit into their box. My brother and I had every right to live our lives as we saw fit and they would just have to deal with it.

The pep talk gave me enough strength to make it down the long hallway to the final room on the left, across from the kitchen. The tall wooden French doors to the dining room were slightly ajar when I pushed them open to find my father at the head of the long mahogany table, my mother to his right, and Theo to his left. They all shifted their gazes toward me and the moment I met my mother's brown eyes, I knew I was in deep trouble.

"It's so nice of you to finally join us, Sarah." Even when my mother was angry she never compromised her manners, but her tone was sharp, cutting through the tense air like a knife.

"Sorry," I mumbled as I slid into the chair next to Theo. I knew that even if I told her about Mrs. Gronemyer being late my mother wouldn't take it as an excuse, so I silently slid the napkin on my empty plate out from the ring and placed it on my lap.

My parents' butler, Calvin, must have been listening through the kitchen door because the moment I was settled he came in with a serving plate of our main course. Steam rose from the roast, potatoes, and carrots. My mouth watered as I realized I hadn't eaten anything since this morning. Not on purpose of course. There were just some days when the bakery became so busy I forgot to take a moment to feed myself.

Once the table was fully set with the meal and my dad said grace, we dug in. I was thankful for the initial silence as we all savored the delicious food their chef prepared.

But then the questions started and I could feel Theo tense beside me as our dad said, "I heard that Stephanie decided to delay college a year to help out at your bakery."

My throat was dry as a bone as I tried to swallow the bite

of roast I'd just taken. Not even five minutes in and the accusatory judgments had already begun.

"Yes. The first year she worked for me, she was trying to save money so she wouldn't have to take out as many student loans. She mostly worked the register, but over the last six months she's started to help me in the back and she's been enjoying it. So she decided to stay with me another year to see if she'd rather work with me or for another bakery instead of pursuing college."

Stephanie was my cousin on my father's side from his sister. My Aunt Beatrice was similar to Theo and me in that she went against her parents' wishes and fell in love with a mechanic. My grandparents were a lot harsher when it came to their expectations of their children, so when Aunt B got married, her parents withdrew her trust fund, leaving it all to my dad. Stephanie was offered a full ride to any university she wanted from my grandparents, but she turned it down knowing just how poorly they'd treated her mother. So, her only options were to compromise her morals and take their money or save up for college on her own.

I stole a glance at my mother who'd barely taken a bite of her food. She held the stem of her wine glass, letting it hover to the right of her face as she assessed me. I immediately looked away.

"It's such a shame that my sister ruined any chances of being able to support her daughter financially. All so she could marry that man who spends more time turning a wrench under cars than he does at home."

Here we go.

I'd only been around my Uncle James a handful of times growing up because my parents didn't want Theo and me to be influenced by him. The few times I did get to spend time with him, I could see why they would be hesitant because he was everything they feared. He was raised by a single father after his mother passed away from cancer. He didn't have a penny to his name when he met my aunt, but he exuded happiness more than anyone I'd ever seen. He was the kind of person who would stop on the side of the road just to smell the wildflowers.

Seeing that he was happy without all the money and everything that came along with it had always been exciting for me to witness. And maybe my parents were right to fear that his presence would leave an impact on me…because it had.

But I knew better than to disagree with my father. My only plan for tonight was to get through dinner unscathed with my dignity intact.

Unfortunately for me, Theo had other plans. "I don't think it's a shame. Aunt B and Uncle J have one of the best marriages I've ever seen. They love each other a lot and they've raised a daughter who has a good head on her shoulders. I'm sure she'll be able to make her own way in the world."

I lowered my chin and closed my eyes. *God, Theo. Can you* not *poke the bear tonight?* I wanted to ask him, but I kept my mouth shut as I slowly opened my eyes.

My father set his fork down on his plate, gearing up for a fight. "So, you think it's a good thing that your cousin will have no monetary support for the future?" It was a calculated question.

"It wasn't Aunt B's decision to have her trust fund taken away. Grandma and Grandpa made that decision for her out of spite."

Oh, shit. The hairs on the back of my neck stood on end. Theo wasn't just searching for a fight, he was out for blood. I thought we were supposed to be a unified front tonight. Doing whatever it took to make it through with little damage. Clearly between our conversation the other day and today, he'd changed his mind.

"There are consequences for every action we take, Theodore. My sister knew the consequences of hers well before she decided to marry James. She was told on many occasions what marrying him would mean for her future and she did it anyway. Now, her daughter is paying the consequences."

Theo's lips parted with a retort, but I smacked the side of his leg under the table and he, thankfully, closed his mouth.

My dad's eyes lingered on Theo for a few moments before he reached for his glass of wine, seemingly satisfied with Theo's silence.

Just as I thought we were in the clear, my mother chimed in, "I just certainly hope you aren't making the situation worse, Sarah."

"What's that supposed to mean?" I didn't hide the edge in my voice.

"Well, it sounds like Stephanie was on the right path before spending last year working with you. I would hate for her to be led astray thinking she can make something of herself by working as a cashier in a bakery."

I didn't need a mirror to know my face was beet red with anger. This exact situation was what I'd tried to avoid my entire life. Prior to me foregoing college and deciding to give my dream a shot, I had done everything my parents asked of me. I got straight A's in school. I stayed away from drugs and alcohol. Hell, I had even planned on saving myself for marriage until I quickly realized that I was almost thirty years old and had no real prospects. But they didn't need to know that.

I did one thing outside of their requests and they've been punishing me for it for years.

I promised myself I wouldn't engage in their antics. That I would keep my head down and just get through the night, but I couldn't. Not when she was attacking the one thing that made me feel joyful and fulfilled.

"I'd hardly call working in a bakery being led astray, Mother." She hated it when I called her mother. "She's building a great skillset in public service and has started to take on more responsibilities in the kitchen. If baking is what she wants to do then she has every right to do it."

Words were our swords and the dinner table was our battleground and just as my mother was about to take another swing at me, Theo jumped in to save me.

"Just like I decided to take a detour from becoming a lawyer and will start training at the Carnelle's ranch on Monday."

I held my mother's stare up until the moment she shifted

her attention to Theo. She looked at him like he was an alien. Like there was no possible way he could be the perfect son she'd always praised for doing the right thing. I wanted to scream at her. Tell her to stop shooting daggers at my brother when he'd already sacrificed so many of his years doing what she wanted, even if it meant being unhappy.

As though her disappointment in him was too much, she simply shook her head and took a long swig of her wine.

I wondered what she would say if I told her that was improper. But I decided to save myself the headache and kept my mouth shut.

"Yes, son. That's quite the turn of events. I can't say I'm happy with your decision, especially after all the money your mother and I paid for your education. And to end up at the Carnelle's ranch of all places. I wish you would have at least chosen another place to train given the Carnelle name has been sullied."

"I figured you and mom would want me back home and being at their ranch was the only option I had."

"You could have stayed at law—"

"Of course we're happy to have you back home, honey. Obviously, we wish it would have been under different circumstances, but if this is what you have chosen to pursue then I am glad you will be close to us while doing it." My mom shot my dad a look that said the conversation was over. I knew she didn't approve of Theo's decision to leave law school, but she'd always shown favor towards him. I tried not to think too much about it, simply chalking it up to him being her firstborn.

At least her intervention gave us a small respite so I could finish my food. My dad updated us on his medical practice and mom gave us details about the renovation she started on the back patio area and rose garden. By the time we were done with the apple pie Calvin brought out to us, I was well into my second glass of wine and ready for sleep.

I gave both my parents quick hugs before Theo and I made our way out front, feeling thankful the verbal assaults only lasted a short while and I'd made it through the night with my dignity still intact.

"Well, that could have gone a hell of a lot worse," Theo's breath misted in the cold autumn air.

"Yeah. Thanks for jumping in. I thought I was going to lose my shit when they started talking about Stephanie not having a viable path in baking and that owning a business before I was thirty was equivalent to throwing my entire life away because I'm not a doctor or lawyer."

"I know they've always been on your case about that, but I want you to know that I couldn't be a prouder brother. Not just for having your own successful business, but for going against the grain. There aren't many people in this world who would have the balls to do that."

"I'm still ball-less, but I appreciate the sentiment," I laughed.

"Good point," he chuckled.

"How're the ribs?"

His hand moved over his ribcage. "They're healing nicely. I can breathe a lot better, so that's a plus."

"Breathing is good," I teased.

"Not sure how well they'll hold up this week, but time doesn't stop for no man."

I cringed. "You are so lucky mom didn't just hear that. She would swat you with a ruler for bad grammar."

He flicked the tip of my nose and I swatted his hand away.

"Just promise me you'll at least try to take it easy until you're fully healed."

"Promise."

"Good. Well, I'm going to head home and get some rest. I have an early morning tomorrow."

"Night sis." He pulled me in for a side hug before we made our way to our cars.

With the windows down and the cool air whipping my hair around, I replayed Theo's words in my mind. He was proud of me. Even though I didn't have my parents' support, having his was truly a gift.

Chapter 7

Sarah

The quiet of my home was doing nothing for the thoughts that kept running through my mind. I rolled over and checked my phone on my nightstand.

Eleven twenty-three. Ugh. I had to get up in just over five hours, but I'd already been rolling around for the past two hours with no success of feeling even an inkling of fatigue.

I grabbed my phone.

Are you awake?

Three dots appeared in the lower left of the screen.

Deacon

Yup. Just working on the cabin.

Can I come over? I need a beer.

Sure. Just drive straight out to the cabin. It hasn't rained in a while so you should be able to make it over the hills without a problem.

Okay. See you soon.

I closed my car door and looked up at the moon hanging brightly in the sky. Countless stars were shining down on me and I wished I had chosen a home where I could see them the way I could tonight. My house was everything I dreamed of on the inside. A bright white kitchen with plenty of space for me to make a mess. The living room was cozy with a large hearth where I watched the flames of fire dance on sleepless nights. But the street lights in my neighborhood made it nearly impossible to see the stars at night.

A chill settled over me and I wrapped my coat tightly around my middle before heading toward the cabin. A faint light shone inside and I could hear the sound of a hammer pulling something apart. Careful to miss the rotten floorboards on the porch, I hopped around them and clung to the doorknob as I teetered on the one good plank right in front of the door.

"You sure you shouldn't be working on the front porch

first?" I asked as I swung the door open, seeing Deacon on my left pulling wood panels off the wall. I wondered how the hell he was shirtless with the temperature being in the low sixties tonight, but then I noticed the glint of sweat shining from his skin under the work light.

He wrapped gloved hands around the wooden frame and tugged. Dust flew everywhere as the piece came loose and he tossed it onto a pile of them on the floor. Waving my hand in front of my face, I tried to keep the dust particles away from me but ended up hacking up a lung anyway.

"Sorry," he grunted before leaning over to turn on the standing fan next to him. "Come stand over here. The fan will keep the dust away from you."

I made my way over to stand next to him and the fan while he grabbed a beer from the cooler on the kitchen counter. As his arm stretched across, I noticed a brutal scar that ran from his right collarbone down over his pectoral muscle and under his ribcage area. The skin was tight and puckered with peaks and valleys. It looked like a burn and I'd only seen it once before when we had a party at the lake a few years back.

"Thank you," I said as he twisted off the top and handed me the bottle, distracting me from the thoughts of his scar.

I took a swig as I looked around the small space. The kitchen was to my left. The vinyl countertops were stained an unfortunate shade of yellow and most of the edges were peeling away. There were two empty spaces where the fridge and oven should have been and most of the tiles on the back-splash were cracked.

The rest of the place was fairly empty except for a small fireplace on the wall next to the back door.

"Um, where's the bathroom?"

"The original owners never put in plumbing even after the first renovation. There was an outhouse next to it, but I think one of the winter storms did it in because it was only a pile of broken wood when I bought the place. I'm going to get someone to come out to put in plumbing and then I'll build a small bathroom in that corner." He pointed to the opposite corner.

"And you're doing all this to turn it into an Airbnb right?"

"Yup. Badger Creek has a ton of great fly fishing. I figured this could be a good way to share a little more of our town and culture."

Deacon didn't grow up in Pebble Brook Falls like most of its residents, but he'd found a home here and I was thankful for it. We'd become good friends. The kind where there was little pressure to be anything but ourselves. And the fact that he loved our little town as much as I did made me happy he'd found peace here after being in the military and working as a firefighter.

"I think that's a great idea, Deacon. Is there anything I can help with tonight?"

"Nah. I was just wrapping up. Wanna go sit by the creek?"

"Sure!"

He grabbed the cooler and his beer while I held the back door open for him. The steps leading to the back open area were just as precarious as the front porch, but I managed to get down them without breaking a leg.

I took a seat in the oversized Adirondack chair next to Deacon's on the small dock built along the edge of Badger Creek.

"Okay, let's hear it."

I blew out a long breath, the moisture clouding in front of my face. "We had family dinner tonight. The first time in years."

"I take it things didn't go so well."

"Yeah. My parents basically insisted that I was leading my cousin, Stephanie, down the wrong path because she decided to forego college and spend another year learning the ropes with me in the kitchen. They said that I was pushing her down the wrong path."

Deacon whistled. "Damn. That's a pretty harsh statement to make. It's not like you gave her a bag of heroin or something."

"I might as well have. They've always looked down on people who don't have savory professions."

"I don't get it. You're not even thirty years old and you own a business. How is that not savory?"

"According to them owning a business without some kind of doctoral degree is risky and irresponsible. If I don't have a title with fancy letters behind my name, I'm not good enough." I spit out the words, feeling the flame of anger and resentment eat at my insides.

Deacon took a pull from his beer before resting the bottle

on the armrest of the chair. He was silent for a few moments and then he asked, "Does it bother you?"

"Most of the time I think I manage it pretty well. Knowing that I'm nothing but a disappointment to them. Sometimes I think I imagined my entire childhood because I remember a time when they didn't care what I was interested in. They never gave me doctor kit toy sets or anything like that." I laughed to myself. "The ironic thing is that my mother actually gave me my first Easy Bake Oven for Christmas one year and now she can't stand the thought of me being a pastry chef.

"I just want to live my life without judgment. I want to be free to make whatever decisions are right for me without feeling like I'm disappointing someone."

The moonlight illuminated Deacon's face and I could see the way his eyes narrowed slightly, like he wanted me to pay attention to what he was about to say. "There will never be a day on this Earth when you aren't judged for what you do, Sarah. That's the nature of being human. If you're in the presence of someone else, they will have their thoughts about how you live your life, the actions you take, and the words you say. The only thing that's in your control is whether or not you allow other people to dictate how you feel."

"I don't think I let them dictate how I feel a lot of the time."

"Yes you do," he said firmly.

I looked away from him, watching the churning water rushing over the rocks. Was Deacon right? Did I spend too much mental energy taking in what others thought of me?

As I thought back to the past year, I realized there were a lot of moments when I felt upset about my mother intervening on the biggest baking account I'd ever had. Any time I heard a customer complaining to Stephanie about one of my baked goods, I took it like a bullet to the heart. And I always made sure to do my hair and makeup before leaving for work, even if I was bone tired and needed the extra sleep.

"Okay, yeah," I said, feeling deflated. "I guess I do take on people's judgments and let them impact how I feel."

"What're you going to do about it?"

"Since you're so smart and insightful, why don't you tell me?" I raised a brow at him and he snickered.

"Well, I think you're doing good with the bakery to start. But what's something else you want to do? Something that would be just for you?"

I chewed on my bottom lip as I thought about it. The very first thing that came to mind was Ranger Adams and his delectable lips. God how I wished I could kiss those lips and feel his hands run through my hair as he pushed me against a wall and…

"Sarah?" Deacon's voice cut through my thoughts.

I cleared my throat. "I think there might be one thing."

He looked at me expectantly. Heat crawled up my neck. "You have to promise not to make fun of me."

He bobbed his head back and forth like he was playing with the idea. "Mmm. Okay. Fine. I promise not to make fun of you."

I swallowed against the knot in my throat. "I think there

might be a guy I'm interested in asking out. Or maybe not ask out, but I want him to ask me out."

"Who?"

"Ranger Adams," I whispered like my mother might hear his name all the way across town.

"He came to my bonfire two summers back, right"

I nodded.

"He seems like a standup guy. Why wait around for him to ask you out? Just do it yourself?"

"That wouldn't be weird?"

It was his turn to raise his eyebrows at me. "I thought the whole point of this exercise was to not care what others thought."

I groaned. "Why do you have to be so obnoxious?"

He shrugged. "It's what I'm good at. But seriously, if you like the guy stop fucking around and ask him out."

"Just ask him out," I repeated, mulling over the words in my mind to get used to the idea of them. "Yeah," I said after a few moments. "I can do that."

"It's settled then."

"So, I just go up to him the next time I see him and ask him out on a date?"

"Don't think too hard on it or you'll talk yourself out of it. You've made up your mind. This is what you want. Now, do it."

"Okay." I felt my head bob up and down as my mind tried to make sense of what I just agreed to. "Not going to overthink it."

"Exactly."

The look on Deacon's face told me he was sure of the decision I made and there was no reason for me to think he'd support me doing something stupid, so I let it rest. Ranger Adams was the man I wanted and if I could go against my parents and build an entire business from the ground up then there was no reason why I shouldn't allow myself to pursue Ranger.

I settled back in the chair feeling at peace with the decision. Deacon opened the cooler and grabbed himself another beer.

"How're you still shirtless? It's freezing."

"It's in the sixties," he deadpanned.

"Yes. Us normal folk consider that cold."

"Compared to the Middle East desert in the middle of winter, this is nothing."

As he leaned back, my gaze found the scar on his chest. "Are you ever going to tell me the story behind that scar?"

"Nope." He took a long pull from his beer.

Deacon never really talked about his time in the service unless he was around Johnny. Even then, they usually just made jokes about the other branches and poked fun at one another. They never talked about the pain of it all—at least not around me. So, I respected his privacy and found comfort in knowing that I had a friend in Deacon. I knew he valued that just as much as I did and the best part was that there was no pressure to talk about things we didn't want to. We could just be.

And so we spent the rest of the night sitting side-by-side staring up at the sky and at the rushing water below.

Chapter 8

Ranger

I'd lost myself in the subtle click of the tagger and hooves on dirt. We were a few days into tagging the new calves and Miles and I had found a stride. It felt like old times, working long days under the bright blue sky until every muscle in my body ached from the effort.

There was little to do in prison and even less if you wanted to stay out of trouble. Most of my days were spent working out, trying to stay strong, knowing that I would be coming home to some of the hardest work there was. The rest of my days were spent in the library working for pennies. But it helped pass the time and I was thankful to have a distraction on the hard days.

The months leading up to my release were some of the hardest. Every day dragged by for what felt like an eternity. I leaned on the visits with Miles and Callie Rose. On remembering what the fresh air smelled like. The quiet sounds of the main house first thing in the morning, when I was the only one awake and had the entire world to myself. How the colors of the sunrise melded into one another. Oranges, yellows, and reds painting a striking canvas above my family's land. My sister's laughter and my best friend's smile.

Every fucking day I clung onto those memories like they were the air in my lungs and the blood in my veins—the only things keeping me alive.

When shit went down, my first thought was hoping I survived long enough to be in this very moment with the dirt beneath my feet surrounded by the only place I wanted to come back to. Then I was out. No more time left to my sentence. No more days to count down to.

Freedom.

Hunger clawed at my stomach as I lifted my knee from the calf's shoulder and watched him trot off toward the herd.

"Ready for lunch?" I asked Miles, dusting the dirt off my jeans.

"Yeah, man. I'm starving."

We made our way to the main house where I pulled out all the fixings for turkey sandwiches, arranging them in an assembly line of sorts so Miles and I could take turns grabbing all the ingredients.

When he reached for the mustard I scowled. "Man, I don't know how the hell you can eat that shit. It's rank."

He smacked the bottom of the bottle and squirted the mustard on both slices of bread. "No, you just don't have good taste. Mustard is by far the superior condiment. Even your sister agrees."

"What?" I glared at him. Callie Rose had never eaten

mustard in my presence. She told me she hated the stuff just as much as I did.

"Yeah. While you were gone, I convinced her to try it one day on her sandwich and now she eats it all the time."

"Wait." I held up my hand. "You're telling me that while I was in prison, you corrupted my baby sister and brain-washed her into liking mustard? Fucking bastard."

He laughed before raising his mustard-laden butter knife at me and said, "I did not *corrupt* her. I merely showed her the error in her ways. I opened her eyes to the joy one has when they use mustard on their sandwich."

"Oh my God." I shook my head, feeling completely betrayed. "Just make sure you brush your teeth after you eat that foul shit. I don't want to have to smell it all day."

He snorted. "Like you have a nose good enough to smell mustard on me from that far away."

"Dude, it fucking stinks!"

Miles just shrugged before he piled up the turkey and cheese and we headed out to the front porch. We both sat in the rocking chairs my grandpa had made for him and my grandma. The walnut had held up over the years with only a few dents and scratches that made them all the better in my opinion.

The sun was straight overhead in a cloudless sky that surrounded the rolling green hills of my family's land. My mind brought me back to that night thirteen years ago. The night that almost stole this land from me.

Something heavy sat in my chest and my voice sounded thick as I spoke. "Hey, man. I don't think I've ever told you how much it means to me that you took care of this place while I was away. I don't think I'd be sitting on this porch right now if it weren't for you stepping up."

Miles just smiled at me like it was no big deal that he'd put his life on pause to make sure Callie Rose and I had a home while I was gone. "This ranch might have your name on it, brother. But this is just as much my home as it is yours. There was no way in hell I'd let us lose this place. Not as long as I had air in my lungs."

He was right. Miles had grown up on this ranch with me. I still remembered the first day I met him. I was nine years old when my father had taken me on a fishing trip to the lake when this scalawag-looking boy came barreling through the trees onto the shoreline. He was barefoot and covered in dirt, wearing only jean shorts that were cut off at the knees. He used a stick and an old rusty hook as a fishing pole that I'd thought would break the first bite he got.

But he ended up catching the biggest bass of the day and from that moment forward, we'd been best friends.

He lived with his dad who worked the night shift for a road construction company and he didn't have a clue where his mom had gone off to. His dad never liked to talk about it. So he spent most of his days on the ranch with us, learning from my dad what it meant to be a good rancher.

When my dad died, Miles took it almost as hard as I did. We had our first fistfight as two angry teenage boys who needed to get out all the hate we had towards the unjust world. We pointed it at one another for a total of five minutes before Callie Rose started yelling at us and sprayed our feral spirits down with the water hose.

Every important memory I'd ever had was with Miles.

"And it'll always be your home," I replied. "I just wanted you to know how much I appreciate what you did, taking all this on by yourself. I know it wasn't easy and there's not a whole lot I can do to repay you for that."

He rested his hand on my shoulder. "Just make sure I always have a chair on this porch and that will be repayment enough, brother."

I smiled, feeling the heaviness in my chest dissipate. "That I can do."

We sat in silence for a few moments before I leaned forward, my clasped hands falling between my legs.

"How's Callie Rose's orchard coming along?" he asked.

"It's fucking impressive. She's taken really good care of it and we were able to get all the wires set up last week, so she should be good to go for a while."

"That's awesome. I guess she has some pretty big plans for it, huh?"

"Yeah. She wants to eventually build a large barn to host wine tastings and maybe some smaller weddings. It'll be a few years before she gets it up and running, but I know once she gets the vines healthy enough to produce wine, it'll be a big hit."

"I think she told me the closest vineyard is about an hour away."

"She told me that too. All the biddies and fancy folk will love having a winery close to town. The perfect place for them to spend all that cash since there's not a place to do it downtown. Joanne's Tavern isn't exactly the place those people want to spend their Saturday afternoons."

Miles chuckled, extending his legs out so he pushed the rocking chair all the way back. "We'll have to make sure Callie Rose puts a decent price on those bottles when she gets started."

"Oh, I'll make sure of that."

Miles pulled his legs in and leaned forward to look at me. "Speaking of rich folk…Callie Rose told me about LeRoy being back in town." His gaze was steady and I already knew the question he had before he asked it. "Why didn't you say anything to me after she told you?"

I stretched my arms out and interlaced my hands behind my head before leaning back in the chair. With a deep breath, I tried to still the anger that always had a habit of immediately rising to the surface at the mention of LeRoy Cummings.

"Honestly, I just wanted to forget about it. I've avoided going to town ever since she told me last week because the thought of running into him makes me so damn angry, I worry about what I might do if I see him. It's not exactly the state I want to be in, but here we are."

Miles took a moment looking out at the fields before he turned back to me. "What do you think it will take to forgive him?"

"Forgive him?" I spat.

"Yes," he answered, a shadow passing over his face.

"Why the hell would I forgive him? He put me away for ten years, Miles."

"That's exactly why you need to forgive him. He's already taken so much from you. It's been thirteen years since everything went down and you're still harboring anger towards him. All that time you were away are years that you'll never get back. If you stay mad at him, he will continue to rob you of your present and your future."

"How am I supposed to do that? How am I supposed to let go of everything he cost me? All the years of my life that I missed out on moments just like this? Moments I lost with my sister?" My voice cracked. From anger. From sadness. Shit. I didn't know anymore. The only thing I did know was that I was starting to lose the grip I had on my dignity.

My eyelids opened wide and my nostrils flared as I sucked in a deep breath, doing everything I could not to lose my cool. I was hanging on by a damn thread and the tension was about to snap it in two.

"I know. He's a piece of shit elitist asshole who has never had to pay for the consequences of his own decisions. And I hope karma comes around and bites him in the ass one of these days if only to prevent other people from dealing with the fallout of his bad behavior. But forgiving him has nothing to do with him and I'm not saying it'll happen overnight." He pointed at the center of my chest. "It's for you, Ranger. So that you don't have to walk around with this chip on your shoulder for the rest of your life thinking that the world is out to get you or that people can't be trusted. When you forgive him, you'll be able to set all that shit free."

Free. The word clanged around in my mind. Such a simple word that had countless meanings depending on who you asked. For so long I attributed the word to the physical sense of not being bound to a cage. But maybe there was more to it. That what Miles was saying eluded to the deeper meaning. Freedom wasn't just about being able to come home again and drive my truck downtown whenever I wanted.

I hadn't realized that I'd built my own prison in my mind. Caged by anger and resentment. I tugged on the bars, but they just weren't ready to come loose yet.

"I want that," I whispered. "And I'm thankful to have you in my life to point out the fact that I need to work towards it. But I'm not there yet. I'm not even sure what it will take to get me there, but all I can do is hope that I will know when the moment comes."

He clasped my shoulder again. "And I'll be right by your side hoping with you, brother."

Chapter 9

Ranger

After a week of avoiding town, I found myself at The Roasted Bean because Callie Rose decided to drain my house of all its coffee last night when she decided to pull an all-nighter harvesting and cleaning vegetables for the weekend's farmer's market. Thankfully, Miles and I had finished tagging the new calves and I could afford to take the morning a little slower.

The small café was filled to the brim with patrons. I tried not to make my discomfort look too obvious as I stood close to the door after placing my order. Crowds had always been difficult for me and they were made even worse when I was in prison as they often meant trouble. I had to remind myself that I was a free man, no longer held behind iron bars. And these people were not a danger to me, even if some of them did look at me like I might be a threat to them.

"Ranger!" the barista called over the noise of the crowd before setting my coffee down on the counter.

Navigating my way through the bundle of people gathered by the counter, I tried not to bump into anyone.

With a quick, "Thank you," I grabbed my coffee and headed out the door. The weather was perfect with the sun shining brightly in another cloudless sky and the air was cool against my skin. Just enough to make me feel alive, but not cold enough that irritation gripped me.

Winters in the foothills were harsh and the weather forecast suggested this one was going to be rough. There was only so much fleece-lined leather gloves could do for my hands while working in the frigid temperatures.

I should have headed for my truck to get back to the ranch, but instead, I found myself walking through the door of *Sarah's Bakery*. A bell chimed above the door as I stepped across the threshold and the entire group of patrons seemed to stop and stare at me at once. I recognized several of them from my time in school, but there were a lot of faces I didn't know the names of. But the only face my gaze settled on belonged to a beautiful woman standing behind the glass case of treats. Her long brown hair was tied in a messy bun on the top of her head, loose strands of curls framed her face as she unpacked a tray of cupcakes into the case.

Something squeezed in my chest as I took in the slight rosiness of her cheeks—flushed from working hard, no doubt. I watched her delicate hands as she reached in and out of the glass case, setting each cupcake in a perfectly neat row. I wondered if it was genetics or her upbringing that made her so detail oriented and I found myself wanting to ask her. To spend the rest of my day getting wrapped up in her luscious voice as she told me about herself.

"Are you in line?" Startled, I looked down to find an elderly woman with bright red lipstick and a little too much blush on her cheeks staring up at me. Her short black hair was curled tightly to her head in ringlets that were streaked with gray.

"You can go ahead of me," I offered.

A deep scowl settled into her face as she looked me up and down before she ambled toward the checkout counter. If looks could kill, I'd be a dead man.

I took my place behind her and found myself looking for Sarah again. It was a bad idea, getting wrapped up in a woman knowing that our worlds were vastly different. She was the cream of the crop and I was just a man trying to make enough of a living to keep my ranch.

But dammit I couldn't stay away from her. Not when those beautiful lips split into a wide smile that had my heart banging against my ribs. Disappointment flashed as I watched her disappear through the swinging door behind the counter with the empty tray in her hands.

Fuck.

She was probably heading back to work on her next batch. The young girl at the cash register looked similar enough to Sarah that they could be related. With long dark hair, a pert nose, and rosebud lips. But she wasn't the woman I wanted to talk to. She didn't have the rich brown eyes that made me feel like I could conquer the whole fucking world when they settled on me.

"Do you mind waiting here for just a minute?" The girl asked the man standing in front of her. "I'll go ask Sarah when the next batch will be ready."

"That's fine, sweetheart," the man at the counter said as he leaned his weight onto his cane.

The girl disappeared through the door for a few moments and when she came back, Sarah was trailing right behind her. Those brown eyes found me and the world shifted as she stumbled to a stop. I took a step forward, my hands instinctively reaching out to catch her even though she was several feet away and there were three people and a counter between us.

The most beautiful shade of red blossomed on her cheeks as she tucked her hair behind both ears. The other girl said something to her that snagged her attention away, cleaving the moment like an axe slicing through wood.

Whatever Sarah said to the elderly man was lost on me because the only thing I could focus on was keeping my feet planted firmly on the ground. The only thing they wanted to do was move closer to her. It was a pull I'd never felt toward anything in my life. The need I felt to survive and make it back to my ranch wasn't even as strong as this and it suddenly dawned on me how fucking terrifying that was.

Time seemed to drag as the man stepped to the side of the counter, clearly waiting for something. And the woman in front of me finally placed her order before it was my turn. I glanced behind me to see if anyone was waiting and loosed a breath as I noticed it was just me tailing the line.

"Stephanie, do you mind checking on those cookies? I can take his order."

The girl, whose name was Stephanie, looked at me with a wide smile before saying, "Sure," and scurrying through the door.

"Hi," Sarah looked up at me through thick lashes, that deep blush on her cheeks remained and I felt myself wanting to reach out and feel the heat of her skin against my palm.

Instead, I dove my closed fists into my jeans pockets and said, "Hey, looks like you're pretty busy today."

She looked around the bakery, taking notice of all the tables filled with patrons. "Yeah, it's kind of surprising to be this packed on a weekday."

"Your sweets are hard to resist."

Those brown eyes widened at me and I could see the flecks of green and yellow dancing in her irises, like changing leaves on a tree falling to the earth.

"You liked the blueberry muffins then?" Her voice was barely above a whisper, but the sultry tone had my cock twitching against the fly of my jeans.

"They were the best I'd ever had. Just don't tell my sister. She prides herself in her baking skills and I wouldn't want her to feel bad." I winked at her and the smile she shot me back nearly knocked the breath from my lungs. This woman was gorgeous, but I had a feeling there was more to her than what met the eye and that meant trouble for me because I wasn't the guy a girl like her dated. Even if she did blush in my presence.

This is fun, I told myself. And that's all it could be.

She pinched her thumb and forefinger together before running them over those perfect pink lips. “My lips are sealed. I won’t tell a soul.”

For some reason, I believed her.

“What can I get you today?”

Leaning back, I looked at the case of treats even though I already knew what I wanted. “How about another dozen of those blueberry muffins?”

“Sure thing.”

I followed her to the case where she carefully crafted the box and started filling it with the muffins. “I think I saw your sister at the farmer’s market last weekend.”

“Yeah, she started taking her harvest there to sell to help fund her winery.”

“She’s opening up a winery? Here in Pebble Brook Falls?” Her voice rose an octave.

“I just finished helping her run the wire last week and she did her first pruning. I think she’ll be ready to start making wine by next fall.”

“Oh my gosh, that’s amazing. A winery would do so well here. Is she planning on offering tastings?”

“Probably not right away, but it’s definitely in her plan. She’s even talking about building an event barn to host weddings and some other events.”

“She sounds like a girl after my own heart. Who doesn’t love wine and weddings?” The moment the words left her mouth her cheeks flushed again and she looked away from me, focusing on filling the rest of the box until she placed the final one in, folded the lid down, and handed it to me.

"Thank you. And you're right you know."

She raised her eyebrows.

"About wine and weddings. Anyone who doesn't love both those things is a fool." Her entire face lit up like a sunrise breaking through the fog of a hazy morning. Beautiful. So damn beautiful.

A noise that sounded like a hog grunting caught my attention and I turned around to find the line had picked up again and all the soured faces told me if I didn't move my ass a riot might break out.

I turned back to Sarah and swiped my card. "Thanks again. The last box didn't make it through the day and I'm sure this one won't either."

"It was good to see you, Ranger." When she said my name, something in me cracked wide open like a dam breaking loose after too many years of holding the weight of rushing water. It was so startling I caught myself standing there—completely unable to move as I stared at this bright wonderful woman.

The only thing running through my mind was that if I came too close to her light, I'd ruin it. My shadows were too dark. Too fucked up.

So, I murmured another thank you and walked out of her bakery.

My pulse was quaking. I could feel it in my head, my throat, my wrists. Fuck.

I was halfway to my truck when I heard someone shout my name behind me. "Ranger!" I turned to find the very woman I was trying to avoid running directly at me. Her soft curls caught the sunlight and shimmered streaks of gold and auburn.

I shifted toward her, feeling that magnetic pull that seemed to have more control over my body than my own mind had.

When she stopped in front of me, she put her delicate hands on her hips and sucked in a lungful of air that had her dainty nose flaring slightly.

"I…um…I was wondering if I could ask you a question."

"You can ask me anything." The words were out before I had a chance to stop them.

"Would you like to go out on a date with me?"

Not the question I expected. Not even in the slightest and maybe that's why I found it difficult to speak. Or maybe it was because this woman was doing strange things to me. Making me feel like I wanted to take chances and put everything on the line.

But there was always the risk that I could lose it all. It happened once and it sure as hell could happen again. I wasn't the kind of man who had an easy go at life. Even now when the ranch was doing well, I had this feeling in my gut that it wasn't going to last long. Some ill fate would come along and swipe my slate clean. Forcing me to start over, just like I had to when I got out of prison.

There was no way in hell I was going to put this girl through that. Not a chance.

I gave myself one touch as I reached out and tucked her hair behind her ear, letting my hand trail down the side of her face. Her eyes fluttered for a moment before I pulled my hand away.

"You don't want anything to do with me, Sarah. I'm no good. Especially for a woman like you."

The devastation on her face nearly did me in, but I knew this was the right call. Sarah Williams was a well brought up woman and I was a rancher with a blighted past. She was everything I wanted, but as I turned my back on her and walked away, I knew I'd made the right decision in saving her from all the things I couldn't be for her.

Chapter 10

Sarah

After the most humiliating rejection from Ranger, I spent the rest of the week licking my wounds. Fatigue had gripped me and I was barely keeping my eyes open from throwing myself into my work. Most of my nights involved countless hours in my bakery's kitchen making way too many cupcakes. I was pretty sure I got a contact high from all the powdered sugar in the air tonight when I started talking to myself about how stupid I was for asking Ranger on a date.

"You don't want anything to do with me, Sarah. I'm no good. Especially for a woman like you."

I was embarrassed to admit how many times his words had run through my mind. *Especially for a woman like you.* What the hell did that even mean? Was he suggesting that I was a rich bitch because of my family? But then he said he wasn't any good…so, maybe he was worried that I would judge him for his time in prison.

Honestly, I wasn't sure which one was worse. Him

making assumptions about me because of my parents' money or assuming I would make assumptions about him for his time behind bars.

I made a mental note to call Deacon later and make sure he knew just how dumb his idea was. Asking a man out on a date had gotten me nowhere and it was his fault for talking me into it. I went after what I wanted and was now sitting on the floor in my living room with a half-empty bottle of wine waiting for Willow to get here so we could start working on wedding details.

Yeah. There was no way I would take Deacon's advice ever again.

The turn of a key sounded at my front door. I slowly rose to my feet, careful not to tip over the wine on my white rug as I made my way to the door.

"Sarah!" Willow bellowed as she swung the door open. Her arms were full of glossy magazines and a wooden box sat at the very top of the pile.

"Oh my God! How'd you make it in here with all that?"

She peeked at me over the top of the box and said, "Very, very carefully."

We both giggled and it felt *good* to have my friend here. She was always the best distraction and I was sorely in need of one tonight.

I took the top half of the pile from her and we set them down in the living room before I snagged her a wine glass from the kitchen. When I walked back into the living room she held up the bottle of wine and arched a brow. "Looks like you already got started without me."

"Sorry. It was a rough week and the wine was calling my name." I handed her the empty glass and she poured herself some.

We sat cross-legged across from one another with the magazines between us. She handed me the bottle and I topped my glass off before settling in.

"Okay, before we get into the magazines, I need to give you something."

"Okay," I drew out the word.

She grabbed the wooden box from the top of the magazines and handed it to me. On top of the lid in hand-painted letters was: *I can't say "I do" without you.*

Tears pricked at my eyes as I realized what this box meant. "Go on. Open it," she whispered and I could hear the emotion in her voice too.

I slid the top off and nestled in a bed of crinkle paper was a beautiful wine glass and matching champagne flute that had deep reds, yellows, and greens blown into the surface with a gold rim on the top. Beside them was a burgundy jewelry box and a stationary envelope lay just below it. I opened the card, blinking away the tears so I could see better.

Sarah,

It's hard to believe just how far we've come in life together. I will never forget the first day I met you and how I was sitting all alone in the lunch room and you decided to take a chance on me. I will never be able to repay you for the kindness you showed me as a little girl, knowing just how different I was from you. But I promise to love you as my best friend every single day. It would be my honor to have you stand next to me as I marry Johnny. You believed in our love, even when I didn't and there's no one else I'd rather have by my side.

Love,

Willow

I was full-on ugly crying as I looked up at Willow. She had the same tears running down her face as I set the box aside and tackle-hugged her. "Of course I'll be there with you!"

We both laughed, rocking back and forth as we hugged each other fiercely. I wiped the tears from her face and squished her cheeks between my palms. "I'm so freaking excited, Willow! You're getting married! And I get to be the sexy bridesmaid standing next to you." My hands fell from her face. She caught them, cradling them with her own in the space between our crossed legs.

"Bridesmaid? No." She shook her head. "You're my maid of honor, Sarah."

"Well, shit. I like the sound of that. Maid of *honor*. Yup. Definitely has a ring to it." We both laughed again before settling next to each other, our backs leaning against the edge of the sofa.

I grabbed our glasses of wine from the small serving tray on the floor and handed hers to her. She took a long sip, eyeing me over the rim of the glass. "Alright. We need to catch up before we do any wedding stuff. I feel like I've barely seen you lately."

"I know," I groaned. "The bakery is doing great. Even during the weekdays, there seems to be a never-ending flow of people. It's awesome."

"That makes me so happy! I remember how bummed you were when you lost Tommy's birthday account. I still can't believe your mom called his mother and told her she should get his cake done by someone else."

Heat crept up my neck. "I haven't even told you about Sunday night's dinner last week."

Willow's nose scrunched. "Sunday night dinner? I didn't think y'all still did that."

"We don't. But the moment Theo came back to town, my mother decided it was going to be a thing again."

Her eyes widened. "How is Theo by the way?"

"If you disregard his three broken ribs, I'd say he's doing great."

"Holy shit. Three?"

I nodded as I took a sip of wine. "I don't love that my brother is doing something so dangerous, but he looks happier than I've ever seen him and I know he would have been miserable if he completed law school."

"Yeah, he's never really been the intense type. I'm

surprised your parents pushed him to pursue that when it's so obvious he doesn't have the personality for it."

"I don't think they've ever taken us into consideration when they started planning our lives. But at least he's doing what he wants now instead of pursuing something that would never make him happy."

"I think you showed him that path, Sarah. When you went against everything you knew and followed your heart, it showed everyone in your life that nothing was impossible. I think Theo saw your success despite having no support from your parents and decided he wanted that for himself too. What you've done is inspiring." She gripped my hand.

"It still makes me so angry that they can't accept it. We basically spent the entire dinner fighting about how they think I'm leading Stephanie down the wrong path because she decided to stay here and pursue baking instead of going off to college." I rolled my eyes, feeling the frustration from that night simmering in my chest.

"It's not right that they're blaming you for that. Especially when it's Stephanie's decision to make, not yours. The only thing you've done is provide her support."

"Yup." My lips popped at the word. I stretched my legs out in a V shape as I rubbed my open palm along the top of my thighs.

"Did your mom bring up the dating thing again?" Willow asked.

I shook my head. "Thankfully, dinner had wrapped up before then."

"Well, that's good at least."

It had been a while since my mother brought up my dating life because the last conversation we had about it in the early summer months had turned into a drag-out fight. She didn't have to tell me that it was abnormal for a woman to be without a partner at my age. Or that I should be focusing on finding someone suitable. My loneliness was something I was very much acquainted with and her pointing it out had been too much. I didn't like the fact that I yelled at her and stormed out of her house, but I couldn't take it anymore—all the judgment and disappointment I felt anytime she looked my way.

"What's wrong?" Willow asked.

"I asked someone on a date," I said quietly, picking at a loose string on the edge of the sofa cushion.

Willow scooted closer. "Um, tell me more."

I sighed heavily, setting my glass of wine on the tray. "Do you remember Ranger Adams?"

"The guy who was released from prison?"

"Yeah."

"Mmhmm. I remember him. You asked him out?"

"Yeah."

A smile spread across her lips. "And…?"

"And he rejected me."

Willow leaned back like my statement had felt like a slap in the face. "He rejected you?" she repeated.

"Yeah. He came into the bakery yesterday and I don't know…I thought I felt something between us. It felt like he was interested, but when I chased him down the street and asked him on a date he said no."

"Was that all he said?"

"He said something about him being no good for a girl like me. I mean what the hell does that even mean?"

Willow draped her arm over the sofa cushion, settling her chin in her palm as she thought about it. "I don't think it was a personal attack against you. If anything, it sounds like he was ragging more on himself than you, which I kind of understand. He's the town's badboy and you come from a notoriously blue blood family. He probably thinks there's no way you'd actually be into him."

"That's a good point. I didn't think of it that way."

"But he's still lame for not accepting your date offer." She leaned toward me, grabbing both my hands. "I know you'll meet your match soon. I can feel it."

I didn't have the heart to say out loud that I thought I might have met my match with Ranger. Not that I knew a lot about the man, but I'd always felt intrigued by him. Almost like there was some intangible pull toward him and I thought for sure that he felt it too.

But maybe Willow was right. It wouldn't be the first time someone assumed things about me because of my last name.

"Thank you for saying that." I smiled at her. "But enough about me. Let's talk about your freaking *wedding*!"

"Eek!" we both squealed in unison before we grabbed the piles of magazines and started flipping through the pages where she showed me the color palette she was thinking of and some different cake ideas.

"Do you have any idea what kind of flavors you and Johnny are thinking about?"

"He said he wants something with strawberries in it and you know how I feel about strawberries." She opened her mouth and stuck her finger in while making a gagging noise.

I couldn't help the snort-laugh that came out of me. "To be fair, it's his wedding too. You have to give the man something."

"Yeah. I know." She rolled her eyes dramatically. "But I'm obsessed with your cookies and cream icing."

"I can do different cake and icing flavors for the different tiers you know."

Her eyes lit up. "I hadn't thought of that! So we can do alternating tiers?"

"Yeah," I laughed.

"See. This is why you're my maid of honor. There's no way I would have thought of that."

"I still think you should both do a tasting. I've been working on some different flavors that I haven't released with my cupcakes yet."

"Okay!" she beamed. "That's going to be Johnny's favorite part of the entire planning process."

"The food usually is."

We spent the rest of the night giggling over wedding details and where they might go for their honeymoon. And for the rest of the night, I didn't think about what I was lacking or how I didn't have a love like hers and Johnny's because I had my best friend and that was enough.

…for now.

Chapter 11

Sarah

Un-freaking-believeable.

Willow and Johnny weren't able to make our annual trip to the state fair because their dog, Asher, decided to eat a poisonous skink and was barfing all over the place. She assured me he would be okay, per the vet, but that he was pretty dehydrated and they didn't want to leave his side.

Groaning, I laid my head back on my car seat headrest. I couldn't believe that little stinker ruined our tradition by eating a shiny lizard. The next time I saw him I was going to have a talk with him about his dietary habits.

Not that I could be too mad. As far as dogs went, Asher was the most beautiful yellow lab I'd ever seen with big golden eyes that would make even the toughest of hearts crack.

But still my night was ruined.

The stark reality of my loneliness was hitting me square in the face as I sat in my car in the grass parking lot of the state fair. When Willow had come back to Pebble Brook Falls two summers ago, we'd established a yearly tradition of going to the state fair together. Corny as it was, the fair was one of my favorite events. It symbolized the fall season with the bright lights, obnoxious sounds, caramelized apples, and cute animals in the petting zoo.

I'd gone every year since I was a kid and I was looking forward to having another year with my closest friends.

Even Deacon had to dip out because of some issue with the cabin that he couldn't delay fixing.

For several minutes I just stared at the entrance of the fair, watching all sorts of people walk through. Groups of teenagers huddled together while young parents tried to keep their toddlers from running too far. There were even some elderly couples, linked arm-in-arm, making their way through the line.

"Screw it," I mumbled to myself as I grabbed my small crossbody and headed toward the entrance.

My phone pinged and I grabbed it from my purse to see a text from Willow.

Willow

I promise we won't miss your birthday celebration at the apple orchard. Sorry again about tonight.

It's okay. I decided to go by myself. Send me updates on Asher!

Will do. Eat a funnel cake for me!

Oh, I most certainly was going to eat a funnel cake. And just because I was here all alone, I might even have two.

After I paid for my ticket, I found the first food stand selling funnel cakes. "Can I have a little extra powdered sugar on top?"

The booth attendant looked irritated by my request, but I shot him a warm smile and he piled on the sugar. I was usually able to resist sweet treats since I was normally elbow-deep in batter and icing most days. But there was something so special about eating funnel cakes at the fair—I couldn't resist them.

With my sugary fried batter in hand, I made my way through the alleys of the fair. Joy filled my chest as I took in the bright lights and felt the crisp air against my cheeks. Fall was magical and even though I was alone amongst a sea of people, I felt like I belonged here. Like this moment was mine to savor.

Maybe that was how I found myself face-to-face with my childhood arch nemesis, the Ferris wheel and felt invigorated to take on the challenge of facing my fear of heights. I didn't let myself overthink it, I just showed the attendant my ride band around my wrist and wound through the zigzag line.

I arrived just in time for the next round of people to board.

"Are you alone?" The second attendant asked me right before he looked over his right shoulder and spit on the ground.

I cleared my throat, trying to prevent myself from gagging. "Yup," was all I could manage to get out.

With a sweep of his arm, he directed me to the next open cab. As I slid across the bench seat, nerves fluttered in my stomach from the swinging of the cab.

This was a bad idea, I thought as I made the grave mistake of looking up and realizing that I would soon be at the very top of the Ferris wheel.

Just as I turned to the attendant to tell him I wanted to get off, a large body slid next to me.

Ranger.

Holy shit. Ranger Adams was sitting next to me on the Ferris wheel. How the hell did he sneak in? I didn't see him anywhere in the line.

The attendant pulled the bar down and latched it into place, forcing Ranger to adjust as his large thighs were nearly hitting the bottom edge of the bar.

I squeaked as the Ferris wheel jolted forward and our cab, which I quickly assessed to be a little rusted and unkempt, was starting to sway forward and backward. There was no getting out of this now.

"Nervous?" Ranger's husky voice was close to my ear. Grasping onto the bar, I settled back, feeling my shoulders meet his outstretched arm that was draped along the back of the cab. It was the first time I'd seen him without his cowboy hat since two summers ago at Deacon's bonfire. Dark curls fanned out underneath his backward baseball cap. A black letter F outlined in white was stitched into the center of the red back strap. I wondered if he was a

Falcons fan or if it was just a hat someone else gave to him.

I felt myself settle into his warmth as I looked up into those stormy eyes. "I'm, um, not the best with heights."

His throaty laugh wrapped around me like a velvet blanket. "Why would you choose the Ferris wheel of all rides to get on alone then?"

We were still only a few feet from the ground as the attendant was loading people into the cab behind us, but my stomach still felt uneasy. "I thought I was feeling brave, but now that I'm here, I'm finding myself regretting my decision."

Maybe it was my anxious mind playing tricks on me, but I swore he leaned towards me as he said, "Don't worry, Sarah. I won't let anything bad happen to you."

The crinkles on the edges of his eyes softened and I found myself unable to look away from him. From the beauty and pain that reflected back at me. Ranger Adams was the most incredible man I'd ever seen. It was true when I was a teenager and it was true now.

Countless questions clamored through my mind. I wanted to know this man. To understand what made him tick.

But the only words that stumbled from my lips were, "I'm sorry I asked you out the other day."

The faint smile on his lips was clouded by the shadow of a frown as he turned away from me, staring at a random spot in front of us. Worry that I'd said the wrong thing clawed at my insides, making the already present anxiety much, much worse.

Just as I opened my mouth to take it back, I felt Ranger's thumb skim the top of my shoulder and then he turned those blue eyes back on me.

"I shouldn't have walked away from you like that. You deserve better. Better than I could ever give you."

Willow was right. When he'd denied me, it had nothing to do with me at all. Ranger didn't think he was good enough and knowing that made my heart hurt because he was so blindly unaware of just how much I wanted him.

"How do you know what you can give me if you don't even try?"

"I'm not like the people you grew up with, Sarah. I spend most of my days in dusty old boots, herding cows. Until recently, I wasn't even sure if I was going to be able to keep my family's land. I don't have anything to give you."

"The only thing I want from you, Ranger, is *you*."

"Sarah…" My name was a prayer on his lips and when he stroked his fingers along the crook of my neck and shoulder, chills bloomed over my entire body.

I closed my eyes, soaking in the feeling of his palm splaying against the back of my neck, his fingertips playing with my hair. I had no idea it could feel like this. A simple touch that brought my entire body to life as though I'd never truly felt anything until this very moment.

When I opened my eyes, devastation was written across his face. Emotion made my words feel thick on my tongue as I reached for his other hand, feeling just how small mine was compared to his. "Please tell me you feel this…this, *pull* between us. And if you don't, I promise I won't ever ask you out again or make this a big deal."

Back and forth, my gaze searched his and I realized this was the bravest I'd ever been. Braver than when I distanced myself from my family to pursue what made my heart happy. Braver than facing any of my basic fears, like getting on this damn Ferris wheel.

Laying myself bare to someone I felt such a strong connection toward with the risk of being rejected a second time felt…*terrifying*. But here I was, doing the damn thing because I could see how I affected him by the way he looked at me with such adoration it knocked the air from my lungs.

I could see the battle playing out in his mind—for reasons completely unknown to me, he was fighting this and I hated it.

When he finally spoke, I let loose the breath I was holding. "Sarah, I can't pretend that I haven't been through some shit in my life and a lot of those things have left scars on me that I'm not sure will ever go away. I've been fucked up in ways I can't even pretend to understand. I'm not the kind of man your mother would want you bringing home." He ran his fingers along the bottom edge of my jaw, his gaze dropping to my parted lips for a single moment before he looked at me again. "If you can honestly say you can look past all of that, then I'd be fucking honored to take you on a date."

Elated words were on my tongue just as the Ferris wheel slammed to a halt and our cab swung wildly back and forth, back and forth. I felt my eyes go wide, realizing just how high we'd gotten during our conversation. All the fear that had somehow taken a backseat came rushing back, making my stomach do somersaults as I made the fatal mistake of looking down.

"Oh. My. God!" With one hand, I grabbed the side of the cab that was still rocking out of control and my other hand landed on Ranger's thigh.

Oh no. That is not *his thigh.*

My cheeks flamed red as I looked at where my hand had firmly grasped his crotch and beneath my palm I could feel his reaction to my touch flexing.

"Ah!" I yanked my hand away, covering my face that I was sure rivaled the red of a bell pepper. But when I looked down again, the swirl of fear had my heart bursting from my chest.

"This was a bad idea. Bad. Bad. Bad," I murmured to myself over and over again, frozen in a swinging metal contraption with a man whose crotch I invaded because I can't handle heights.

"Sarah," Ranger said, tightening his arm around my shoulders.

I was too embarrassed to look at him so I settled for squeezing my eyes shut so I didn't go into a full-blown panic attack.

"Sarah," he said again, gentler this time. Then I felt a calloused palm against the side of my cheek as he slowly angled my face to the right.

"Open your eyes, beautiful."

I took a moment to focus on his voice, letting it calm my

nerves before I slowly peeled my eyes open to find him smiling at me.

When I shifted to look down again, he whispered, "No. Just look at me."

Those blue eyes dipped to my lips and maybe it was the adrenaline spike that had me doing crazy things, but I kissed him. His lips were firm at first like I'd completely taken him by surprise, but then they softened and butterflies soared through me as he pulled me in close, wrapping his strong arms around me.

Soft curls met my fingertips as I wove my hands around the nape of his neck, drawing him closer as I opened myself to him. The warmth of his tongue against mine had me pressing my thighs firmly together as heat pooled in my center. As if a strike of lightning struck me from the sky, I felt electrified by his touch.

The swinging of the cab, the bright lights of the fair and the murmur of the crowd below us drifted away. He was the only thing that existed in my world and I didn't want it to end.

Chapter 12

Ranger

Sarah's lips weren't made for this earth with their softness and taste of sweet honey. If heaven ever existed, it was right here with this woman who smelled of powdered sugar and spice. My own special treat, like nothing I'd ever had before.

My hands shook as we came up for air. Her lids were heavy with the same emotion I felt taking hold of my entire body.

"Wow," she whispered. "That was incredible."

Pinching her chin between my thumb and forefinger, I tilted her head back and pressed my lips to hers once more.

So sweet.

Everything about her was decadent. I found myself overwhelmed by it all. It wasn't supposed to be this good because simply kissing a woman never had been before. But Sarah was different. *I* was different when she was around and there was no more denying that. Hell. There was no more denying that I couldn't stay away from this woman, no matter how scared I was that she was going to use me up and toss me to the side once she took longer than a moment to see who I truly was.

I stomped those thoughts out though because the fear didn't matter anymore. Sarah lassoed my heart with that kiss and I'd follow her down whatever path she wanted to lead me.

"Ride's over. Time to get off," the attendant shouted a little too close and when he tried to unlatch the metal bar, I shot him a look that told him to think better of it. Eyes wide, he took a step back with his hands up.

I looked back to Sarah. "Ready?" I asked.

She just nodded with a smile that touched a part of my heart I wasn't sure still existed. Wrapping my hand around the back of her head, I pulled her close to me and pressed my lips to her forehead before I reached to my right and unlatched the metal bar. I kept the cab steady as she made her way off the ride and towards the crowd.

She looked back at me, that smile broadening. "Come on."

When I got to her, she slipped her hand in mine and I was sure nothing else had felt so right in my entire life. That voice in the back of my head told me to be wary. That this wouldn't last long because nothing good ever lasted for people like me. There would certainly be something that stole her away from me and I would be left to pick up the pieces, just like I always was.

For this one night, I could give myself the freedom to

enjoy it. Even if tomorrow meant she would wake up and realize the mistake she made in wanting me.

"What brought you to the fair tonight?" she asked as we wove through the throng of people dashing toward the rides and various game booths.

Normally, I would have made up some generic response, but those big brown eyes were filled with genuine curiosity and I couldn't resist her. "When I was in prison, I made a promise to myself that, once I got out, I would make the best of my life. I wouldn't sit around and sulk over the years I lost. If there was something that came along that I felt I wanted to do, I would do it."

"Except go on a date with me." She arched a brow and narrowed her eyes on me, making me laugh.

"Yeah, you got me there. I did deny myself a date with you."

She stopped walking. "Why? Why would you break the promise you made to yourself?"

"Because you terrify me, Sarah."

"Terrify *you*?"

I tucked a lock of hair behind her ear. "Yes." I ground my molars together. "I don't know what it is about you, but no matter how hard I try I can't seem to stay away from you. Ever since I saw you at Deacon's bonfire two summers ago, I've done everything in my power to keep my distance."

"Why would you do that?" She grabbed my hand and held it to the side of her face.

"Because the thought of having you means there's a possibility that I can lose you. And for some reason, the idea of losing you makes me feel fucking crazy. So, I stayed away for as long as I could. Letting myself admire you from a distance. But…"

"But you couldn't stay away anymore."

"Exactly."

She stepped toward me and the entire world seemed to slow around us. Rising onto her tiptoes, she placed an open palm on my chest that sent a cascade of heat through my body. "I'm glad you didn't stay away, Ranger," she whispered, her lips grazing my ear. "And I don't care what people might say about us because I want you too."

When she nipped the edge of my earlobe with her teeth, I almost picked her up, threw her over my shoulder, and ran back to my truck. But I remembered what she'd said to Deacon a few weeks ago when I walked into her bakery. If she was telling him the truth about being a virgin, I was going to have to walk a fine line because there was no way in hell I was going to let myself ruin such an important experience for her even if my dick was straining so hard against my jeans I thought it might fall right off.

"It's settled then."

"What is?" she asked.

"This will be our first date."

She threw her head back and laughed. "Oh no. This"—holding my hand, she extended her arm and did a little twirl—"is not our first date, Ranger. This is a happy coincidence. If you want me, you're going to have to take me on a real date."

"Is that right?"

"Mmhmm."

The balls of her cheeks tightened as she bit her bottom lip, trying not to smile. She was so damn cute, I wanted to eat her up.

I tugged on her hand until she fell into me. When she was pressed against my chest, I slid my hand along the side of her neck, rubbing my thumb along the edge of her jaw.

"Sarah Williams, will you go on a date with me?"

A single, breathy word left her lips. "Yes."

I pressed a kiss to her temple. "Now it's settled."

"Indeed."

With a tilt of her head, those lips I dreamed of were merely an inch from mine. "And now it's time for me to kick your ass in some arcade games," she challenged before leaning away so I couldn't kiss her.

"You're going to be the end of me," I groaned as she slipped her hand back in mine and we started walking.

"No, Ranger. I think I'm going to be your beginning."

The flutter in my heart told me she might be right.

"I don't understand how you're so good at this." I shot Sarah a questioning look as I handed the attendant a five-dollar bill.

"This time I'm going for the big tiger." She'd already won five medium-sized stuffed animals that she traded in for an extra-large dolphin.

"There's no way you're going to win this one. Those clowns are all rigged." She tossed the red ball into the air in front of my face before catching it again. This was the last game on her list and I knew from experience it was basically impossible to win. The balls weren't nearly heavy enough to knock down the clowns that were filled with sand. It would take serious speed and hitting them in the exact spot to knock them over.

"Watch and learn, cowboy." She winked at me before she wound up her arm and threw the ball like a fucking softball star, nailing the first clown pin just above where the neck tapered. It went down with a thud.

"Shit," I muttered.

Within thirty seconds the other four clowns were toast. The attendant looked irritated, rolling his eyes at Sarah as he reached for the long pole to unhook the huge tiger hanging from the wall.

Sarah jumped up and down, clapping like a fiend as the attendant gave her the stuffed animal.

"See?" She waved the tiger back and forth. "Told you."

I chuckled as I grabbed her dolphin from the counter and we started walking off. "Who taught you how to throw like that?"

"My older brother, Theo. Do you remember him from high school? I think he was in the grade right below yours."

"Yeah. Blonde hair. Looks like a Viking giant?"

"Yup, that's him."

"I remember him playing almost every sport there was in high school."

She nodded. "He was good at everything. Still is. When he got into football and baseball, I was his throwing partner. He would get so upset when I couldn't throw the balls straight to him. He taught me so he wouldn't have to chase them all over the yard. When I got the direction down, he helped me gain some power behind the throws."

"You're full of surprises." I draped my arm around her shoulders, pulling her into me as we slowly walked toward the exit.

"What's surprising about a girl throwing a ball well?"

"Not a thing. I think it's sexy as hell." She looked to the side with a demure tilt of her lips.

"I'm just surprised that it wasn't your dad who was helping Theo with his sports training."

The corners of her lips drew downward and her shoulders sagged under my arm.

I stopped, placing my hands on her shoulders, I turned her so she was facing me. "Hey, if there's ever a question I ask that you don't want to answer just give me the word."

Familiar with the weight of other people's assumptions and prying, I never wanted to make her feel like she didn't have to appease me by responding. But I hoped she would trust me.

"No, it's okay. I want to tell you." She sighed as she twirled a strand of her hair between her fingers. "It's just that I didn't have the easiest relationship with my parents growing up. Actually…nix that. I *still* don't have the best relationship with them."

When she reached for my hand and intertwined her

fingers with mine, something eased inside of me. And when she started walking toward the exit again, I followed.

“Theo was always an active kid. Like you said, he played every sport available and he was great at everything. But our parents had a plan for him and becoming a pro-athlete was not part of the plan. The only reason they let him play sports was because he made a deal with them. If he didn’t get straight A’s in every class, he was banned from playing altogether.”

“Damn. That’s a pretty intense stipulation to put on a kid.”

She huffed, her tiny nostrils flaring slightly. “You have no idea. I can still remember walking into his room in the morning and his face would be glued to an open textbook. He worked himself into the ground to uphold his end of the bargain.”

“I’m guessing they did the same thing to you?”

“They still do it. If they had their way, I wouldn’t be working as a bakery owner. Instead, I would have letters behind my name or I would be married with three children to someone who did.”

“You wouldn’t be happy living like that.” This was the first night we’d spent together and I already knew my statement was true. Sarah was sweet and kind, but I could see the wild behind those dark eyes—like a stallion wanting to run the plains.

“No,” she said with a breath. “I wouldn’t.”

“I can’t say I fully understand what you go through having parents who want you to be something you’re not.

But I can tell you that there's freedom in chasing after who you are and I hope you never lose sight of that."

"Wow." She smiled widely at me.

"What?" I laughed.

"I think I really like you, Ranger Adams."

I swallowed hard and pulled her into my chest. I didn't have the courage yet to tell her how much I liked her too because guys like me never ended up with girls like her. There was no disputing the constant reminder in the back of my mind telling me that this was fleeting and to hold onto her for as long as she'd let me.

Chapter 13

Sarah

I had no idea how I got here in such a short amount of time. I'd gone from a lonely single woman who was desperate enough to consider asking her best guy friend to pop her cherry to riding in a classic Chevy truck with a tall dark and handsome man who smelled like leather and fresh-cut grass.

I was in heaven.

Willow and I had gushed over Ranger when she came to my house tonight to help me get ready for our first date. I told her about the kiss and how I felt like I was floating on clouds ever since. She laughed, of course, and asked for every naughty detail. Then I told her to thank Asher for me because if he hadn't eaten that skink, I probably wouldn't have experienced the best kiss of my life.

"Where are you taking me?" I asked Ranger because the roads were starting to look unfamiliar.

He slid his gaze toward me and my stomach did a flip. "It's a surprise."

"I'm not very good with surprises," I grumbled.

His deep, raspy laugh made my heart squeeze. "Why not?"

I sighed, dramatically. "It's the anticipation. It eats me alive."

"I think I like getting under your skin." He shot me a wink and I turned to puddy in his passenger seat.

After a few more turns, we ended up on a dirt road with no street lights. About a half-mile down, there was a large cabin-looking structure with a bright neon sign that read *Cowboys*. The parking lot was filled with pickup trucks and a few motorcycles.

"Oh my God! Are we going line dancing?" I squeaked, sitting tall in the seat to get a better look through the hazy windows of the establishment.

"Cats out of the bag." He found a spot at the end of the lot and came around to open my door. "Are you excited?" He looked at me under the brim of his black cowboy hat, the boyish grin tugging on his lips pulled at my heart-strings.

"I've always wanted to go line dancing."

"You never have before?"

"Nope. My mother always told me that real ladies don't line dance, they waltz."

Ranger snorted. "I'm pretty sure that sentiment is outdated, sugar. I can promise you, there will be plenty of *ladies* in there line dancing."

Sugar.

The man just called me sugar and now my entire body

felt like it was taking flight—lifted into the air on butterfly wings with a simple word.

"Ready?" he asked.

"Mmhmm," I replied, even though I had no idea how I was going to make it out of his truck without falling because my legs felt like they were tingly all over. I had no idea how one person could have such an impact on me, but here I was completely enthralled by his charm.

I didn't have to worry about my legs spontaneously deciding to stop working because Ranger grasped my waist, picked me up, and set me right in front of him like I was just a barrel of hay that he could maneuver easily. His calloused palms stayed on my hips, grazing over the sliver of skin between my jeans and my flannel.

My core clenched when his tongue darted between his lips, those stormy blue eyes growing hazy.

"Kiss me," I whispered, needing to feel this man's lips against my own.

He studied me for a moment before he took off his cowboy hat, his black curls falling into his face. I stepped into him, feeling the heat from his body as I rose onto my tiptoes and draped my arms over his shoulders.

With a hand on my lower back, he brought me closer until I could feel the steady rise and fall of his chest against my own. His heartbeat clamored against his ribs, matching the wild rhythm of my own heart.

When his thumb found my bottom lip, a shooting star couldn't rival the burning heat of my body when his lips met mine. He took his time, holding me tighter like he was afraid I might disappear if he loosened his grip.

Somehow I knew that this was what I had waited for. I hadn't simply chosen to be alone to focus on my career. I was waiting for a man to come along who made me feel like I wouldn't survive without his touch. When Ranger's hands came to grasp each side of my face as our lips parted, I knew this was what I'd wanted all along. And maybe my younger self knew it too as I watched him from a safe distance. Waiting for him to see me too.

The space between us grew shorter as he inhaled deeply, his broad chest widening. "I wish I could do that all night," —he tucked a piece of hair behind my ear—"but I promised you a date."

"Right," I grinned, burying my face in his chest. "Maybe we should go do that."

He reached around me to grab his cowboy hat from where he placed it on the passenger seat before taking my hand and shutting the door.

"Is this your first time line dancing?" His large hand enveloped mine as we started walking toward the entrance.

"I used to do it a lot with my sister. We learned from our parents when we were kids. Almost every night, they'd turn up some country music while my mom cooked dinner and they'd always end up dancing around the kitchen. When my dad passed away, Callie Rose and I kept up the tradition until I went away. I haven't danced since I got out."

My heart broke for him, hearing that prison had stalled something he clearly loved. I only knew what the townsfolk whispered about him because I tried my best to stay away from the news. Watching it had always made me feel angry and sad. But now I wished I had paid better attention to his trial all those years ago because while there were certainly people who thought he belonged behind bars, I couldn't help but feel they were wrong about him.

The questions bounced around in my mind. I hoped I would get the chance to hear his side of the story one day, but I wasn't going to ruin our first date by probing about his past.

So I squeezed his hand and said, "Thank you for choosing to dance with me tonight."

He let go of my hand and wrapped his arm around my shoulders. "I'm just glad you said yes."

I bumped him with my hip. "You knew I'd say yes. I was the one who asked you out first."

He winced. "Why don't we just pretend that I did the right thing and asked you on a date the morning I bombarded you at your bakery?"

Through tight lips, I sucked in a lungful of air. "I don't know if I can give you that one. I think you might need to live with the regret for a little while longer."

His laugh was warm. "I can handle that."

Sweat trickled down my spine, a wide smile parted my lips and I was almost out of breath as *Watermelon Crawl* came to its final note and the DJ started with Tim McGraws's *Something Like That*.

"I need a drink!" I shouted over the rising music to Ranger. A sliver of his tan chest peeked through the V of his flannel where the top two buttons were undone. Sweat glistened on his skin and I found myself wanting to press my tongue against him to see what he tasted like.

He grabbed my hand and guided me through the crowd to the bar and I admired his tight ass the entire way. I couldn't help but wonder what it would feel like to have him deep inside me while I reached around and dug my fingernails into one of his firm cheeks.

Shit.

I was already sex crazed over this man and the only thing we'd done so far was kiss. But those kisses had blown my world to bits and I only wanted him to show me more of what he could do.

"What do you like to drink?" Ranger asked as his hand slid around the curve of my waist, his fingers wound through the belt loop of my jeans. Every bit of my concentration went to that small area of my body where his thumb started roaming over my hip.

I cleared my throat, trying to knock myself from the daze his touch brought over me. "I'll have ginger ale and Captain Morgan."

"A rum girl?" Those bright blue eyes shone with amusement like I surprised him.

Avoiding the heat of Ranger's gaze, I looked to the bartender as she made her way over to us. "The combination tastes like cream soda."

"Two ginger ales with Captain Morgan, please." He shot me a wink before sliding his credit card to the bartender. "And you can close it out."The bartender nodded as she grabbed his card and started on our drinks.

"Having fun?"

He leaned an elbow on the bartop and settled his foot on the footrest at the bottom of the bar. I couldn't help myself as I took in the full power of his stature. Even though the bartop was high and deep, Ranger made it look like it was child-sized and I found myself wondering what it might be like to be held beneath that much power. If the tingling sensation between my thighs was any indication, I suspected it would be fucking amazing.

"I am," I smiled up at him. "I feel like I've been missing out on something special my entire life."

His laugh skated over my skin like velvet as I watched his Adam's Apple bob up and down. "Next time you see your mom you'll have to tell her that ladies do, in fact, line dance."

Rolling my eyes, I snorted. "I don't think that would go over too well. Best to keep this secret between us."

When I looked back at him, his eyes were questioning and a flurry of nerves took over me as I realized what I'd said. My mother was the last person I wanted to think about tonight and I silently hoped he wouldn't find the need to start asking questions.

His hand shifted upward from my hip along the edge of my rib cage, leaving a trail of fire in its wake before I felt the rough callouses of his palm settle on the nape of my neck. He pulled me into him, the brim of his black cowboy hat grazing my cheek as he leaned his lips to my ear. “Here’s to hoping we have a lot more secrets to share.”

Shivers coursed over my entire body as his lips found the bottom of my neck. When he pulled away, his eyes had shifted from vivid blue to a stormy gray so beautiful they rivaled the winter clouds hanging over the Blue Ridge Mountains.

“Here you ago.” I jumped at the sound of the bartender’s shrilly voice and backed away from Ranger’s warmth.

“Thanks,” I muttered, wrapping my hands around the cool glass as I tried to reel myself in. But there was no use as Ranger gripped my right hip, rotating me around until my back was flush against him. He draped an arm over the side of my shoulder, letting his hand settle on my opposite hip. I was trapped against him and yet I’d never felt more alive as I let myself settle into his hold.

I let my head fall against his chest as I slowly sipped on my drink, wondering how in the hell it had taken me this long to realize what a pivotal piece of my life was missing. If this was what it felt like to fall for someone, I didn’t want to stop.

I’d chased a singular dream for the better part of my life, never letting myself want for anything else. Maybe I thought it was too selfish. To have grown up with such privilege and have the ability to start my own business. But this moment, feeling Ranger's strength surrounding me…feeling the need to be even closer to him went way beyond the thrill of defying my parents' wishes for me. There was a thrum in my blood that had never been there until Ranger came back into town.

I was thankful that despite all the hell this town shot his way, he decided to stay.

"Let's go dance." His chest rumbled against my back with his words. I couldn't turn it off. The acute awareness of every place his body met mine. I wasn't even sure what song was playing as I leaned back and pressed a gentle kiss to the stubble along his jawline.

"Those lips are going to be the death of me, woman," he growled before nipping my earlobe, sending me squealing into a fit of giggles.

"Right back at you, cowboy." I flicked the rim of his hat and he winked at me.

His hold on my hip tightened before I felt him moving us forward. Unwinding our tangled limbs, he reached for my drink and set them both on the bartop before he grabbed my hand and led us toward the dance floor.

A loud smack sounded behind me right as a hand came down on my rear. I was so shocked it took me a moment to register that someone had smacked me on the ass. In public. When I didn't know their name. And while I was very clearly with Ranger. But even if I hadn't been. A fucking douchebag stranger had just smacked my ass.

Ranger went deathly still in front of me.

Shit.

If there was a look in someone's eyes that indicated they were about to commit murder, Ranger had it. All the joy and ease had left him. Those blue eyes that stole my breath away were honed steel, aimed right at the guy I knew was standing behind me because I could feel his presence like the edge of a razor against my neck. He was dangerous and lacked any respect for women.

But I had something far more dangerous. A man who didn't want his woman to be touched by anyone else.

Ranger gripped my hand and tugged me toward him like we were on the dance floor. Spinning around, I found myself behind him, nestled safely against the edge of the standing bar that surrounded the dance floor.

The guy who smacked my ass laughed drunkenly to his friends, not seeing that the giant in front of him was on a war path for revenge.

Ranger's hands found their way around the man's neck—quick as a snake bite, the man jumped. His body didn't waver far as Ranger yanked his chest toward him.

"Didn't your parents ever teach you to keep your hands to yourself?"

Wide, frightened eyes darted back and forth between Ranger and where I stood behind him. His drunken brain was trying to make sense of the situation. Unfortunately for him, it moved too slow.

Ranger reared a fist back and clocked the guy right on the chin sending him straight to the sticky floor. His large frame bent over the guy and Ranger stabbed him in the chest with his pointer finger. "If you ever touch a woman without her consent again, I'll find you and finish what I started. I don't give a fuck if you leave town and try it somewhere else. I'll know and I'll fucking hunt you down and remove your meaty hands so you won't be able to do it ever again."

The entire bar was silent, listening to Ranger's tirade before he rose to his full height and stalked toward me. His breaths were heavy, but so were mine.

He draped his arm over my shoulder. Pulling me in close, he kissed the top of my hair as I slid my hand into the back pocket of his jeans.

"Let's get the hell out of here," he said as I looked up at him, the wild still tingeing his eyes.

Chapter 14

Ranger

I worked really hard to keep my anger under control after going away. The day I was sentenced to ten years I made a promise to myself that I would never allow my emotions to get the better of me. Time was a valuable currency and I didn't want to give any more of it away. I had my sister to look out for and the ranch.

But the moment I heard that asshole's hand make contact with Sarah, I lost all sense of control. I was wild for the woman and the thought of some other man touching her set my blood on fire. But seeing a drunken piece of shit do it without her consent was next level.

The cold night air made my sinuses burn as I heaved in another lungful of breath. Sarah's hand was small in mine as I led her to my truck, the distant hum of the music from the bar was the only sound around us.

"Are you okay?" Her voice was soft, like she was

worried if she spoke too loud it might break the fragile thread of sanity I had left.

"No." I yanked my hat off and raked a shaking hand through my hair. "I'm not okay."

She spun around, leaning her back against the tailgate before she took the edges of my flannel in her small hands. I wrapped my own around hers.

"Talk to me, Ranger. What's going on?"

That rage was so damn consuming, I thought I might burst into flames from it.

Breathe, I told myself. *Just fucking breathe*.

My throat was thick as I struggled to get out the words, "That asshole deserves a lot worse for putting his hands on you, Sarah. He shouldn't be able to walk out of that fucking bar after what he did."

Understanding flashed across her face as she let go of my shirt and slid her hands around my waist. "You're right. He's not a good guy. But I'm okay, Ranger. I promise I'm okay." She kissed the center of my chest with a gentleness that cleaved my heart in two. "I'm okay," she said again as her cheek rested over my heart.

Sliding my arms around her, I held her tight against me. Letting the warmth of her small body seep into all the hardened parts of my heart.

It was so easy with her…so easy to let my guard down.

Tilting my chin downward, I whispered against her hair, "I…I didn't want to scare you, Sarah. But there's one thing you need to know about me. I will *never* allow another man to put his hands on you ever again. I should have put you in front of me when we were walking. I should have made sure nothing like that could have happened to begin with."

I could just make out the chocolate hue of her eyes as she looked up at me, a ghost of a smile on her perfect lips. "Ranger, as hard as you might try you won't be able to protect me from everything in this world. I hate that you're even having the thought that you could have prevented that asshole from doing what he did. You can't be responsible for everyone's actions. Only your own." That ghost of a smile turned into a real one. "But I'm thankful you came to my defense."

Her gratitude churned something inside of me that I'd rarely felt before. For so long it had only been Callie Rose, Miles, and me. Three kids with broken families coming together to survive. But looking at Sarah's beautiful face made me feel like I might have the chance to do more than survive. I could *live*.

The idea of that terrified me because if I was already starting to feel this way about her, what the hell would it be like if I lost her? I'd been through a lot in my life, but losing this with her was something that terrified me more than time being stolen away.

Having her this close felt too good to let fear win. So I stomped out that thought, burying it deep in the back of my mind.

"Tell me what happened." I felt the muscles of her face move against my chest.

I didn't have to ask to know what she meant.

"You didn't watch the trial?"

Her fingers moved in slow circles against my chest. The feeling was a balm to the heat of my anger—squelching it like a breath to a flame.

"The entire town was talking about it. But…I don't know. I'd always had this feeling that what they were saying wasn't the whole story. Two of my best friends were made out to be people they weren't just because others decided to talk negatively about them. I didn't want to fall for the picture LeRoy's lawyers were likely painting you out to be. I…wanted to form my own opinion."

Shock and bewilderment hummed through my body. Sarah was full of surprises and it seemed that with every new thing I learned about her, I found myself more in awe of the woman she was. And more than that, she wanted to give me the opportunity to tell my side of the story completely unbridled.

"I have to say, I think you're the only one in this town who even considered thinking about my side."

"Will you tell me?" Her big eyes were a glassy reflection of the moon hanging above us and I realized at that moment I would tell her anything she wanted to know.

"It's a long story. Are you sure you're up for it tonight?"

"Mmhmm." She nodded, the curls she'd made in her long brown hair bounced with the movement of her head. My palm ached to wrap those strands around my hand and pull her head back so I could claim her lips. I stretched my fingers, letting them splay wide so I wouldn't give in to the temptation.

I unlatched the tailgate of my truck and pulled it down

gently. Sarah let out a breathy sigh when I gripped her hips and lifted her onto the tailgate. I wondered if that was the same sigh she might make as I buried myself between her legs.

I never considered myself a lucky man, but I sure as hell wished I was lucky enough to one day have the pleasure of tasting her.

"Wait," she grabbed my bicep and the feel of her touch sent a lightning bolt straight to my crotch. I stopped just before I was about to hop onto the tailgate with her. She gave me a cute tilt of her lips and then she stretched her legs out, doing a funky little maneuver until her right leg hooked behind me and pulled me into her.

Her tongue darted out between her lips before she said softly, "I want you right here." And then she tucked her fingers into the front pockets of my jeans. I went still as a stone. Feeling her hands that close to my cock had me about one second away from letting my self-control snap and taking her on the bed of my truck and making her come so hard she screamed my name into the cold night air.

This woman is going to be the end of me. That thought should have scared me, but I was starting to realize there was nothing normal about my reaction when it came to Sarah. She had a way of making me want to be better. A way of giving me hope that there was more to this life than I could ever dream of—that I ever *let* myself dream of.

"This is where you want me, sugar?"

"Yeah, cowboy." The smell of something sweet mixed with nutmeg and clover had my mind spinning as she pressed a tender kiss to the edge of my lips. "Now I can look in your eyes when you tell me your story."

I leaned my hips into her as her hands dove deeper into my pockets. "And how, exactly, am I supposed to concentrate on the story when I have you this close?"

Her fingertips flicked against the lining of my pockets. "You're a strong man, Ranger. I'm sure you can figure it out." Then the little devil winked at me like she knew exactly what she was doing.

Somehow the nerves I'd felt earlier when she asked me to tell her what happened had gone away as I thought of where to start. When I looked into her eyes, I had a feeling all the flirting and close call touches weren't just because we were on a date. She was trying to distract me.

I wanted to praise her for it.

With a long sigh, I placed my hands on the top of her thighs and tried not to read too much into the shiver that ran over her or there was no way I'd get through the story she was asking me to tell.

"My sister was looking at colleges to apply to for dual enrollment. She was always the smart one in the family. Too smart for her own good sometimes," I chuckled, remembering all the creative ways she would reel our parents in and get *me* into trouble for something *she* did.

"So, in her junior year of high school, I brought her to Atlanta to tour one of the universities that has an Agricultural Business major. We spent the weekend there during the second week of September. Looking back now, I wish more than anything that I'd chosen another time to go."

"Why's that?" Sarah's head tilted to the side with curiosity brimming her eyes.

I shook my head. "I didn't know it then, but we were touring the school in the middle of the sorority and fraternity rush. There were kids everywhere. Lines of girls chanting as they walked in high heels across campus and the guys were even crazier."

"Yeah, I've never been the biggest fan of those institutions. I've always found the idea bizarre. But each to their own." Sarah shrugged.

"It was definitely bizarre." I thought back to seeing those poor girls stumble across campus, their feet bright pink with blisters as they tried to maintain their smiles.

"On our final night there, I left Callie Rose in the hotel room while I went out to pick up pizzas at one of the universities's restaurants. As soon as I left our room, I had a feeling that something was off. I can't explain it, even now. But it was the same feeling I had right before our mom told us our dad had died in the war. And like a dumbass, I ignored it. Chalked it up to thinking about Callie Rose being on her own in such a big city. Not listening to my gut that night cost me ten years of my life."

Sarah didn't say a word as she removed her hands from my pockets and placed them over mine, giving them both a gentle squeeze. Sadness was etched into the lines of her face. Sadness and…understanding.

The look in her eyes gave me the strength to continue. "It was pretty late when I headed out. There was hardly anyone on campus when I found them in a dark alcove between buildings." Flashes of that night made my head spin. "I noticed the sounds first. Drunken slurs mixed with fists meeting flesh. When I turned the corner and saw what was happening, my instinct just took over. Like a blanket of rage that couldn't be stopped.

Her grasp on my hands tightened.

"Three guys were looming over this poor kid, each one of them taking shot after shot at his face. Telling him if he wanted to join their fraternity, they needed to beat the bitch out of him. That he was too weak of a man and the only way they'd let him in was if he proved he wasn't a pussy."

"Oh my God," Sarah's hands moved to cover her mouth as tears welled in her eyes.

"When I saw how bloodied his face was, I didn't think. I just acted. I told the kid to run while I took them on. When he stumbled away, I let that rage fly. Giving them the instant karma they had coming. Once it started, I couldn't stop. Every time I hit one of them, all I saw was that poor kid lying on the ground getting ganged up on by three older guys. It was so fucked up, Sarah. But what I did was worse."

Her brows scrunched together. "What do you mean?"

My chest tightened. "I didn't stop." The words came out in a whisper. "I took advantage of them being drunk and I didn't stop until every single one of them was a useless heap on the ground. It wasn't until then that I recognized LeRoy Cummings. When I'd finally given them enough, he'd looked up at me through swollen eyes and I knew he recognized me too.

"It was only a few days after Callie Rose and I got home that the police showed up at my door and took me in."

Sarah was looking down at where our hands were joined. I slipped a finger under her chin, tipping her head back so she was looking at me.

"I understand if it's not enough. If my reason for doing what I did doesn't make sense to you and you want to walk away from this before we get too deep, I understand."

Gentle fingers clasped around my wrist. Her thumb rubbed over my pulse. "Here's the thing, Ranger. I'm already in too deep. And I don't think there's anything you could do that could stop me from falling."

For a moment, I looked up at the blanket of stars wondering which one sent this angel to me. When I looked back at her, I snaked my hand around the back of her neck, letting my fingers tangle in the silken strands of her hair. "I don't deserve you." I pressed a kiss to her forehead.

"When you stop thinking that is when you'll finally have me. The only thing getting in your way is you."

I couldn't help but chuckle. "Smart woman."

She shrugged. "I've been told that a time or two."

When I nipped her lip she hummed and pulled me toward her, drawing my face close so her lips were near my ear. "Thank you for telling me what happened that night. I can only imagine how difficult dealing with the aftermath must have been."

"You're the first person I've talked to about it since I was released."

Her throat moved as she swallowed. "I…I didn't realize.

"No." I took her face between my hands. "Don't do that. Don't question yourself with me, Sarah. I told you my story because I trust you and I want you to feel the same. If you have a question, I want you to feel comfortable asking it."

It was the truth. But the part I didn't say was that I would tell her anything she wanted to hear. There wasn't a single part of myself that I wasn't willing to cut wide open for her to see.

"Okay," she replied with a demure smile before she let her head fall against my chest.

"Okay," I repeated, my voice a hushed whisper as my hands moved to cradle the back of her head. I held her there for what felt like hours of precious moments.

I'd never been one to get lost in the moment. I was always looking too many steps ahead. But tonight I let myself be consumed by her. The little movements of her chest rising and falling with each breath. The way loose strands of her hair fluttered in the night breeze, tickling the edge of my jaw. How, with every inhale, I felt like I was breathing in the comforting scent of my favorite fall spices. And how she fit perfectly in my arms.

By the time I drove her home, I knew I was a goner. There was nothing I wouldn't do for her. And I fucking loved it.

Chapter 15

Sarah

If a person could float on a cloud without falling through to their early demise, that's what I was doing. Floating.

Two nights had passed since my date with Ranger and I couldn't stop the euphoric feeling that filled my chest. If this was the beginning of what love felt like, I was mad at myself for not pursuing it earlier in life.

It didn't matter that my mom had blown up my phone yesterday, sending me text message after text message saying she had something important she wanted to talk to me about. I ignored every single one of them, not wanting anything to take away from the high I was riding.

For so long, I'd hidden myself away in my work, letting it be the only thing I focused on because I couldn't afford not to. Failure wasn't an option. Because failure meant I would have to crawl back home to my mother and father and let them claim victory. Even more than that, it would mean they were right and that pursuing something of my own wasn't a viable option.

There wasn't any time to focus on the idea of falling in love. Of giving part of myself to another person. That was until I saw Ranger at Deacon's bonfire two summers ago and a seed was planted. The man I'd had my eye on since I was a teenager had come back to town. More handsome than I could even remember. But it was more than that. Like kindred spirits, I was drawn to his presence and Saturday had confirmed that.

The seed was growing, giving space for a new way of life. Maybe I didn't have to go at this all alone. Maybe there was a chance for me to have it all, just like Willow and Johnny did.

I couldn't let myself think too much about it though. If I did, I'd probably talk myself out of how I was feeling and I didn't want to do that.

"Willow and Johnny are ready for you," Stephanie popped her head through the door of my bakery's kitchen. It was the day of their cake tasting and I wanted everything to be perfect for them.

"Give me just a minute and I'll be right out to get them."

"Okay, I'll let them know."

The door swung shut as I quickly placed two forks next to each miniature cake, making sure they were aligned with precision and there weren't any drops of extra frosting on the plates.

This was the first time I was hired for a wedding and even though it was for my two best friends, I still had a reputation to uphold. While I loved having my bakery, it was only the first step in my long-term plan. Weddings and private events were where my heart was at and this was the first chance I had to showcase my talent with not only wedding cake design but taste.

"Alright you two! If you're ready, we can head on back," I said to them as I opened the door, excitement blossoming in my chest.

Willow clapped her hands together as she bounded toward me. "Eek! I'm so excited!" She gave me a big hug and Johnny placed a hand on my shoulder.

"This is the best part of the wedding planning in my opinion." He grinned at me before he slid his arm around Willow's waist and they followed me through the door.

Willow gasped as she caught sight of the six rows of miniature cakes. "Oh my gosh! They look so beautiful, Sarah."

I couldn't help but laugh because they were only ensconced in white or chocolate buttercream.

"I appreciate your enthusiasm, but I promise the actual cake will have a lot more details. I have a few sketches to show you both. Do you want to see them before or after the tasting?"

"Before," Willow said at the same time Johnny said, "After."

I threw my hands up and giggled. "I'm leaving this one between you two."

Willow turned to Johnny and I for sure thought she was going to try talking him into seeing the sketches before they tried the flavors. But she surprised me. "I know you've been really excited to taste the cake, so we can do that first."

He snaked his arm around her shoulders and kissed her neck. "This is why I love you."

"Because I let you eat before I torture you with design choices?"

"Exactly," he hummed.

We spent the next hour moving our way through all the cake flavors until Johnny finally decided on the vanilla with strawberry jam filling and Willow chose the chocolate cake with my cookies and cream icing. It was precisely how I thought the appointment was going to go, both of them compromising on the alternate cake tiers so they could both have what they wanted on their special day.

"Okay, so I have three design choices for you to look over. We can make any changes you want to them, they're just an idea of some different directions we can go in." I spread the three pages in front of them.

"This first one is called a semi-naked cake. It's very simple and rustic looking. The icing will be a thin layer on the outside so you can still see parts of the cake sponge beneath it." I pointed to the next page. "This one is a more traditional style with a cascading floral effect. We can use whatever flowers or objects you want for the cascade, it doesn't have to be what's in the picture here. And the final one is a little funkier. The sheen you see on the outside is a metallic edible glitter. I'm not sure that it's the best fit for you guys, but I wanted you to see the full spectrum of what we can do."

Willow looked up at me with glassy eyes and my heart sank.

"What? Do you not like any of them? I can work on some other sketches if you—"

"No, Sarah. They are all *perfect*. I knew you were talented. But I had no idea you could do something like this. These designs are more than I could have ever hoped for."

"Willow's right, Sarah. They're amazing," Johnny echoed.

The tension in my stomach lessened as butterflies began to soar. "Thank you for trusting me with such a special order. I know I'm just starting with wedding cakes, but I appreciate you both taking a chance on me."

Willow wiped under her eyes. "There's no taking a chance when the mockups look this good." She shifted toward Johnny. "What're you thinking, babe?"

He considered each design carefully, taking the papers into his hands and switching back and forth between them all. Then he turned to Willow and said, "Since we're getting married at the cabin I think the semi-naked one would look best with the color palette you picked out and the rustic nature around the cabin."

Willow could have stopped the world from spinning with the smile she gave him. "I think so too."

My heart ached as I watched two of my best friends fall deeper in love while planning out the details of their wedding. It made me long for Ranger and the way he made me feel when I was near him.

I cleared my throat, trying to ward the emotions away. It

wasn't my moment, it was Johnny and Willow's and I didn't want my feelings getting in their way. "Okay. I'm going to have you two take this mockup and give you a week to think about the flowers you might want on it. Let me know by the end of the week so I can get a final sketch over to you to approve so there's plenty of time to have the florist order them."

"Will do," Willow mused as she took the mockup and headed toward the door. "Oh! And don't forget, I made a reservation to go apple picking in two weeks for your birthday."

"Right!" I started clearing the remaining miniature cakes from the island. "Is it okay if I bring a plus one?"

"Of course it's okay, it's *your* birthday."

I blushed. I was still brand spanking new to the dating world and wasn't sure what the etiquette was when it came to bringing a man around my friends.

"Plus"—Willow winked at me—" that will finally give me a chance to vet Ranger and make sure he's up to snuff."

"Easy there tiger," Johnny rubbed his hands up and down her arms. "Sarah's got a good head on her shoulders. I'm sure if she's bringing him around, she's already done the vetting herself."

Willow stuck out her bottom lip. "Fine. But if he hurts her, I'll hurt him."

Johnny laughed before pressing a kiss to Willow's cheek. "Noted. Now let's get out of here so Sarah can get back to work."

"Bye, y'all. I'll see you both soon."

They both tossed me a smile before heading through the doors and without a second to breathe or take in the fact that my first wedding cake tasting had gone incredibly well, Stephanie barrelled through the doors with a stricken look on her face.

I immediately stood upright, ready for whatever pastry catastrophe was likely waiting for me out front. "What is it?"

She swallowed. "It's your mom. She's here."

Well, I definitely wasn't ready for this. I couldn't recall the last time my mother had been inside my bakery. Honestly, I wasn't completely sure she'd ever come to see what I'd made of myself.

The sigh that blew past my lips revealed the exhaustion I already felt and I hadn't even spoken to her yet.

"Can you send her back here? I really don't want the patrons seeing an HBO special of Daughters with Over-bearing Narcissistic Mothers."

Stephanie nodded. "Don't worry, I've got you."

The door closed and I stole a few deep breaths, trying to steel my nerves. It was one thing to talk to my mother over the phone. There was power in that bright red button that could end a call. Not that I'd ever hung up on her before, but knowing I could made me feel a lot better than being trapped in the small space of my work kitchen with only one exit. I also hadn't responded to her messages over the weekend, so she was likely going to come in with guns blazing.

The moment I saw her face when she came through the doors, I knew I was in deep trouble.

Great.

“Hey, mom.”

“Hi, sweetheart.” She drew out the last word as she took in the mess of my work kitchen. If I’d known she was going to show up I would have scrubbed it from top to bottom if only to prevent the disdain that showed on her perfectly made-up face.

A quiet voice in my mind told me I was being ridiculous. It was the middle of my work day with three dozen cupcakes in the oven. Any bakery kitchen would look the way mine did right now with splotches of flour everywhere and drips of icing along the island counter. But that stronger voice—the one that had been ridiculed by the woman before me—was chastising. Telling me that I should be better.

I fidgeted with the tie of my apron, not knowing what to say. I was alone, cornered, and I didn’t have my big brother or anyone else to help defend me.

Thankfully she broke the silence. “I’m sure you remember my dear friend, Mrs. Campbell.”

I nodded, keeping my face pleasantly neutral. *Where is she going with this?*

“Well, her son Jones is moving to town. He’s going to be taking over his father’s real estate business. I think it would be good for the two of you to meet.”

I stifled the groan building in my throat. Southern propriety took the wind from my sails once again.

“I don’t k—”

She held up a hand and my lips immediately zipped shut. With a small sigh and a flicker of her eyes, I knew I was already testing her patience and I'd barely gotten more than a few words out.

"You've been obstinant since you were a young child. Always chasing after frivolous dreams and leaving important traditions behind. Your father and I have tried our best to take a step back and let you sew your wild oats, but there has to come a time when you grow up and start making adult-like decisions, Sarah."

Every inch of my body felt cold and hot all at once. I was frozen. Unable to move when my body was screaming to run away. To not allow her to drive me to that place of quiet darkness. And yet, I was flaming on the inside as anger flushed my cheeks.

I hated that she did this to me. I hated that I couldn't have a normal relationship with my mother because she refused to give me freedom, even as a grown adult.

Pinching the bridge of my nose, I tried to calm myself down. Allowing her to frustrate me wouldn't end well and I had too much to do today to get to that point.

"Mom, I appreciate what you're trying to do but I'm perfectly fine on my own." There wasn't a chance in hell I was going to tell her about Ranger right now. Not when she had an agenda.

Her long delicate fingers graced the side of her hips, her lips pursed and I swallowed hard. "I'll throw in a little sweetener for you since you've clearly refused to shed even an ounce of your obstinance. If you go on a date with this young man and give him a fair shot, your father and I will endorse your bakery."

I crossed my arms. She took her shot and it hit me in the only weak spot I had. "You and dad would seriously do that?"

A subtle lift of her chin. "Yes. But I want to see a real effort from you, Sarah. Time is ticking and you won't be this young forever."

There it was. The truth behind her mission. Theo and I were getting older which meant her chances of having biological grandchildren were becoming less and less in her favor. It was just another thing for her to dictate. Another area of my life she wanted to control.

Little did she know that I had no intention of allowing her anywhere near my children—if and when I had them.

But knowing the influence my parents had in this town… it could be life changing for my career. Their support could mean the difference between me reaching my goals or not. I'd worked so damn hard. Since I was eighteen, I had a vision for what I wanted my life to be, but there was always an obstacle in my way, preventing me from reaching the next level.

This could be it. The opportunity I needed to start landing big accounts. To become a true wedding cake designer.

Ranger. His name clanged through my heart like a lightning strike. In such a short amount of time, he'd become someone important to me. More than just an adolescent crush. I *felt* things for him that I'd never felt before.

I bit the inside of my cheek, weighing the options in my mind. I knew there was no way she'd let me think about it.

My mother had always been ruthless in her negotiations. This time was no different. If I let her walk out of my kitchen, the offer would no longer stand.

"Okay," I said quietly. "I'll meet him."

"And give it a good effort?"

"Yes." I resisted the urge to roll my eyes.

"Wonderful." The way her face lit up made my heart ache because I wished she would look like that from watching me pursue my dreams instead of doing her bidding.

"I will refer your number to him and we will talk soon, dear."

I didn't have the strength to say anything more and as I watched my mother walk out the door, I couldn't help but feel like I'd just made a deal with the devil.

Chapter 16

Ranger

The tune singing past my lips was a familiar one. A whistle rendition of a song my mother used to play for Callie Rose and me on her guitar.

It had been a long, long while since I allowed myself to remember those times with anything but hate and sorrow in my heart. But Sarah…she was opening up something inside of me that hadn't been visible to anyone in years. That glimmer of hope. The smallest kernel that had kept me going all these years.

When I rounded the bottom of the staircase into the kitchen, I found Miles and Callie Rose staring at me with confused looks on their faces.

Miles's brows bunched together, creating an angry caterpillar above his eyes. "Were you just *whistling*?"

I didn't miss how Callie Rose elbowed him in the ribs before she said, "I think hell just froze over."

I shot them both a bird. "Busybodies."

Callie Rose snorted. "Um, you're the one coming in here all chipper which, by the way, is completely unlike you. So forgive us if we're a little confused."

I glowered at my little sister. "Shouldn't you be glad for your brother when he's in a good mood?"

The stool she sat on squeaked as she rotated her seat, following me with those piercing eyes as I made my way to the coffee pot. "Yeah. Sure. But usually when something shifts like this it means there's trouble on the horizon."

Setting the coffee pot back down I turned to face her and I saw the worry written on her face. My mood immediately soured. Not because of her prying, but because I hated that my sister had experienced such pain in her life that she struggled to let a good thing happen without worrying about the other shoe dropping.

Miles must have sensed the tension because he gulped down the remainder of his coffee before saying, "I'll see you at the barn."

"Actually,"—Callie Rose held up a hand—"I need some help with the chicken coop before he heads out."

Miles simply tilted his chin at her in acknowledgment before heading out. She was the woman of this house and despite Miles and I being more than twice her size, she kept us both in line. Held us together. When she spoke, we listened.

I knew the conversation wasn't over, even when she hopped off the stool and made her way out the front door. I ate my eggs straight from the pan before I grabbed my black cowboy hat off the wrung and stepped into the biting cold.

One of the roosters let out a loud crow on my approach to the coop. Callie Rose was already herding some of the hens to a smaller holding pen. With the morning light hitting her face, she looked so much like our parents. Our mother's button nose and bright hazel eyes. And her long black curls were a match for our father's. Something clanged in my chest, but I shoved it aside as she righted herself and looked over at me.

"So, I take it your date went well?" Her breath clouded in front of her.

"It did, yes."

"Tell me about her." Something shifted in her gaze. Softness perhaps? Replacing that cold steel that had gotten her through all the losses in her short life.

I grabbed the leather work gloves from the back pocket of my jeans and slid them on. Silence took over me for a few moments, not knowing where to begin.

Then, finally, "She reminds me of the first flower to rise in spring after a long harsh winter. I can tell she's been through a lot in her life. Maybe not similar to what you and I have gone through, but her own mess. Her own pain. Yet, she fights the grip of that pain and still chooses to be bright and kind and courageous."

My sister stopped unwinding the chicken wire and shifted toward me.

"What?" I asked.

"I don't think I've ever heard you speak about someone like that."

I shrugged. The feelings inside of me became overwhelming. I didn't know what to do with them all, so I remained quiet.

Callie Rose went back to unwinding the wire so I could nail it to the bottom board.

"Do you think she likes you?" This time my sister kept working, kept pulling hard against the metal.

I chuckled. "I hope so. She seemed to have fun the other night before—" I cut myself off, not wanting to talk about the asshole who'd almost ruined our first date. But more so not wanting to worry Callie Rose.

"Before what?" When I glanced at her, those eyes—our mother's eyes—were trained on me.

Shit. There was no getting out of this one now that I'd slipped up. I could see it now. Spending the next several days under her fire of peppering questions until she finally wore me down and I told her what had happened.

Saving myself days of misery, I decided to tell her now. "There was a guy at the bar, drunk off his ass. When we walked past him and his buddies, he decided to put his hands where they didn't belong." I flexed my right hand, remembering what it had felt like for my fist to meet his face. "He paid the consequence."

"Fucking hell, Ranger," she spat. "What were you thinking?"

My spine stiffened at her tone. The fear that laced the anger.

My mouth popped open with a retort I knew I'd regret, so I slammed my lips shut.

"Do you have any idea how easy it would be to get sent back to prison after already being found guilty of a violent charge?"

Frustration zipped through me as I stood, no longer able to remain in the small space. "You don't think I know that? *I* was the one sitting behind those bars, Callie Rose. I know the risk."

She took a step toward me, anger crumpling her face. "Then why do it? Why take the risk for someone you barely know?"

"Because!" I threw my hands in the air and she flinched. Not because she was afraid, but because I'd always had a leash on my emotions. Always controlled. Always unfeeling.

My chest heaved from the cold air hitting my lungs. "Because for the first time since mom and dad were gone and I fucked up my entire life…I finally feel like there might be a chance for something more. And I can't tell you why she makes me feel this way. But she does. And just like I'd lay my life down for you and Miles, I'd protect her from the evil of this world. Even if it meant sacrificing myself."

She stared at the dirt for a long while until I wasn't sure if she was going to respond at all. Then she turned to me and the look on my sister's face nearly broke me as she said, "But who protects *you*, Ranger? We don't live in a fair and just world where the good guy gets to walk away unscathed. Our world is fucked up. You're not invincible. You can't go around protecting everyone. Because when you do, there are consequences. Very *real* consequences." Her voice broke, along with my heart.

"Maybe Sarah is everything you've ever wanted. Ever needed in a partner. And maybe it's selfish of me to say this, but I don't want you to be betrayed by *those* people again. Sarah…she's part of that world. She grew up as one of them."

I shook my head. "She's not like them, Cal. She's not."

She took another step toward me, taking my gloved hands in hers. "Maybe she isn't. God"—she closed her eyes for a moment, her ebony hair shimmering as her head shook side-to-side—"I hope she's not like them. But her parents are. What will that mean if you let this go on any further?"

I stared back at my sister. Seeing the pain of my decisions etched into the planes of her beautiful face.

Emotions. Too many emotions swirled through me. I'd learned to handle the anger. Deep breaths and all that shit. But *this*.

Everything Callie Rose said was right. Sarah came from a blue blood family and it wasn't a secret just how far their prejudices ran against people like me. I wasn't a lawyer or a doctor. I grew up nearly poor as dirt. I was a fucking cattle rancher for Christ's sake.

Logic was barking at me. Warning me to stay away. To listen to my sister because even though that guy had just been a drunken bastard in a bar, he could have easily been someone of influence. Someone with more money and resources than me. It wouldn't have changed what I'd done because any man who touched a woman without her permission was on my permanent shit list. But my sister was right. One punch could have landed me right back in prison.

The thought of gray stone walls and iron bars had me grinding my molars together. I couldn't go back. *Wouldn't.*

And yet.

Sarah had quickly become the light leading me from the darkness. I was probably crazy by normal people's standards. We'd only truly known one another for a short time. But there was no denying the connection we had. Maybe there was a feral side of me that wanted to protect the people I loved. And maybe being with Sarah put me at risk of giving into that side of me. But the thought of letting that light blink out, of not giving it a chance, had my stomach forming a pit.

Dropping my sister's hands I grasped her shoulders. "I know you're afraid of me being taken away again. I can't tell you how much I wish I could go back in time and change what I did. Call the police or just grab the kid and run. But that time isn't now. I promise that I will try harder to do things differently. To prevent myself from getting in trouble. Because you're right. The world isn't a just place. It never has been." The image of our father leaving our home for the last time flashed across my mind. Coming and going like a swift wind.

"But I will do my part in making this easier on you, okay?"

Those hazel eyes darted back and forth between mine like she was trying to see if I was being sincere.

"Okay," she said with a whispered breath.

I brought her in for a bear hug and tussled her hair with

my gloved hand. She swatted me away and I loved seeing her like that. Wild hair pointed in all directions, a childlike smile on her face. It reminded me of simpler times. Before… *everything*.

We went back to working on the chicken coop. Me hammering and her holding the wire tight. We were halfway done when she asked, "And what about Sarah?"

Crouched, I settled my elbow on my knee, letting the hammer hang from my hand. "I would love for you to get to know her. See what she's really like. I think you'll come to like her a lot."

Callie Rose stared out at the rolling fields. When she looked at me, the worry was gone. Replaced with a joyful smile, moisture gathered in her eyes. "If you care for her this much already, then I think you're right. I'll probably like her very much."

Something lessened in my chest like I was finally letting go of a weight that I'd been carrying for so long I'd almost forgotten just how heavy it was.

Chapter 17

Sarah

Jones Campbell was the epitome of a Southern blue blood. Citrus smelling pomade kept his blonde waves perfectly sculpted against his scalp. Bright blue eyes stared back at me and I was pretty sure he had a mouth full of veneers because no one's teeth were that perfect. The collar of his button-down peeked over the edge of his sweater—the perfect tie-in for a gentleman's fall ensemble.

He was clean…almost *too* clean.

I wondered if he'd spend more time getting ready for date nights than I would. The thought immediately shifted my focus to another man. One with rugged, dark features and callouses on his hands that felt good when they scraped against my skin.

Blinking the image of Ranger away, I cleared my throat and tried to focus on the man in front of me. The one I was supposed to be giving a fair shot so my parents would support my small business and catapult me toward my dreams.

Just laugh and smile and pretend you're having a good time, I told myself.

"So, how're you liking Pebble Brook Falls?" I asked him right after the waiter took our drink order. When he'd texted me about going on a date, he'd offered *Sauvage*—the fanciest restaurant in town. It made sense given that it was one of my mother's favorite spots. She probably told him I would love it because it was what *she* loved. There wasn't anything wrong with the place per se. It just reminded me of all the things I didn't live up to.

"It's perfectly fine." His Southern accent was smooth and melodic. For some reason, it grated on my nerves. "Nothing compares to the city in my mind, but I think this town is suitable to set down some roots, find a wife, and build a family."

I nearly choked on the sip of water I took. *...find a wife.*

"Certainly sounds like you're on a mission."

Jones's smile was wide, but the sincerity didn't quite meet his eyes. For a moment I wondered if he felt the same pressures from his family to follow a certain path.

He unfolded his napkin into his lap and said, "I think it's time for me to grow up. I've sewed my wild oats. Went through the typical partying stage. After a while, I started to realize how lonely that life was. It didn't take me long to know it was time to shift my focus. So, I followed my parents here and will be taking over my father's real estate business. Everything feels like it's set in my life. Everything except for having a partner by my side."

There was a subtle shift in the way he looked at me. For the life of me, I couldn't quite read what it was. But the words he'd said about wanting a partner. Someone to do life with. I found myself liking the idea of that.

"Well, there are plenty of eligible bachelorettes in Pebble Brook Falls. Most of them were brought up to be the perfect housewife and partner. I'm sure you'll find exactly what you're looking for in no time."

"And what if I'm looking at the woman I want right now?"

Crimson heat crept up my neck. I was still fairly new to this whole dating thing but I didn't think most men were this forward. His blue eyes bore into mine like I was the most interesting thing in the world. It was intimidating. Yet, I found myself staring right back at him. The heat of his words trailed to other places.

Looking away, I cleared my throat. "I guess we'll just have to see." My voice was smaller than I wanted it to be. I couldn't figure out how he made me feel or what I even thought of him. I wasn't sure if that was because my mother had set this date up and the idea of her being right about anything to do with my life seemed off the wall. Or if it was because my mind kept wandering to another man—one that was wild and untamed and made me feel like I could take on the world by his side.

Just give him a chance. Feelings aside, I couldn't negate just how much was riding on my interactions with this man. There was no doubt my mother would acquire a report of how things went between us, even if I wasn't the one to tell her.

Remembering the dream that always tugged at the back of my mind, I squared my shoulders and sat up a little straighter. If Jones thought I was attractive, I could lean into that.

"Tell me more about yourself, Jones. Where did you go to college?"

"I went to Hightower University in downtown Atlanta. Some of the best years of my life were at that university."

"I've actually never been to the city before."

"Is that right?"

I nodded.

"Why is that?"

I paused as the waiter approached us with our sweet teas and took our orders. Shifting a little in my seat I finally said, "I think I knew what I wanted to do with my life from a young age. The minute I turned eighteen, I took some of the allowance my parents had given me throughout the years and started learning how to bake and decorate cakes." I giggled to myself thinking of that time. "It quickly grew from a hobby to an obsession. When I moved out of my parents' house, I started an online business in my kitchen. Baking cupcakes mostly until I had enough saved up that I could rent the storefront I have now."

"A self-made woman," Jones said.

"I guess I had to be. My parents took away my trust fund when they discovered I was on a path for destruction as they like to put it."

"They didn't help you at all?"

The pang in my chest was still almost as strong as the day they had both sat me down and told me that they couldn't support my 'crazy' idea. That the only thing they could think to do was discipline me by taking my trust fund away and dangling it over my head every chance they got for when I might decide to make better decisions for myself.

Little did they know, their discipline would only drive me further away from them and closer to accomplishing my dreams. Even if I had to do it on my own.

"Not in the way I would have hoped. I guess you can say they helped me because they gave me a pretty lofty allowance growing up and I was able to buy everything I needed to learn the craft. But no. They didn't help me once I moved out and started the business."

His hand was warm as he reached across the table and covered mine, giving it a gentle squeeze. "Sarah, I'm sorry you didn't have the support you wanted from them. I can imagine how difficult that would be."

I blinked away the tears that stung my eyes as his words hit me right where the wound was still sore. I hated feeling this way. I absolutely hated that I didn't have parents whom I could be close with. Most of the time I was able to keep the anger and sadness at bay. I could focus on everything I was trying to build for myself. But the moments like this, when I was reminded of just how messed up our relationship was, I found myself drowning in the sorrow.

The tightening of my throat was hard to speak through, but I had to change the direction of this conversation. There were prying eyes everywhere in this place and the last thing I needed was for one of the town's busybodies to report to my parents that I was grovelling with tears streaming down my face on my first date with Jones.

I cleared my throat. "Did you always want to go into real estate?"

Thankfully, Jones rolled with the abrupt transition without pause. "I've always been good with people. I have a knack for knowing what people want to hear and what they need. Real estate seemed like a good fit since you're helping people convince themselves that making the single largest purchase of their life will be worth it."

Jones continued talking about his journey into real estate when a woman with long black hair caught my eye. She was slowly walking past the large picture windows of the restaurant on the sidewalk. It took me a moment to recognize her as Callie Rose—Ranger's younger sister. I'd seen her quite a few times at the farmer's market, selling a variety of seasonal harvest vegetables.

She was always the quiet one in school, mostly keeping to herself. I'd never paid her much attention. I never thought that maybe I should go out of my way to say hi or be friendly with her. As she turned the corner, out of sight, I realized there were so many questions I wanted to ask her about her brother.

What was he like when he was a kid? Was he always so broody or was there a time when he enjoyed laughing? How did he have the strength to fight every single day for ten years, knowing that he'd been the one to do the right thing and was paying the price for someone else's actions?

"Sarah?" Jones's voice broke through my thoughts and I shifted my gaze back to him, blinking away the thoughts I was just having.

"I'm so sorry," I whispered, leaning back against the velvet cushion of the chair. Jones had been talking this entire time and I'd drowned out his voice, letting my thoughts roam to another man and his family.

"Are you alright?" His gaze narrowed on me and I could tell he was frustrated but was also trying to be polite.

"Yes. I…I just saw someone I know walk by outside and I got distracted."

His lips tilted downward. "Would you rather go be with them?"

Alarm bells rang in my head at his sharp tone. "No." I shook my head, startled by his response.

"Okay," was all he said as the waiter finally brought us our meals.

I stared at the plate of pasta in front of me, not sure what to say or do after that exchange. The insecure girl who had always been reprimanded for making the smallest of mistakes had me rounding my shoulders and zipping my mouth closed.

This isn't me. This isn't me anymore. I kept repeating the words in my mind. Over and over again. But no matter how many times I said them to myself, I couldn't find the courage to get up and leave the table.

I was silent for the remainder of our dinner. Only taking a few moments here and there to ask Jones questions about his real estate ventures and whether he'd found a house he liked in Pebble Brook Falls yet.

It didn't take me long to realize that he enjoyed talking about himself more than engaging in a reciprocal conversation. The beginning of our dinner date was likely him buttering me up with feigned interest.

"Would you like to come back to my place for a nightcap?" he asked as we stood outside the front doors of the restaurant.

"I'm sorry but I have a big day at work tomorrow, so I need to turn in early."

For a moment, I thought he was going to push the issue. My heart thundered in my chest. All I wanted to do was get to my car.

Thankfully, he said, "No problem. It was nice to meet you, Sarah and I hope I can take you out again."

Not having a single word to say, I simply smiled at him. I stiffened in his arms as he pulled me in for a hug and when he tried to kiss me, I shifted my head to the side, giving him my cheek instead.

We said our goodbyes and I nearly ran to my car. When I was tucked away inside, I didn't fight back the tears that spilled over my cheeks.

I was stuck. So damn stuck between a rock and a hard place. Jones was wrong. Totally and completely wrong. But he was the one thing standing between me and my dreams if my mother had anything to do with it. And it wasn't just that thought that had me spiraling. If I didn't play by the rules of her game, there was no telling what she might do to try to sabotage me.

Sobs of frustration wracked my body for what felt like forever until I was finally able to get myself together enough to drive home.

Chapter 18

Ranger

Miles turned away from me, walking towards the only door of my cell. He didn't look back as his hand turned the knob and he stepped through it. I screamed after him. "Don't leave! Please, Miles! Please…don't leave." My throat was sore. Hoarse from the number of times I yelled his name.

Then Callie Rose appeared. Looking the same as she did the day I was sent away. Her long black hair in soft curls framing her face—our mother's face.

"You did this," she whispered. Her voice sounded like it was far, far away.

"I'm sorry," I cried. "I'll do better. I promise, Cal."

Her eyes were vacant. Like what I'd done had robbed her of all the joy she had left. It was my fault. Everything was my fault. She'd already lost so much in life. First, our father. Then, our mother. Now, by my own stupid actions, she was alone again.

There was something eerie about the way she was

looking at me as I called out her name. Begging her to stay with me.

Her head tilted to the side slightly as if she was assessing me. "You're going to be alone in here forever because of what you did. You ruined us. You ruined the only family I had left." Black tears rolled down her face before her body started to lose its opaqueness.

I leaped for her, trying to keep her with me. I didn't want to be alone. I didn't want her to suffer anymore. By the time I reached her, she was already gone. Her body turned into a swirl of mist around me.

The door Miles had walked through shimmered away and I was left in a dark gray box made of cold stone walls.

Alone. *I was completely alone. Hurtling toward the wall, I led with my shoulder. I slammed into it and crumpled into a heap on the ground, my shoulder splintering with pain.*

"No!" I screamed, again and again. Until finally, the walls started moving toward me.

"You'll die here." Callie Rose's voice echoed against the walls.

I squeezed my eyes shut, curling myself into a ball like I'd done when we found out our father had died.

"No," I whispered this time. And the walls swallowed me whole.

"Agh!" I jolted forward. Breaths heavy. My heart banging against my chest like a war drum. My fists were tangled in sweat-sodden sheets as I slowly oriented myself to my bedroom.

My breaths were ragged. I tried to slow them down. One breath in. One breath out. Over and over again.

Home, I told myself.

I was home and I wasn't in jail anymore. I'd gotten out. My sister was here and I had Miles too. I was okay.

"Fuck." I scraped a hand over my face before I untangled my legs from the sheets and slipped out of bed.

Moonlight spilled across the wood floor. I looked through the window and guessed it was probably around one o'clock in the morning by the location of the moon.

It had been a while since a nightmare haunted my sleep. When I first got out, it was almost a nightly occurrence. Wrenching myself free from that cell had been hard enough in real life. It was even harder in my dreams when I was confronted with my worst fears.

I switched my boxer shorts for another pair and tugged on some sweatpants and a sweatshirt before heading out to the back deck.

There was no way in hell I was getting any more sleep tonight. Not when the image of Callie Rose's body misting away was still planted firmly in my mind.

I found my heavy winter coat hanging on the coat rack downstairs and slipped on my boots before I opened the door to the back deck. My breath fogged the air in front of me on the first step out. To my right, Callie Rose was bundled up in a quilted blanket, sitting in one of the Adirondack chairs around the firepit. Embers glowed as smoke billowed toward the open night sky.

"Couldn't sleep?" I asked, sitting in the chair next to her.

"Not tonight." She took a sip from her steaming mug. It was probably hot cocoa if the mound of whipped cream was any sign.

"Did you have another nightmare?" she asked.

I stared into the bright flames as they flickered and danced about. "Yeah. It's been a while since the last one. Tonight kind of hit me by surprise."

She shot me a look that said she knew exactly why I'd had a bad dream. I chose to ignore her.

"Tell me about it."

I took in a deep breath and watched the air cloud in front of me as I let it loose. "It's not really something I want my little sister thinking about. Especially when she has troubles of her own."

She snorted. "Are you going to treat me like a child forever?"

I laughed. "Being a child isn't a bad thing." It was simpler. Easier. I often wished I could harness some of the childlike wonder I had about the world and let it wash away all the fear I experienced now.

"We share. It's what we've always done, Ranger." The fire reflected in her eyes. Such a stark contrast to the vision of her in my nightmare. Lifeless. Dull.

What she said was true though. Losing our parents had

forced us to become close. We'd been one another's confidants.

Things had shifted when I came back from prison. There was a part of me that had missed out on so many years. My wrong-doings had prevented her from having the big brother she deserved. So, I'd kept my demons to myself. Not letting her see the bruises hiding beneath the surface. But she did see. Even when I didn't want her to.

And maybe that was the power of love. It doesn't matter how hard we try to hide. Love exposes us to the ones who care. The ones who are willing to look beyond the facade.

"It was a different version of the same one I used to have. I was locked in a cell without bars. There was only one door and Miles turned his back on me and left. Then you…" I swallowed against the knot in my throat. "Then you appeared and told me I was going to die alone. That I'd be stuck in there forever."

"Fuck," she hissed. "Why do our brains torture us?"

I settled my right ankle over my left knee and sat back in the chair, looking up at the endless cascade of stars. "I'm not sure. All I know is that mine is a relentless fucker that doesn't know how to turn off."

That earned me a laugh. "Did the walls cave in on you this time?"

"Every. Fucking. Time."

"Maybe we can get brain transplants or something. You know?" She sat up and turned towards me, eyes bright with mischief.

“A brain transplant?” I deadpanned. “Then we wouldn’t be who we are.”

“No. It would totally work. Our brains aren’t *us*. They’re the weird organ machine that controls everything.”

I chuckled. “I think you’ve lost a little too much sleep, sis.”

With an oomph, she sat back in her chair and stuck out her bottom lip. “You just crushed my dream of getting a new brain that’s not fucked up. I thought I’d solved all our problems and there you go, ruining everything.”

I winced. “Sorry for crushing your dream.”

Digging my hands deep into my coat pockets, I reached for any warmth I could find from the frigid air. We were quiet for a while. Only the wind whistling through the tree branches and the crackling of firewood sounded around us. My mind was loud and silent all at once. A stream of thoughts rushed in and then they were met with utter numbness. Like my nightmare had taken all the energy I had to give for the night.

“You never asked me what my nightmare was about.” Callie Rose was staring straight up at the stars, her words were gentle.

“I didn’t know you had one tonight,” I replied.

“It was about everyone in my life leaving me. In some form or another. Mom. Dad. *You.* It never feels like you three want to go, but something steals you all away and I’m left wondering why it had to be me.”

“I didn’t want to leave you, Cal.”

Her eyes were lined with red and I knew she was fighting

back tears. "That's not what I mean when I tell you it hurts, Ranger. This world…it's brutal and unfair and humans are the worst of it. If people didn't fight over their beliefs then our father wouldn't have died in a war and our mom wouldn't have left us stranded. If money didn't corrupt, then my brother wouldn't have spent ten years of his life locked behind bars for defending a young kid who was ganged up on and beaten in an unfair fight. And I hate it. I fucking hate that this world favors evil."

She was breathless when she finished and I could feel the fury rolling off her in waves. There was so much emotion wrapped up in her tiny figure and it didn't take me long to realize how much we were alike. The anger that led me to seek vengeance on those three guys was the same anger that had my little sister burning as bright as the fire before us. And that brightness only led to one thing—burning out.

I waited a minute or two until she'd calmed down enough that she could hear me through the rage. "I know it must feel like these things were done to you. Like you had no control over your own life or when people came and went. I know you must be scared that it will happen again." I reached across the space between our chairs and placed my hand on her forearm. "But believe me when I say that living your life in fear is no place to stay. It's lonely and only bitterness can come from it."

She snorted and rolled her eyes.

I chuckled. "I get it. I don't have much room to talk. I haven't exactly been setting the best example since I got out."

Her brows shot up as she said, "You hardly left the ranch for the first six months after you got out."

"Okay. Yeah. So maybe I was an awful example of how to live your life without fear. But I'm sick and tired of people in this family running away from the fight of life. There's so much good in this world and who better to fight for it than us?"

A smile split her face and then she laughed. "What on earth has Sarah Williams done to my brother? You sound like an infomercial for a self-help book."

I wasn't sure if I could attribute the change to Sarah since we'd only been out together twice. But my sister was right. There was a shift happening in me. I was trying. And I couldn't remember the last time I'd done anything but simply get through life. For so many years, I took each day as it came and tried not to go crazy behind those silver bars. And maybe it was even before then, when I was just trying to help Callie Rose feel like a normal kid.

Now…now I wanted more for myself. I wasn't sure if the feeling would last. If I was honest with myself, I was still terrified that it would go away and I'd be left being the same miserable asshole who could hardly do much else than be around cattle all day.

"I don't know," I responded. "But I hope it doesn't go away."

"I hope it doesn't either," she said quietly before patting the hand I'd placed on her arm.

A few silent minutes ticked by and then, "Thank you for tonight. I think I needed to get everything out of my head—"

"And leave it to the wind," we both said at once. It was the saying our mother told us anytime we were upset as kids. She would tell us to shake it off, or sometimes dance it off. Then she'd kneel to our level and press a kiss to each of our cheeks before telling us that the wind would always carry our worries away if we were willing to let go of them. There were even a few times when I saw her doing the same thing to our father when he was stressed about the ranch. And it worked. Every time.

"What do you think they'd say about us now?" Callie Rose's words turned to fog in the cold air.

I took in a deep breath before I looked over at my sister. "I think they'd be proud of us."

The warmth of her smile—so much like our mother's—stayed with me for the rest of that bitterly cold night.

Chapter 19

Sarah

"Um, did you put an advertisement in the paper or something?" Stephanie asked, peeking her head through the cracked door.

I rubbed the sweat off my forehead with a tea towel. Every one of my ovens were on and I was still running behind and it wasn't even noon yet.

"No. But it's crazy, right? All the people out there?"

Her eyes grew wide as her head shook up and down."I don't think we've ever had this many people in the shop at once."

I yiped as the top wire rack caught the edge of my wrist as I pulled out a sheet of cookies. "Damnit," I hissed, sliding the baking pan onto the island countertop before I dashed for the sink and ran cold water over the burn.

"Sorry," Stephanie whispered. "I didn't mean to distract you."

I bit my bottom lip as the tan color of my wrist started to

turn bright pink from the burn. Thankfully I was quick enough that it didn't look too big, but it still hurt like hell.

"No, Steph. You're fine. I'm just moving a little too quickly this morning," I glanced over my shoulder at her concerned face and shot her a smile.

"Okay." She smiled back. "I'm going to get back out there. But I wanted to let you know that the biddies are in full force today. It's like they all crawled out of their knitting caves to come here. So we will probably need some more scones soon."

"Thanks," I laughed. "I'll get started on a batch right now." The biddies had a hankering for my blueberry and orange scones and the last thing I wanted to do was piss one of them off by not supplying their demand.

I heard the kitchen door snick shut as Stephanie went back to manning the cashier. I carefully dried my injured wrist and grabbed some Neosporin from my emergency medical kit before I gently wrapped it with some gauze and tape.

Leaning against the cool metal counter, I stole a few deep breaths. Today was wild and even though I told Stephanie that I didn't take an ad out in the paper, I'd neglected to tell her that it was all my mother's doing.

Stephanie and I had always been close as cousins, but I didn't want anyone to know that I had given in to my mother's demands and gone on a date with a man of her choosing. Especially when that date had gone awry. When I'd left dinner with Jones last night, I was feeling so awful that I almost called my mother on my way home to tell her that the deal was off. I couldn't continue faking my feelings when I knew without a doubt the possibility of me falling for Jones was zilch.

But I stopped myself when I thought of what her influence and support could do for my dreams. I told myself that I'd just see if she was going to be true to her word before I made any hasty decisions.

My bakery had done fairly well over the years, but there was no doubt that today's payout would likely be almost as much as I normally brought in over a week. The numbers were huge and all I could see was it turning into a giant leap toward my bigger goals.

Maybe I was selling my soul to the devil, but that little girl inside of me still ached for her mother's approval. That part of me saw beyond the dreams of becoming a famous wedding cake designer to an ever bigger dream of having her mother be proud of who she was. It was a quiet dream. One that I kept only for myself. And I was probably an idiot for even thinking it could happen. That someday she'd look at me with love in her eyes and I would know that I'd finally done something right.

I hoped for that day and yet I had a feeling deep down that it would never come.

There was about a thirty-minute lull in the late afternoon before the early evening rush hit and I was pretty sure I had about every baking ingredient splattered somewhere on my body when Ranger Adams walked through my kitchen door.

I stilled as I took in his large frame. His cowboy hat was missing today, but those dark wavy locks had me desperate to run my hands through them. There was no stopping the immediate reaction my body had to seeing his exposed forearms flex as he shut the door behind him. I hardly registered the flowers he had in his hand as he strode toward me and extended his hands.

Bundled together in a twine wrapped paper bouquet was a mixture of vibrant wildflowers with shades of deep purple, bright yellow, and pink.

I reached for them, but quickly remembered I had frosting all over my fingers from the round of cupcakes I was frosting before he'd come in. Feeling my face flush, I raced for the sink and started scrubbing my hands together with soap and water.

When I finished drying them, I turned to face him and smiled. "Those flowers are beautiful." He extended them toward me and when my fingers brushed against his, I felt a jolt run down my arm. I couldn't control how my body reacted when he was around.

Keeping the bundle of flowers in front of me, I tried to hide the mess on my apron. He took two steps closer to me. I backed up, feeling overwhelmed by his presence and insecure with the amount of baking ingredients splattered all over me. I definitely wasn't looking my best and certainly wasn't worthy of this man's presence given my state.

"You don't need to hide yourself from me." His voice was low, his blue eyes piercing. Then he reached out and tucked a loose strand of my hair behind my ear. His fingers were rough as he trailed them down the side of my neck. I loved how I could feel the history of his hands beneath his touch. Like every day of hard work was etched into them and his touch was a glimpse into all those moments.

He leaned down until I felt the heat of his breath against my ear. "You've been haunting my thoughts, Sarah Williams. I couldn't stay away any longer."

"I'm glad you didn't," I whispered as he leaned back and I was able to get the full view of his devastatingly handsome face. He was so different from most of the men I'd grown up around. A life of pain and struggle flickered in his eyes, but there was strength there too. A sheer will to keep going and to find something good.

Maybe I was his something good. It was a dangerous thought for a woman like me. I didn't have much to give with my lack of romantic experience and a life wrapped around a dream that had nothing to do with finding love.

His lips pulled to one side as he smiled and it was nearly my undoing. I had a feeling there were very few in this world who ever saw the vulnerability in the look he gave me now.

"Looks like a busy day today." It took every bit of concentration I had to focus on his words and not how his hands settled on my hips. Just resting with ease, like they belonged there.

I swallowed, remembering *why* my bakery was filled beyond capacity today. I'd gone on a date with another man to please my mother's wish for me to find a suitable partner.

Right.

I was a piece of shit coward who gave in to my mother's demands instead of standing up for myself. I went on a date with a guy I wasn't even attracted to when the man standing in front of me was everything I'd ever wanted. And I wasn't going to tell him. I couldn't. Not when he looked at me like I was the answer to every problem he'd ever had. Not when my body was desperate for him to claim mine.

I couldn't ruin my chances with this. And I couldn't let my dreams slip away either.

Piece. Of. Shit. Coward. My mind was relentless and all the heat I'd felt just moments before had been doused with a bucket of ice water.

"Yeah," I croaked. When I looked into his blazing blue eyes, I could feel the words stinging on my tongue. I wanted to tell him everything. How I was terrified of how quickly I was falling for him and how I was likely making one of the biggest mistakes of my life by giving in to my mom's wishes. I wanted to tell him that I felt like I had no other choice but to go on dates with Jones for fear that my mother's wrath would destroy everything I'd built for myself.

So close. I was so damn close to spilling everything right then. But instead, I said, "I think everyone is just looking for some warmth from the cold outside."

"Your baking does have a way of warming one's soul."

I beamed at him and I decided that I would tell him what

was going on with my mom and Jones. But not today. Not right now when he was being so sweet. I didn't want to ruin it.

"I think that's probably the best compliment anyone has ever given me."

His fingers threaded through my hair as he wrapped the back of my head with his palm. He tilted his head an inch closer to me, eyes flicking toward my lips for a brief moment. "I'm glad I was the one to give it to you then."

His lips were soft and bold as he pressed them against mine. Kissing Ranger was like coming home after a long day of work. It was the only place I wanted to be. Comforting and safe. Yet, the spark he ignited in me was wild and unruly. As he deepened the kiss I opened up for him, relishing the feel of his tongue moving smoothly over mine. I was on fire for this man. Burning so bright I thought I might combust.

There was no comparison in how he made me feel. Not to Jones or any other man I'd come to know.

Ranger made me want to live life without abandon. I wanted to be wild with him. To not give a fuck what other people thought of me. He had a way of tapping into that side of me that had the guts to walk away from a fortune and life of privilege so that I could chase after what felt right in my heart.

When he broke the kiss, I whimpered from the loss of contact. "Please, don't stop," I pouted.

His laugh was like falling into a velvet blanket. Rich and warm. "Trust me. The last thing I want to do is stop kissing you." He tucked a strand of hair behind my ear before his thumb trailed the side of my neck until his hand came to rest on my shoulder and collarbone. I wondered what it might feel like to have his large palm move a few inches to the left, cusping the edge of my throat.

Watching porn while I put my vibrators to work over the years had given me a wealth of fantastical ideas. Many of which I wanted to put to good use once I finally broke the threshold of my virginity.

"When can I see you again?" he asked, breaking through my debaucherous thoughts.

I breathed in, trying to think of my schedule for the next few weekends. "I'm not sure if you'd feel comfortable hanging out with my friends just yet. Especially since you tried to run away from me when I asked you out on a date."

His nostrils flared as his eyes rolled into the back of his head. I decided I liked teasing him. The thought of getting under this man's skin was a major turn-on.

"Are you ever going to let me forget it?"

My nose crinkled as I shook my head. "Mmm. No," I laughed.

"I guess that's fair."

I played with the edge of his open flannel as I said, "But if you are okay with it, we're going apple picking at *Harry's Orchard* for my birthday next weekend. I'd love to have you join us."

Something like hesitancy flashed in his eyes and I wasn't quite sure what to make of it, but I found myself suddenly nervous that maybe I was expecting too much too soon.

"It's totally okay if you don't want—"

"No," he said, firmly. "I'd be honored to share your birthday with you. Just text me the day and time and I'll be there."

"Okay." I grinned.

"I hope you have a good rest of your day, beautiful and I'll be seeing you soon." His thumb gently rubbed against my cheek as he brought my forehead to his lips and kissed it. I breathed in the scent of leather before he stepped away and left me standing by myself in my kitchen.

It wasn't two minutes later and Stephanie came back in through the door with a large bouquet of red roses and baby's breath cradled in her right arm.

"Did Ranger bring those too?" I asked, confused.

Stephanie bit her bottom lip like she was trying to fight back a smile. "Um, no. These are from a guy named Jones Campbell. I told him you were overwhelmed in the kitchen because I thought it might be bad for him to walk in on you and Ranger. Do you want to tell me what's going on here, cousin?"

I pinched the bridge of my nose as I exhaled loudly. *Shit.*

"Nope. Not today," was all I could manage to get out.

"Okay." She laid the flowers on the island and walked back towards the door. "If you ever need to talk about it, I'm here for you."

I let my hand drop from my face and looked at her. "Thank you."

The door closed behind her and once again I was left alone with the very big mess I'd made.

Chapter 20

Sarah

Moisture clung to the fall air, covering the rolling hills of *Harry's Orchard* in a blanket of fog. There was something deeply romantic about the scene that made my heart ache.

A reminder of what I was fighting for and what my circumstances forced me to fight against. Sleep had evaded me since Ranger showed up at my bakery and gave me what had to be the best kiss any woman on this planet had ever experienced. He was so tender like I might break from the contact. But I could feel the wild in him lurking beneath the surface, desperate to break free.

It was the same wild that ran through my veins. I'd tampered it down over the decades of my life to satisfy my parents—to *belong*. Being near Ranger had it roaring to be let loose. To finally run without anything in its way.

Maybe I'd let myself get there one day. Live life without abandon. To stop caring what my parents would think of me. I'd already made it this far. Forgoing my inheritance to open a bakery. I could still see the look on my mother's face the day I'd told them I made enough money from at-home baking to open a brick-and-mortar location.

The way her eyes narrowed on me and her lips twisted downward in a scowl. My father just stared at me blankly, like his brain couldn't even process that *I* was his child.

I was furious at the part of me that still longed for their approval. The little girl who wanted nothing more than to have her parents look at her with love and tell her how proud they were of her.

Anger stung my eyes as I wiped the rogue tears away. *No*. Today was my day and I wouldn't let them get away with ruining it.

I checked myself in the visor mirror of my car. Satisfied that the tears hadn't done too much damage to my mascara, I got out of my car and walked up to the large renovated farmhouse to sign in for apple picking.

"Happy birthday, bestie!" Willow's voice reverberated through the space and I turned to see her just as she'd walked through the door Johnny was holding for her. Arms spread out wide, she started running towards me and I couldn't help but laugh.

"Ooph!" I huffed as we collided in a mess of giggles, hellos and I missed yous.

"Happy birthday, Sarah." Johnny squeezed the two of us together before we all parted with smiles on our faces.

"I just checked us in, so all we have to do is grab our bags and we're good to go."

"As long as you remember this one's on us." Willow winked at me.

I rolled my eyes. "Yes, Willow. I do remember that you are forcing me to be spoiled this weekend and there's nothing I can do about it."

She tapped me on the nose with her pointer finger. "Good! As long as that's settled, then I think we're good to go." Willow twisted to turn toward the other set of doors leading out to the orchard entrance but stopped mid-step and shifted back toward me. "I almost forgot to ask. Are we waiting on a special someone? Or maybe a few special some-ones?" Her lips tilted into a mischievous grin and I could feel the heat of my cheeks flaming. I knew I was bright red without looking in a mirror.

"I don't know what you're talking about," I whispered, looking around the large open space where dozens of our fellow townsfolk were eating apple cider donuts and drinking hot chocolate at the picnic tables scattered throughout.

Willow sided up next to me, looping her arm through mine before she leaned close to my ear and said, "I think you know *exactly* what I'm talking about."

She directed me toward the doors where Johnny was casually holding one open, doing his best to mind his own business while Willow tried to coax the details of my love life from me.

"Listen, you know there is no judgment here. You could date four guys at once if you wanted to."

"Willow!" I jabbed her lightly in the ribs.

My left arm rose with hers as she shrugged. "What? I'm just saying that it doesn't matter to me what you do, as long as you're being true to yourself."

I sighed heavily before I leaned my head on her shoulder, burying myself closer to her as we hit the cold air. I looked over my shoulder where Johnny was keeping a few paces back and I knew he was trying to give us some privacy.

"You promise you won't judge me?"

She stopped walking and her bright blue eyes turned serious. "I swear to you."

A lump formed in my throat. Not because I didn't trust her. But because I knew she wouldn't judge me and it was so incredibly rare to find that in life. To be fully loved by someone else that it didn't matter what you did, even if it was as shameful as fake dating one guy to get in your mother's good graces when you were really falling hard for someone else.

I told her everything, though. How I was embarrassingly still a virgin, which she informed me that she already knew because we'd never talked about how I'd lost it. And the way Ranger made me burn every time he was near. Like a moth drawn to a dangerous flame, but it was too damn beautiful to avoid. But worst of all, that I was betraying *myself* by dating Jones to appease my mother.

"You're living in fear, Sarah." Our hands were bound together between us. She squeezed mine.

"I don't know what else to do. I've already agreed to her deal and if I go back on it…you know what she's capable of, Willow."

She chewed on the inside of her cheek as she mulled over the point I'd made. "You're right. I do know what she's capable of." She gave my hands another squeeze and winked at me. "But I also know what *you* are capable of. It sounds like you have the beginnings of something really special with Ranger. I don't think I've ever seen you this smitten with someone before. So, when the time is right you'll know what you need to do. Until then, I've got you, girl. If shit hits the fan, you have backup."

I snorted. "Thanks for that."

"I'm just kidding." She nudged me. "But seriously. I think you're being too hard on yourself. Everything will come out in the wash as long as you stay true to yourself."

I knew she was right. I couldn't keep this up for much longer. Not when my feelings for Ranger were growing by the second. It would be better to rip the bandaid off with my mother. The longer I kept this charade up with Jones, the more she would expect the relationship to move forward.

I just hoped I had the strength to cut it off.

"Both of you are too much." I rolled my eyes at Johnny and Willow as they broke apart from their makeout session.

Johnny smacked her on the butt and Willow went squealing down a row of apple trees before Johnny started chasing after her.

"I'm leaving you two love birds!" I called out after them before heading down a different row.

My small burlap bag wasn't even halfway full as I started eyeing some honey crisps. Their swirls of red, pink, yellow, and green were striking against the gloomy fall clouds that hung high above the orchard.

I plucked one off the tree, watching the droplets of dew splatter to the ground as the limb shook the leaves on the rebound. I brought the apple to my nose, smelling the faint crisp scent and nearly tasting the turnover I planned to make with it later today.

Baking was one thing. But I had a fondness for baking with fresh fruit I'd picked myself. There was something special about seeing the apples come directly from the tree to my kitchen.

After dropping the apple into my bag, I wandered further down the row of trees until I spotted the largest honey crisp I'd ever seen.

"You are mine," I whispered at it. Well…I thought it was going to be mine until I got closer and realized it was nearly at the top of the tree and completely out of my grasp.

I reached for it anyway. Grunting in frustration when my stupid arm wouldn't extend further. I started hopping up and down doing my best to grab the large apple, but there was no use.

Frustrated, I placed my hands on my hips and glared at it,

trying to figure out if the owners would kick me out for climbing their tree just as a very masculine arm extended past my shoulder, toward the apple I was longing for.

"Hey! That one's—" I whirled on the sneaky fucker who was trying to take my apple to find myself face-to-chest with Ranger.

"Oh!" I breathed.

Behind me, I heard the faint rustle of leaves moving and a small *pluck* before he brought his hand down between us.

"Is this the one you were after?" he asked, his voice a deep rumble.

I swallowed. Already feeling the heat from his presence take hold of me, casting the words in my mind far, far away.

I nodded and he grabbed the burlap sack from my hand, placing the apple inside. My heart thudded as he bent toward me and placed a kiss on the edge of my ear. "Sorry, I'm late, sugar. We had some issues with a few of the cows this morning and I had to handle it before coming over."

"That's okay." I smiled up at him, thankful my brain found its ability to form words again. "I'm just glad you were able to make it."

He took my hand in his like he'd done it a million times before as we started to walk deeper into the orchard. His hand was so big compared to mine, but the way our fingers interlaced felt like I was made for him. They fit so perfectly together. I wondered if it was a sign. That soulmates' bodies were created to form to one another like the shaped edges of a puzzle aligning without gaps between them. I'd never thought much about the idea of soulmates. Then again,

Ranger had a way of making me wonder about life in a way I'd never done before.

"I got you something for your birthday," he finally said as we neared the far end of the row, no one else was in sight.

"You didn't have to do that." I stopped and turned to face him. His eyes were molten hues of blue and gray today. Matching the dark swirl of the clouds overhead as the sunlight tried to peek through the thinner layers.

"I wanted to," he replied as he reached behind him into his back pocket.

I wondered if the man ever got cold in this frigid weather as I watched his corded forearm flex with the movement. The sleeves of his flannel were pulled up to his elbows, revealing tanned skin dusted with dark hair.

My mouth popped open as he revealed a small leather jewelry box. Handing it to me, I opened it with shaking hands to find a beautiful gold necklace with a vertical bar pendant with the word *dreamer* engraved on the surface. It was perfect. Not because it fit my sense of fashion to a tee, but because the word he chose represented the truth of who I was. Somehow, this man who I was just getting to know, saw that I was more than my family's name. That I had a vision to chase after and I'd stop at nothing until I saw it come to fruition.

Tears burned the back of my eyes. I blinked wildly as I whispered, "I love it, Ranger. It's perfect."

He took the box from me and gently unwound the necklace from the cushion it was resting on. Placing the box back into his pocket he gestured for me to turn around. When my back was to him, I lifted my hair and felt him step closer. He placed the necklace over my head, the pendant falling just below the center of my collarbone. The brush of his finger-tips on the back of my neck sent a jolt through me. My breath hitched as I closed my eyes, letting the feeling of his warmth seep into my skin.

When he was done, he palmed the back of my neck, his grip tightening slightly right before he spun me around, my front becoming flush with his. Our breaths were heavy as his forehead came down to meet mine.

"Don't ever forget what you are, Sarah." He grasped the pendant between his thumb and forefinger. "I hope this reminds you of your strength and that no matter what anyone else thinks, your dreams are worth chasing after."

His stormy eyes were hooded as I looked up at him through my lashes. Without a second thought, I grasped the back of his neck, weaving my fingers through his long curls, and pulled his lips to mine.

Nothing else in the world mattered in that moment. It was just us, completely lost in one another. His knuckles skirted down the center of my back until his open palm grazed my backside. He gripped me firmly, lifting me with ease until I wrapped my legs firmly around his center.

I could hardly breathe with the feel of his hands cupping my ass, his thumbs digging into me with hungry need. He moaned as I ran my tongue along the edge of his bottom lip, giving it a gentle tug with my teeth.

"Careful with that bite," he growled. "I don't think the

townsfolk would take kindly to me tainting their favorite good girl in the middle of the apple orchard."

"But what about what I want?" I breathed, not fully recognizing my own voice. "It's *my* birthday."

He nipped my earlobe as he gave my ass a smack on one side. "Sugar, when I claim you we'll need to be miles away from anyone else so they can't hear you scream my name."

I whimpered, feeling the heat building in my center. My body ached for him and I couldn't help myself as I ground against his stomach in a desperate attempt to find friction against my aching clit.

"I want that, Ranger. I can't tell you how badly I want that."

A loud cat-call rang through the orchard right as our lips met again. We pulled apart, but he still held me tightly against him as he shifted toward the entrance of the row where Willow and Johnny were smirking at us.

"Oh my God," I groaned, dropping my head against Ranger's chest to avoid him seeing me turn tomato-red. "I'm going to kill her."

His breath was warm against my neck as he laughed before he gently lowered me and my feet met the ground. He bent down and whispered so only I could hear, "I'm not finished with you yet, sugar. Don't you worry." Then he smacked my ass, jutting me forward with a yelp.

Hand-in-hand, we strode toward my best friends. Willow had a wicked gleam in her eyes and I knew she was about to put Ranger through the ringer.

Chapter 21

Ranger

A large thunderstorm had started to roll in, so we sought out shelter in the orchard's farmhouse building. There was so much concrete—the floors, the block walls, the checkout counter—that I had to remind myself that I wasn't back in prison. I was free with a wonderful woman tucked under my arm.

I hated that I still struggled with the feeling of being trapped. It was like my brain had a hard time differentiating between my past and present.

We headed toward one of the picnic tables where two other people were already sitting. Sarah and I had been alone in the orchard, right before drops of rain started falling from the sky.

I recognized both of them. A petite blonde woman with striking blue eyes sat cuddled up against Johnny Moore—the town's veteran hero who also owned one of the best archery equipment stores in the Southeast. I remembered Johnny from school. He was a few years younger than me, but he was always scrappy in gym class and had a knack for getting in trouble just like I did. His fiancé, Willow, had always been the quiet one. That was until she made a big fuss in the town after going from an orphan to the richest woman living amongst us.

The first year I was out, I didn't get around town much, but Miles and Callie Rose would fill me in on all the town gossip.

"Guys! We already got some donuts and cider. Come sit!" Willow called us over.

"Ready?" Sarah peeked up at me through her lashes, a tinge of pink from the cold dusted her cheeks.

I kissed her hair. "Ready."

We sat on the bench across from them as Willow laid napkins in front of us and opened the box of cinnamon cider donuts. The smell was amazing, but it still didn't hold a candle to the spice and sugar aroma that seemed to always cling to Sarah's skin.

I grabbed a donut for Sarah, placing it on her napkin before I reached for my own.

"Thank you." She rubbed her hand up and down my thigh. My dick twitched in response at just how close her hand was moving to my inner thigh. I looked at her and could see the mischievousness flickering in her eyes.

The little devil knew exactly what she was doing, so I buried my face in her neck and whispered into her ear, "If you want me to lay you on this table so I can get my fill of you, sugar, just say the word."

When I pulled away, her chocolate eyes were wide. The rose color of her cheeks deepened. And when she tried to pull her hand away from my thigh, I grasped it, planting it right back where it belonged.

"So!" Willow's voice cracked through the air like a whip. Sarah and I both shifted our attention to her. "What is your intention with my best friend, Ranger?"

Sarah's head dipped low as she groaned while Johnny just laughed like his fiancé's question was a typical expression of her feisty personality.

Sitting up a little taller, I cleared my throat and looked Willow straight into her eyes. But before I could say anything, Sarah responded, "Willow, you can't just go around asking people that question."

Willow tilted her head in confusion. "Um, yes I can. You're my best friend and I hardly know a thing about Ranger other than the fact that he was in prison for ten years and owns a ranch."

A straight shooter. I couldn't knock the woman for that. And if *her* intention was making sure Sarah was protected, then I couldn't knock her for that either.

I twined my arm around Sarah's back and gave her hip a small pat to let her know I was fine.

"I think it's a fair question, Willow. If someone with my rap sheet was trying to date my sister, I'd be asking the same thing."

She shot Sarah a look that said *see, it's not a big deal.*

"To answer your question, my intention with Sarah is to only make her happy. For as long as she'll keep me around."

"And what about keeping her safe?" There was no jesting in her tone this time.

I didn't hesitate as I responded, "I'd protect her with my life." And it was true. I thought back to the promise I'd made to my sister earlier this week. That I'd make sure I didn't put myself in another vulnerable position of being sent back and taken away from her again. But if it came between my freedom and Sarah's safety…there was no question that I'd sacrifice myself for her.

Seemingly satisfied with my answer, Willow responded, "Good. Now that that's settled we can get on with Sarah's birthday presents." She clapped her hands together, shifting her attention back to Sarah.

If that was all the chastising I was going to get from her, I considered myself lucky. I had a feeling that when it came to the people she loved, Willow was a bulldog, ready to bite and rip apart whoever she needed to.

Willow rose from her seat and grabbed a large wrapped box that had been hiding beneath her side of the bench. "Happy birthday, Sarah!" she exclaimed, reaching the present across the table.

"Willow, this is huge. What on earth did you do?" I could hear the excitement in her voice as she started to tear the wrapping paper apart.

"Just open it," Willow urged.

I reached for my pocket knife and switched the blade open to cut away at the tape from the cardboard box.

"Thank you." Sarah smiled at me, the sweet look on her face making my stomach do strange flips. It was then that I realized all it would take was a simple look from this woman and I'd be on my knees for her. And there wasn't a single part of me that cared how easily I'd become wrapped around her dainty little finger.

When she opened the cardboard flaps of the box, I watched as her lips parted further, cracking into a bright smile that rivaled the sun.

"No. You. Didn't. Willow!" She let out an excited squeak as she pulled the contraption from the box and carefully pulled at the tissue paper surrounding it. It took me a moment to realize it was a large hand juicer.

"I know how much you love freshly squeezed juices, especially for your fruit tarts. This one has different sizes so you can hand squeeze limes, all the way up to a grapefruit."

Sarah narrowed her eyes on Willow. "Are you sure you didn't get me this for yourself? I know how much you love my lemon tarts."

Johnny let out a roaring laugh as Willow glowered at him. "Of course not!" she defended herself, giving Johnny an elbow to the ribs. "You talked about wanting a juicer all summer." Then her lips twisted into a smirk. "But I definitely won't pass up any tarts you want to bake."

"I knew it!" Sarah threw a ball of scrunched-up wrapping paper at Willow. It smacked her square between the eyes. Willow was shocked for a moment before we all burst out laughing and I wondered if this was what it felt like to be free of my past. If the lightness in my chest would stick around from moments like this or if it would disappear when my nightmares of a six-by-six cellblock came clawing back.

"Did you get the birthday girl anything, Ranger?" Willow asked before taking a bite of her donut.

"Damn, darlin'. Leave the poor man alone." Johnny wrapped his arm around her and pulled her into him. I could tell he was trying to soothe whatever fear had her coming for me, but I admired it. The fierce protection she had for the ones she loved.

It was Sarah who answered, reaching for the pendant hanging just below her collarbone. "Actually he did. Isn't it beautiful?"

Willow leaned forward to observe the necklace I'd bought Sarah. "Dreamer," she said slowly. Turning the pendant side-to-side, the gold caught the reflection of the overhead lights, making it shimmer.

When Willow looked up at me I saw the judgment leave her eyes and something like comfort settled in. "I think you might have outdone me on this one, Ranger."

"Might have?" Sarah snorted before curling into my side. "He most certainly did."

I breathed her in, drawing her closer to me. We all settled into a comfortable silence, biting into donuts and sipping on the hot cider which I had to admit was pretty damn good. Good food was one of the things I'd missed most when I was away. I was thankful that Callie Rose was willing to spoil me when I got out. Every single night, I would come in from working the ranch to a hot homecooked meal waiting for me.

Willow started rambling on about wedding festivities with Sarah and that's when I asked Johnny, "Do you still practice archery now that your store has really picked up?"

Miles had told me that *Faraway Archery* was featured in a national hunting magazine a few months ago, bringing patrons from all over the country to Johnny's store.

He swallowed a sip of cider. "Not as much as I'd like to. The store and the wedding planning have been keeping me pretty busy, but after our honeymoon, I'm planning on getting back to it. If you ever want to come out and shoot, just let me know. We have a practice area set up just behind the store."

"Thanks, man. I might take you up on that offer. My dad was in the military, so he taught my sister and me how to shoot guns for protection but I've never shot a bow before."

Johnny nodded. "It's similar but different. I've drifted away from shooting guns after I got back from the war. But archery still keeps my skills sharp and it's more peaceful. It takes a lot of strength and practice to get it right. How's the ranch doing?"

I heaved a deep breath as his question reminded me of all the work that would be waiting for me when I got back. "It's growing faster than we can keep up with it, which is a good thing I think. But trust doesn't come easily to me, so the thought of hiring someone new to come to my home…it's difficult."

Understanding flashed in his eyes and maybe our trust issues came from different wounds, but I could tell he struggled with it just the same.

"I get that. I think things have a way of working out in the end though. As long as you're open to it when the opportunity comes."

I chuckled. "Yeah. I'm working on the being open part." I took another bite of the donut before wiping the remnants of cinnamon off my fingers with a napkin.

Johnny glanced at Willow before leaning forward a fraction. "I'm sorry she busted your balls. I told her to be gentle, but when it comes to the people she loves, my woman has a dagger for a tongue and she doesn't give a shit about how it comes across."

I smiled. "Don't worry about it. I didn't take offense to it at all." I stole a look at Sarah who was scrolling through her phone now, showing Willow images of florals I assumed were for the wedding. "And I wouldn't blame her for wanting to protect Sarah. I'd do the same thing if I were in her shoes."

Chapter 22

Sarah

I was digging my own grave and I knew it, but the Monday after my birthday weekend, my mother showed up at my bakery to let me know that Jones was very much interested in me and that if I ruined this chance of happiness for myself (*for her*) that she would never forgive me.

The words between her carefully crafted lines were simple. If I didn't continue pursuing Jones, there would be hell to pay. I'd made a deal with the devil and she had come to collect.

So, when Jones sent me *another* text message asking to take me on a date, I'd told him about an ice cream parlor on the edge of town that was truly awful compared to Mrs. Sheehan's place. But I didn't have the heart to show up at Mrs. Sheehan's place when I was living a lie. That woman was the sweetest person in the world, but she had a tendency to say exactly what came to her mind and her intuition was sharper than a knife.

"Ice cream in the middle of fall is an odd choice," Jones said before sitting down at one of the picnic tables out front of the parlor. Drips of chocolate sauce were running down the outside of his plastic bowl of ice cream.

Strike number three. What kind of man insults his date's choice of food?

But I also started to truly question what kind of woman went on a date with a man she had no interest in. Especially when her interests lay with someone else.

"It's my favorite dessert. You could have said you didn't want to come when I made the suggestion."

He blinked at me and I wondered if I was the first woman to ever test him. Given the slight downward tilt of his lips, I assumed I was. Then his face shifted, like he'd pulled out a mask from his back pocket and slipped it on. Now he was wearing a wide smile and his bright eyes shone with interest.

"And give up a chance to see your beautiful face again? No way."

It was a struggle not to roll my eyes, so I distracted myself with a large mouthful of chocolate ice cream.

"I heard your brother is making good progress at the Carnelle's ranch."

I wiped my mouth with the paper napkin. Even if I couldn't stand Jones, I was still a woman raised with manners. "Yeah, I talked to him yesterday and he seems to really enjoy the training they offer there. He has a natural talent for bronco riding, which is great given his late start."

"I was honestly surprised to hear that he quit law school

to pursue a career that's so dangerous. Most men of his caliber tend to go for the sure thing."

I tried to remind myself that Jones carried the same biases that my family did. He was raised with Southern charm and a silver spoon in his mouth. That kind of upbringing meant he was told to think a certain way his entire life. Not all of us were capable of breaking through the barriers of propriety.

But he sounded too much like my mother and father that it grated on my nerves, which were already fried to a crisp.

"Theo is great at whatever he does. I'm sure he'll be able to pull this off as well."

"Of course." Jones's smile was tight.

We both concentrated on our ice cream for a few minutes. The sun shone bright through a cloudless sky and I was thankful for the mid-sixties temperature after weeks of endless cold.

"Do you think you will still be working at the bakery when you have children?" Jones's question washed over me like a bucket of ice water, chilling me to the bone. Mostly because I'd never really considered children. I'd been so focused on my career that I didn't even make time for a boyfriend, let alone think about having children.

But my mind immediately flickered to images of a little dark-haired boy with striking blue eyes running through a field on a ranch I'd never even seen before. I swore I could smell the scent of leather and feel the warmth of Ranger's touch like we were back at *Harry's Orchard* walking hand-in-hand.

Jones may have been the one to ask the question, but it was Ranger who my mind went to. I wasn't sure what I wanted when it came to my career and having children. Having Ranger in my life made me think things could look different from how I'd always imagined them.

I looked up from my mostly eaten bowl of ice cream to Jones with his dusty blonde hair and clean-shaven jaw suddenly feeling protective over my wants and desires. There was no part of me that wanted to share my thoughts with him. I would appease my mother and go on these dates with him until I could find a way out of our agreement without my business taking a major hit. But I wouldn't let him have the parts of me that belonged to someone else.

"I don't know," I smiled sweetly at him. "I'm sure when the time comes for me to have children, I'll know what I want to do then. What about you? Would you mind if your wife was the one to work while you stayed home raising your children?"

A tactical question and he took the bait. "I think a more traditional household suits my wants best. I'd love for my wife to be at home with our children so I can keep the family business going strong. My father's real estate business was passed down from his father and so on. It would be a shame to let all that history go."

"A shame indeed," was my only reply before I asked him more questions about the transgenerational business the men in his family cultivated. A question I hoped would distract him from asking me anything else.

The last thirty minutes of our date-but-really-it-wasn't-a-date droned on as I listened to him tell me of the great men in his family. Which, if I was honest, they did sound like high-achieving people. I had to refrain from asking him about the women out of spite. Mostly because I already knew the answer to my question. The women were there to rear the children, make homecooked meals, and attend to their husbands.

It was an honorable life. One that many women chose with pride. Being a caregiver to those you love seemed like a great way to live life. The problem I had with men like Jones was that they didn't give their women a choice. It was an *expectation*. The men in his family very clearly stood in front of their wives, not next to them.

By the time we'd tossed our empty bowls of ice cream and he'd walked me to my car, I was aching to get away from his monotonous reminders of the life I'd already tried to shed once. I wanted to be in the arms of a man who looked at me like I was the stars in the night sky. To feel the press of his lips against mine as he ruined me for anyone else.

I needed a way out of the mess I'd made by giving in to my mother's deal. And I needed it quickly.

"Would you like to come back to my place for a cup of coffee? I just had a shipment of Blue Mountain Jamaican beans come in yesterday. It's supposed to be some of the finest coffee in the world." He winked at me and I felt my stomach roil. The more time I spent with Jones, the more I felt like he was trying to get to a part of me I wasn't willing to give. He was certainly pulling out all the stops to bring me home, but I wasn't having any of it.

"I appreciate the offer, but I need to get back to the bakery. I don't like leaving Stephanie there to manage everything for too long without me."

Frustration flashed in his eyes and for a moment I thought he might tell me off but all he said was, "I get it. You're a hard-working woman. Next time then."

I loosed the breath I was holding and gave him a small nod. "Mhm," was all I managed to say.

How the hell am I going to get out of this? Jones was proving to be persistent and if I didn't find a way to end things soon, I had a feeling everything was going to blow up in my face.

When he hugged me goodbye, it took everything I had not to be stiff as a board against him. It was all *wrong* and it only made me crave Ranger's touch more. The feel of his strong body against mine as he held me close. How his warmth seeped into my bones, giving me life.

I was thankful when Jones and I parted and I finally found the respite I needed alone in my car. He drove off in his BMW and I watched the tail lights of his car disappear around the bend before I let my head rest on the seat.

Just as I closed my eyes, my phone went off. I dished it out of my purse and saw a text message.

Ranger

Hi sugar, are you free this weekend?

My heart thundered in my chest as my fingers glided over the glass screen.

Yes! What do you have planned for me?

I took a deep breath in, trying to calm my racing heart.

Another surprise. And no, I'm not giving any hints.

Can't wait. 

I slipped my phone back into my purse and turned the key into the ignition. As the engine thrummed to life and I drove back towards town I knew I had to end it with Jones and face my mother's wrath.

There was no way I could do this on my own.

It was time to call in reinforcements.

Chapter 23

Sarah

I'm calling an emergency meeting.

Willow

I had a feeling this might happen.

Johnny

What might happen?

Deacon

When is the meeting?

Willow

I had a feeling Sarah would need this emergency meeting given the status of her love life.

Um, not cool, Willow. But also, very true. My love life is in shambles and I need help.

Deacon

My place, Friday night?

Perfect.

"Wow, this place is coming along quickly, Deacon." The front porch of his renovated cabin had fresh boards with a matching pine wood railing that smelled like heaven.

He tossed me a can of beer and I gently cracked it open, pressing my lips against the lid to keep it from fizzing over.

"Thanks. I've been working on it nearly every day. The plumbing contractor took my deposit and never got back to me, so I watched some videos of DIYers. It was was the biggest pain in the ass. I had to rip out a few of the pipes due to rusting. Fingers crossed I put everything back together the right way."

I grabbed one of the koozies from the pocket of his soft

cooler and sat next to him on the porch steps. He clinked his can against mine with a cheers.

"I hope you did too. It would suck for your first renter to have busted pipes during their visit."

He snorted. "Knock on wood that doesn't happen." Then he wrapped his knuckles against the side of my head.

"Hey!" I swatted at his hand as he laughed at me.

Just then, Willow and Johnny pulled up in Johnny's truck. Their dog, Asher, was the first one out of the cab. His bright yellow body bounced up and down through the tall grass, his tongue lolling out the side of his mouth.

"Come here, cutie!" I cooed at him. His round golden eyes settled on me before he dashed towards my direction. I was met with wet kisses and a body that was much too wiggly to pet.

"Did you guys give him doggy drugs today or something? He's so hyper."

Johnny laughed and said, "No. He's finally starting to feel better after the skink incident and I think he's just happy to be alive."

I scratched just above his tail and whispered to him, "I feel it too, buddy. The excitement of being alive."

"I brought the emergency rum!" Willow called out to us as she hopped out of the truck.

"And some ginger ale I hope!"

She pulled a two-liter bottle of ginger ale out of her reusable grocery bag with a wide smile.

"Perfect," I said, drawing the word out.

"I don't think the two of you drunk on rum with power

tools in your hands is a good idea," Johnny said as he clapped Deacon on the back in a hello.

"Psh. Don't put limitations on us. You have no idea what we're capable of."

"Exactly what Sarah said, babe. I think you're underestimating our talents."

Deacon looked up at Johnny shaking his head. "No worries, brother. All we're doing is painting the inside tonight. I've already hidden the power tools from sight."

I stuck out my lip at them as Willow looped her arm through mine. "Painting is more fun anyway." She leaned in so only I could hear her. "And they'll be sorry for making fun of us when they end up covered in paint."

I snickered.

"What are you two she-demons plotting over there?" Deacon asked, his eyes narrowing on Willow and me.

"Nothing!" We both said at the same time.

Willow's face was covered in tiny speckles of ivory paint. Two drinks in and she was putting *way* too much paint on the roller and it was splattering everywhere as she ran it along the wall. We'd spent the last hour listening to good music and putting some of the final touches on Deacon's cabin.

I realized how much I missed this—spending time with my three best friends, getting lost in building memories.

Over the past few months I'd hardly seen them because we were all so busy. Johnny and Willow with their businesses and wedding planning. Deacon with his cabin renovation and me with my bakery and hot mess love life.

Willow set her roller down in the metal pan before she grabbed her drink and sat on a five-gallon bucket turned upside down. "Okay, Sarah. I think we've earned our right to a little break. Let's get this emergency meeting going."

I swallowed the dryness in my throat as Deacon and Johnny shifted their attention to me from the opposite wall.

I set the paintbrush down in the same metal container that Willow set the roller down and looked at each one of my friends. "I honestly don't know where to start. It all feels like such a mess."

It was Willow who spoke. "Just start from the beginning." She looked over to where the guys were standing before shifting back towards me. "And we all promise there is no judgment here. Only support."

Her words were exactly what I needed to hear in that moment and I was thankful that I had this—the three of them to come to whenever I needed to. My brother was busy carving his path in a brand new career. A dangerous one at that and the last thing I wanted to do was distract him with our family's melodrama and my massive mistake.

A long breath passed between my lips before I finally launched into the story. "I think you all know that I've been dating Ranger Adams for a little while now." They all nodded and I continued, "But what you don't know is that I made a deal with my mother to date her friend's son, Jones Campbell."

I looked Willow, Johnny, and Deacon in the eyes waiting for one of them to wince or show some kind of disappointment, but they all just looked at me with patience. Waiting for me to explain.

I pinched the bridge of my nose for a brief second before moving forward with the story. "I never would have even entertained the idea of dating someone my mother picked out for me, but she offered to support my bakery in a really big way."

Willow's brows rose. "In what way?"

"She told me that if I dated Jones she would tell all of her friends to use my bakery for their needs. Birthdays. Anniversaries. Weddings. She and my father would give me their complete support and would fully endorse me."

"Damn. Talk about a power move," Johnny cursed under his breath.

"Yup." My lips popped on the *p*. "I'd had just one date with Ranger at that point, but I was already starting to fall hard for him. When my mother first told me about Jones I said I wasn't interested. And when she told me she would support my business…I don't know. It was hard to say no to her."

"So, you've been dating both of them?" Deacon asked, concern shining in his eyes. "Does anyone else know about this?"

I shook my head. "Not that I'm aware of. I went on one date with Jones at *Sauvage*, but our second date was at an ice cream parlor on the edge of town. After Ranger came to pick apples with us for my birthday, there was no way I could chance anyone seeing Jones and me in town."

"Do you like both of them?" Johnny crossed the room and Deacon followed. They both leaned against the kitchen bar.

I blew a raspberry. "Jones is about the furthest from my type. He's exactly the kind of man my parents would want me to end up with though. All-American looks. Perfect pedigree. Has a college degree and will be taking over his father's multi-generational business. There's no doubt he comes from a shit-ton of money too if his mom is close with mine."

Willow snorted. "Yeah. Mary Lynne isn't exactly known for hanging out with the riff-raff."

"No, she is not," I replied.

"And it seemed like you and Ranger were getting along really well at the orchard," Johnny said. "Why not just end things with Jones? I'm sure your mom won't like it, but at least you won't have to keep everything a secret anymore. Then you can give things with Ranger a real shot."

"I wish it were that simple," I murmured, suddenly feeling very overwhelmed by the whole issue.

"What aren't you telling us?" Deacon asked.

I looked down at my fingernails and the tiny dots of paint that coated my nails and skin. It seemed so stupid now that I was saying everything out loud, but they didn't know my mother the way I did. Well…maybe Willow understood. She'd been around my house enough growing up that she saw what it was like when my parents started in on me.

I think it hurt most of all that I was even in this position. That my parents not only lacked the ability to accept me for who I was and what I wanted for myself, but they were willing to manipulate me so that I was forced to twist myself into their mold.

I hated that tears hit the back of my eyes as I said, "It's hard to explain, but I saw the look in my mother's eyes when she came to me with this deal. I might have had a fighting chance if I'd been smart enough to turn her down. But if I renege on my end of the bargain, she will make sure I pay the consequences."

"You think she'd be that spiteful?" Anger flashed across Willow's face.

I half-laughed. "There's no doubt in my mind that she would do whatever she could to ruin my chances of taking my bakery to the next level. You saw how easy it was for her to contact Tommy's mom and prevent me from making his birthday party treats. Imagine what she could do for bigger accounts. My parents' reach is far in this state." I spread my arms wide. "Hell, it spans the entire country."

"Money certainly does transcend a lot of barriers," Deacon commented. "But damn, Sarah. To let her rule you in this way with something as personal as choosing who to date." He whistled, the high-pitched sound ending in a low octave. "You deserve a hell of a lot better than that." Johnny and Willow nodded in agreement.

There they were. The three mirrors of my colossal

mistake. I gave my mother an inch and I knew she'd take it a hundred miles if given the chance.

"I can't risk my business y'all. I've worked so damn hard to get where I am."

"And that's exactly why you need to stand up for yourself and end things with Jones." Willow stepped toward me, fire burning in her eyes. "If you let her dictate this part of your life, you'll regret it, Sarah. I saw the way you and Ranger look at one another. There's something really special between the two of you and if your mother gets in the way of that, you'll hate yourself for it."

She was right. Ranger and I were still new, but there was something undeniable between us. I craved his presence like I craved being in my kitchen. It felt like maybe he was the missing piece in my life and if I leaned into what we had, I'd finally be able to let go of the fear that I wasn't enough. Because he always made me feel like I was more than enough.

"What if she lashes out and tells everyone not to use my services? What if the entire town deserts my bakery and I end up going bankrupt? What—"

"Stop." Willow's voice was firm as I stared at her wide-eyed. Every one of my fears tingled on my lips, desperate for release. "One, even if she did become spiteful and told people not to use your services, there's no way anyone could stay away for long when you are the most talented baker and cake designer this town has ever seen. Two, you have the three of us in your corner and even though your parents have sway over some people, your best friend so happens to be the wealthiest woman in this entire state. All the people she has sway over will follow my lead of showing you support. They can't help themselves. Not when it comes to following who has the most money."

Yes. I'd forgotten the power my best friend now had and the influence she could yield if need be. The fact that she would be willing to do that had my eyes burning hotter, tears threatening to spill.

Maybe I didn't have supportive parents. But I did have the most incredible friends—a found family of sorts. The fear started to settle, shifting into something that felt like shaky confidence. If I had my friends to support me through this, then maybe I could face my mother's consequences. Maybe I would have a chance of not totally ruining things with Ranger—the man who made me feel like there was so much more to life than I'd ever let myself imagine.

"You really think I can do this without her destroying my business?" My voice came out softer than I wanted it to.

"Of course." Willow said at the same time Johnny and Deacon replied, "Yes!"

I buried my face in my hands, a hopeful smile tugging at the corners of my lips. I needed this. The confidence they gave me. I needed it more than I knew at the time I called for the emergency gathering.

"Okay." I sucked in a lungful of breath. "How am I going to do this?"

They all started glancing around the room, lost in thought as to the best way to approach it.

Deacon spoke first. "I think you should end things with

Jones in person. The last thing you want to give your mother is more ammunition in how you're failing the laws of Southern propriety. If you let him down gently in a respectful way, you can stand firm knowing you made the right decision in that."

I studied the wooden floors of his cabin for a moment. "Yeah." I nodded. "I think you're right about that. As much as I *don't* want to go on another date with him, he's been nice enough to deserve a proper letdown. Honestly, I don't think I have it in me to end it over text or a phone call even if he was a total jackass."

Jones might not have been my knight in shining armor and he certainly maintained some values that were in complete misalignment with my own, but I wanted to be dignified in how I broke things off with him. If not for him, then for me. There was no reason for me to lower my standards just because he wasn't the right fit for me.

"Okay," Willow said. "I agree with letting Jones down in person. But that will mean giving your mother and whoever else more time to spread the news that you're still seeing each other. Ranger could easily get wind of that information. What are you going to do about that?"

My stomach immediately clinched at the thought of Ranger finding out I was dating someone else while seeing him. Even if there was no connection between Jones and me from the start, I was still omitting the truth and spending time with another man.

"I'm supposed to see him tomorrow at his ranch. I can tell him everything then so he hears it from me and not someone else around town. I'll be able to tell him that my only intention with Jones was to gain my mother's support."

Everything sounded perfect as I said it out loud. It was the right plan with good intentions, but that didn't mean I would be brave enough to say it to his face. I quietly hoped that when the time came tomorrow, I'd be able to tell him the truth instead of running away from it.

Johnny said, "Ranger seems like a pretty reasonable guy. If you tell him the backstory about your mom, he might be a little ticked that you weren't honest to begin with, but I'm sure he'll come around."

"Right." I ran my palms over my jeans to rid them of the sweat that started pooling. "Just tell him everything."

Willow took a final step towards me, bringing me into her embrace. "There's nothing to worry about, Sarah. We've all got your back, even if something does go awry." She let me go and looked into my eyes. "You can do this."

I saw my distorted reflection in her eyes. Fear dancing in my irises. Lips drawn into a tight line. Because the one thing that I hadn't told my friends was that I wasn't just worried about telling Ranger the truth or that my mom might take her revenge out on my business. It was also about that little girl in me finally having a moment when her mother was proud of her for doing the 'right' thing and now I was going to take that away from her—from myself.

Deep down, I was still that child who wanted nothing more than her mother's approval. And I was about to do something that would most certainly warrant her *dis*approval.

Chapter 24

Ranger

Sarah was a cowboy's dream dressed in tight bootcut jeans that hugged her ass so tight I thought the denim might be painted on. She wore the necklace I had gifted her and her long dark hair was curled and bound in a pink bow, the tresses draped casually over her shoulder. I wanted badly to wrap my hand around her hair while I buried myself deep inside her. She was so fucking beautiful it almost hurt to take in the sight of her. My cock twitched and my chest ached. I'd been used to the former experience as I'd only ever sought out physical connections with women.

Call it mommy issues or whatever.

But Sarah churned something deep within me and I found myself willingly giving more and more.

"It's stunning out here." Her breath clouded in front of her as she walked from her car to the barn entrance. I watched the sway of her hips as she sauntered up to me, her gaze dancing around the pastures on both sides of the barn.

"I'd argue that my view is better." I winked at her.

Stopping toe-to-toe in front of me, she placed her hands on her hips. "Is that so, cowboy?"

I slid my hand behind her lower back, drawing her closer. Her pink lips parted with a breathy sigh that struck me to my core as I kissed her. She softened into my touch, hiking one leg up around my own so her middle was flush against my thigh. My hand wove through the bottom of her hair, settling just beneath her ponytail. My instinct was to reck it, letting her chestnut strands fall loose from the bow that secured them. But I restrained myself, knowing we'd have plenty of time for things to get wild.

I lost myself in the sweet taste of her lips and how her tongue melded against my own. There was a banging in my chest, not only from my raging heartbeat but from the awakening that only Sarah brought out in me. That zest for life I'd once had, but the world stole from me. It was a kernel of hope that her presence and touch watered into something more.

I could kiss her forever, but I promised her a surprise. Absence filled the space between us as I broke the kiss and let my hand fall from the back of her neck.

"Is it too soon to say that I've missed you?" she whispered, eyes bright under the fading sun.

"I don't think anything is too soon for us." And it was true. The rational part of me had shriveled into dust when it came to my feelings for her. It didn't matter that we'd barely had time together. She was mine and that was all that mattered.

She smiled at me and I tucked her under my arm, guiding us through the hall of the barn.

“Did you build the barn?” she asked.

“I like to think I helped a little bit, but the true answer is no. My grandfather built it after the old one burned down from a lightning strike. I probably hammered a nail or two, but it was mostly him and my dad.” I caught the emotion feeling heavy in my chest, but not bearing quite the same weight it usually did when I spoke about my dad.

“The woodwork is incredible.” Her head tilted back against my shoulder as she looked up at the exposed wood beams running along the ceiling.

I shifted my eyes upward to study them as she did. “Yeah, it really is.”

“So, do I get to know what we’re doing today?”

I stopped in front of one of the stalls where my sister’s buckskin mare was peeking her head over the door. “I thought I might take you for a sunset ride along the river. But I have to let you know that I don’t have any one-legged saddles with me, so you might have to ride like a man,” I teased, remembering how she talked about her parents not approving of any unladylike behaviors.

She pinched my side making me pull away in a laugh.

“I can ride perfectly fine with my legs on either side, just so you know.”

My mind flashed with the image of her straddling me while riding my cock and as I took in the flame of her cheeks, I wondered if she might have imagined a similar image.

Sarah cleared her throat and asked, "Which horse do I get to ride?"

I turned to the stall behind me and patted the mare on her forehead. "You get to ride Honey Blossom tonight. She's gentle and doesn't like to take her riders on misadventures."

"Hi, Honey. Aren't you beautiful?" Sarah crooned as she let the mare smell her before rubbing her hand over her snout. She turned to me, eyes glowing with excitement. "Is she yours?"

"She's my sister's."

"Oh." Something like worry had her brows crinkling together. "Does she know I'll be riding her horse?"

I chuckled as Honey Blossom whinnied for Sarah to keep petting her. "Yes, she knows."

Sarah's throat worked as she swallowed. "Okay, good. I wouldn't want to ride her without Callie Rose's permission."

I grabbed the lead rope off the hook hanging next to the stall door and latched it onto the mare's harness. Sarah backed off to the side as I swung open the door and led Honey Blossom to the tack room door.

Sarah watched as I saddled Honey Blossom. "This is actually really great, Ranger. I haven't ridden in years and I've missed it a lot."

I looked at her over the saddle and said, "I'm glad I could give you something you've been missing."

Emotion flickered in her eyes like a wild flame. I wanted to know what she felt. What she wasn't saying out loud, but I kept my mouth shut as I led the three of us down to the end of the barn where Hank was already saddled and waiting.

"Oh my gosh, is that a Clydesdale?!" Sarah's mouth popped open in awe as we rounded the corner and she saw Hank pawing at the ground.

"Sure is." I steered Honey Blossom towards Hank and let her reins drop over the holding bar.

"Can I pet him?" she asked, walking over to him with slow steps.

"Of course. But I have to tell you, he's quite the ladies' man. I can't be held responsible if he steals your heart."

Sarah rolled her eyes at me over her shoulder before shifting her attention back to Hank who was more than happy that she was giving him scratches along his neck. Hank curled his head around and tried to grasp her ponytail with his lips which sent Sarah into a fit of giggles. "Quite the ladies' man indeed."

She stepped towards me and said with a smirk, "I don't know if I have room in my heart for both of you. I might have to make a difficult choice."

I grasped her middle and lifted her until her legs were wrapped firmly around me, arms dangling over my shoulders. "Is that so?" I nipped at her neck and I felt her legs tighten around me.

"Mhm," she mused, burying her face in the crook of my neck.

"Then I better show him up."

She leaned back, and even though she had her legs around my waist, she still wasn't eye-to-eye with me. That didn't stop her from scooting up and planting a kiss on my cheek.

"Depriving me of a proper kiss? You're killing me, sugar."

"Kisses are earned, cowboy. If you want one, you're going to have to give me a good time."

My laugh came out raspy as I fought against all the images floating around in my mind of just how much of a *good time* I wanted to show this woman.

"That can be arranged." She didn't take her eyes off me as I walked us the few steps to where Honey Blossom stood patiently. "Ready?" I asked.

"Yeah," she replied before she loosened the hold of her legs around my waist and I guided her right leg into the stir-rup. She swung her other leg over the saddle and settled in.

"Here's her reins. Do you need a quick refresher course or are you good?" I kept my hand on her thigh as she adjusted her seat.

"Does she lead with a command or just reins?"

"Just reins for this old girl. Wherever you want to go, just guide her. And she responds well to heel pressure, so no need to kick."

"Okay, great."

"You look good up there."

"I know." She shot me a wink as she directed Honey Blossom to back away from the barn and toward the trailhead.

I rose into the saddle myself and leaned over Hank's long black neck and whispered, "I think we're in deep trouble with this one, boy."

The sun cast shades of purple, red, and orange across the evening sky as Sarah and I rode side-by-side along the river. She didn't stop smiling the entire ride and her joy brought a lightness to my chest that reminded me of times before I went away.

"Did your parents like to ride?" The question came out of nowhere, but it didn't jostle me the same way it would have coming from someone other than Sarah. With her, everything felt easier. Like I could let my guard down and take a deep breath.

"They both rode a lot, but it was my mom who really enjoyed it. My dad found it as a necessity to keep the ranch going in between deployments."

"That seems like a lot of work on him. Being in the military and trying to keep a ranch going."

I looked out toward the river that ran through most of our property. "It was. He's definitely where I got my work ethic from. But he knew how to have a good time too. Every week that he was home, he'd come up with some ridiculous game for all of us to play. It usually involved some kind of obstacle course that Callie Rose and I had to run through. During the summers we'd always have slip 'n slide races."

I laughed to myself thinking back on those days. "One time, when we were really little—Callie Rose had barely started walking—he created an obstacle course in the yard and he and my mom raced us in wheelbarrows until they were both dog tired and my belly hurt from laughing so much."

Sarah's eyes were glassy, smile serene as she said, "That sounds like a magical childhood."

"It was," I rasped, wishing that I could relive some of those years when my parents were happy and all felt right in the world.

We rode on for a few minutes in silence.

"Did your parents do anything like that with you and your brother?" I asked, carefully.

She huffed, "No. Their idea of fun was putting us in as many extra-curricular activities as possible. Most that neither one of us wanted to do."

It was wild that we came from two different worlds and somehow both experienced pain where our families were concerned. Before my parents left us, they'd gifted Callie Rose and me with love and acceptance. Sarah might have been born with a silver spoon in her mouth, but her childhood home seemed void of the most important thing.

"I'm sorry they didn't give you more."

She knew what *more* meant as she solemnly replied, "Me too."

Her gaze turned west where the sun was sinking behind the distant mountains. "You know, I've always wanted land like this. A place where I can run wild and free without anyone to tell me I'm doing something wrong. Somewhere I can just be *me*."

She was so beautiful at that moment, her body limned

with the bright hue of the setting sun. If I knew better, I'd say she was an angel sent straight from the heavens. Breaking through every icy barrier I'd put around my heart with a simple look or smile.

"You can have it all, Sarah," I whispered and she turned to look at me.

"What?" Her voice was soft.

I wished I could capture it and hold onto it forever. How the loose strands of her hair fell in gentle curls framing her face. The cute bow shape her lips made when she was at ease. And how her eyes shone with curious wonder at all the world had to offer. I wanted to give her the world. I wanted to give her everything.

"My land. My sunsets and sunrises. Anything I have that would make you smile. Hell, I'd give you the air in my lungs and the last beat of my heart if it meant I could die with you looking at me like that. You can have it all."

Chapter 25

Sarah

The way he looked at me cracked something in my chest. It felt like an awakening. A step through a door that would change the rest of my life.

There was so much I didn't know about him. So many questions I wanted to ask, but I also knew that every word he spoke was the raw truth, spoken from the depths of his soul. He was bare, letting himself be completely open to me. Something tugged in my heart.

It was an answer to his vulnerability. Soul to soul, I found my mind skipping forward over all the little moments that could make up our lives. Him celebrating the rise of my business. Us spending our time together riding horseback through his ranch with no one but the stars to see the love we shared for one another.

Is it possible? I asked myself. To love someone I barely knew.

Maybe it was.

Because my heart ached for him. I ached to be in his arms when he was absent or to hear his voice when he wasn't around.

The question seemed trivial as I looked into his eyes, a serene smile painted on his lips like he had all the confidence in the world that I felt the same.

With a subtle shift in my heel, I nudged Honey Blossom forward and stretched my hand across the space between us. When he took it, I let my eyes close for a moment, savoring how his warmth seeped deep into my skin. His touch felt like home.

"If I get to spend the rest of my life feeling like I do right now, then that would be a gift, Ranger. Because you've become the brightest light in my life. What I feel for you…" I swallowed against the emotion swelling in my throat. "I don't think I could ever feel for someone else. When I'm around you, I'm alive. I want things for myself that I've never allowed myself to want. With you, life feels like it's filled with endless possibilities."

I smiled at him, blinking away the tears that lined the rim of my eyes. His laughter was soft and joyous. "Phew. I'm glad I'm not the only one hanging onto their emotions like a lifeline."

A single tear spilled over, rolling down my cheek as I laughed. "Everyone will think we're crazy."

"There isn't a single person's opinion in this entire world that I care about when it comes to you."

For a moment I thought about my parents and the mess I was in with Jones. I wondered what it would be like to show up to Sunday dinner with Ranger by my side and what my parents might say about him. But as I took in the man beside me, felt the callouses of his palms against my own, I realized that I would damn them all if it meant protecting him—protecting what we had.

I knew it for a while now. Somewhere deep in my heart, even before I made the deal with my mother, that there was something different between Ranger and me. Call it fate or divine timing, but I knew Ranger came into my life at the right moment. There was nothing more I wanted than to start building a life with him. Step by step, I wanted to know everything about his world and what made him who he was.

The truth was on the tip of my tongue before I swallowed it down. I would tell him about Jones and the deal I made with my mother that was soon to be broken. For now, I just wanted to live in this moment with him.

"I'm glad to hear we're on the same page." I squeezed his hand, feeling the connection between us buzz like electricity.

I felt Honey Blossom pawing the ground beneath me like she was tired of standing around and wanted to run in the beautiful fields before us. Ranger's gaze tracked the mare's movement before he looked back up at me and said, "Come on. I want to show you something."

"Okay," I whispered.

It was about a fifteen-minute ride to a field at the edge of Ranger's property. His hands were firm around my waist as he helped me off of Honey Blossom. Soreness crept along the inseam of my thighs, but the feeling quickly faded as I took in the view before me.

What seemed like miles of purple and green hues stretched out in all directions as the muhly grass swayed from side to side giving a long rippling effect from the fall breeze. The violet of the grass merged into the pinks and oranges of the setting sun, making the scene look surreal.

My breath caught and it took me a moment to find the words. "It looks like what I imagine heaven might be like."

I felt Ranger take a step towards my back, his warmth was palpable, even through my thick coat. For just a second, I closed my eyes when his arms wrapped around my front. He pulled me in close as I opened my eyes again, taking in the stunning view.

"We have about a hundred acres of the stuff. The cows don't do well with it, so we have it fenced off from the other pastures." He huffed a breath. "Miles has tried to convince me to kill it all so we can plant cow-friendly seed now that the ranch is expanding. Most of the time, it's just an endless sea of green or brown depending on how hot the summer months get. But when fall comes and it blooms…I don't know. I just can't seem to find the heart to mow it all down and replace it."

"I don't blame you." Twisting my neck, I looked up at him. "It's too beautiful to touch."

His eyes darted back and forth between mine, a solemn look on his face. "That's exactly what my mom used to say."

"Was she the one who brought you here?" A tentative question. There were whispers around town when Ranger's mom left him and his sister. Word always had a way of moving quickly in a small town. Unfortunately, the truth often got twisted in the game of telephone as a story bounced from one person to the next. The judgment placed on his family hadn't been kind.

I looked back out at the sinking sun and the river of purple grass before it, giving Ranger the space he needed as silence filled the air.

He shifted behind me, drawing me closer as he finally said, "Yes. She'd packed a picnic for just me and her and told me we were going on an adventure. I remember it being colder than tonight so it was probably in October or November. We rode her horse out here and I don't think I've ever felt as free as I did that night. When I saw the field for the first time I thought we'd gone to a different world. Like a fairytale or something. After we ate our sandwiches for dinner we spent hours running through the grass playing tag and probably some version of cowboys and outlaws.

"She was happy then. Always had a smile on her face." His words were strained like the memory made him smile from joy and frown from sorrow at the same time.

"Do you mind me asking what happened?"

His chest moved closer to my back as he inhaled deeply. "I have to admit, showing you the ugly side of my past makes me nervous."

I turned in his arms so we were facing one another. Sliding my palm over his chest, I let it rest over his heart. “The ugly parts are what make the happy moments so beautiful.”

“I think she’d like you very much if she were here. You both have a way of seeing the good in every situation.” His gaze drifted to the sunset behind me as he continued, “Or at least she did until my dad died.”

“I can imagine losing the one you love changes you in a way no one could predict,” I whispered.

The way his eyes shone made it seem like he was lost in distant memories. “When we received the news that he’d died in combat, my mother didn’t come out of her room for a week. Callie Rose and I took turns trying to get her to come out, but nothing we tried worked. She was inconsolable. Most nights, Callie Rose came into my room to sleep because our mother would spend the waning hours sobbing. Our walls weren’t thick enough to hide from the sound.

“It was hard. Fuck,”—he exhaled loudly—“hard doesn’t even begin to describe it. My dad would always tell me that if anything happened to him I’d become the man of the house and would need to take care of my mother and sister. And I tried.” Ranger’s voice broke and the sound cleaved my chest in two.

“But I was still a kid when he passed and it didn’t matter how hard I tried, losing him was my mother’s downfall. For a long time, I avoided the idea of loving someone. I had Callie Rose and my best friend Miles. They were enough for me. After I went away, the idea of someone loving me for all my faults and mistakes seemed nearly impossible.

"But then I saw you two summers ago at Deacon's bonfire. I knew exactly who you were, but I don't think I ever let myself truly see you until then. I think something in me shifted that night because I couldn't stop thinking about you."

"Why didn't you ask me out then?" I wondered what my life might look like if Ranger and I had started this journey together a year ago.

"Honestly?" He grabbed the back of his neck with a wince. "I'd just been released from prison and I know how this town talks. No part of me thought I had a chance in hell with you. Not with the way you grew up and the prejudice your family would likely have against someone like me."

The truth struck me like a blow to the gut. I wasn't offended by what he said, I was offended that he was right. My parents—and the people I grew up around—would have given me hell for dating him.

"If I'm being honest as well, I don't know if I would have had the mental fortitude to stand up to my parents back then."

"And what about now?"

Tell him. Just get it out.

I opened my mouth to reveal my version of the truth. To tell him how I'd fallen into a trap with my mother and even though Ranger had my heart, I allowed my mother to have dominion over my mind.

But then I sealed my lips, once again. Fearful that the

same prejudice he spoke about my parents would coat his thoughts about me if he knew the truth.

His brows furrowed as his gaze sharpened on me. "What is it, Sarah?"

My heart leaped into my throat and I felt like I was going to be sick. Was I really about to risk everything and tell him about Jones? About my mother?

"Um," I stuttered, my brain not quite knowing what I wanted to say as my heart battled for me to stay silent. To not risk losing this man who made everything seem right in the world.

The warmth of his open palm slid against my cheek and I savored the way his thumb stroked idly against my skin. Patient. He was so damn patient and I was being a coward.

I can do this, I internally whispered to myself. *I owe this truth to him.*

On a long exhale I looked him in those striking blue eyes and said, "There's something I need to tell you, but I don't want to taint this place."

"You could never." Concern shone in his eyes. "Just tell me what's going on."

I brought my hand up to where his was resting on my cheek and covered it. I didn't want this to go away. I didn't want us to end. But Ranger had a right to know what I'd done.

"I've already told you a little bit about my parents." He nodded. "But I don't think I've truly relayed how manipulative they can be."

"Have they done something to you?" His voice was thick

with malice and something primal in me loved how protective he was.

I sighed. "They haven't done anything directly to me, no. But a few weeks ago, my mother came into my bakery—which she's never done before—and offered me a deal."

His thumb stilled on my jawline. "I can't imagine it was a savory one."

My chest tightened. "No, it wasn't." On a deep inhale, I fought against the thudding of my heart and told Ranger the truth. "Her and my father have always been hung up on Theo and me finding the *right* matches. Since we were young, it was expected for us to marry someone of equal or greater monetary status. When I bucked against that and decided not to marry in my early twenties like most other debutantes around here do, I was already fighting an uphill battle against my parents. Just two summers ago, my mother prevented me from landing an account with one of her friends. All it took was a phone call from her and I lost a major opportunity."

Ranger's face shifted to cold stone. "Why would she do something like that to her own daughter?"

I shrugged. "Punishment? Incentive to get me to bend to her will? I honestly don't know why they're so rigid in their beliefs. But it showed me just how far she was willing to go to show me her disapproval of my choices in life.

"So, when she came to my bakery and struck a deal, I knew that if I declined her there would be consequences."

"What was the deal, Sarah?" I could hear it in his voice. That he'd march right over to my parents' house and demand my mother to leave me the hell alone.

I couldn't help the shaking in my voice as I said, "She told me that if I dated a man of her choosing, she would fully support my bakery. That she would encourage all of her friends to book their events with me so I could take the next step toward becoming an exclusive cake decorator."

My next words came out in a rush. "So, I've gone on a few dates with her friend's son. It was after you took me out on our first date and I already knew that no one in the world could compare to you, but I've struggled my entire life to be accepted by my mom and when she told me that she would endorse my dream of becoming a renown cake decorator, I didn't know how to say no." I sucked in a lungful of air and realized I was gripping the lapels of his brown jacket for fear if I let go, I'd lose him forever.

Heat hit the back of my eyes as I continued quietly, "He means absolutely nothing to me and I'm going to end things with him later this week. Not that there's anything to truly *end* because nothing's happened between us and he's actually kind of awful. But I'm going to tell him that I don't want to see him anymore. That I've fallen for someone else."

Ranger's face was impassive. I opened my mouth to say more, to say *anything* that would convince him that I wasn't a completely awful person. But there was nothing else to say. So, I clamped my lips shut and let the silence linger between us.

Cold licked at my skin as the sun finally slinked beneath the horizon, leaving Ranger and me dusted in twilight. A muscle ticked along his jaw and I swore an eternity slipped by as he mulled over everything I said to him.

I couldn't stand the silence anymore. "Say something," I whispered. "Please."

His gaze finally settled on me, his face still unreadable.

Oh no. This is it.

My breath caught as I readied myself for the blow I knew would land as he told me he wanted nothing to do with me. That there was no way he would continue building a relationship with a liar.

Maybe it was my own self-loathing that made me gasp as he framed my face with both his hands. "Sarah, the only thing that makes me mad about that story is the fact that you felt so cornered by your own mother that you went against your better judgment and started seeing a man you had no feelings for. Do I wish you would have told me sooner? Yes. But that's only so that I could have convinced you that giving in to someone like your power-hungry mother will only lead to your demise."

I gaped at him. "Wait, so you're not angry at me?"

His fingers came to grasp my chin and as he tilted my head back, he brushed his lips against mine. "No, sugar. I'm not. I couldn't expect you to fully dedicate yourself to me when we'd only been on one date. That wouldn't be fair, especially since we'd never talked about being exclusive."

He wasn't mad. Maybe I hadn't screwed this up after all.

He kept my chin snug between his thumb and forefinger while he snaked his other arm around my waist, drawing me so close to him I could feel the hard planes of his body even through our coats.

His eyes shifted into a molten storm of blue and silver as

his tone deepened an octave. "But now that we have everything out in the open, let's make one thing clear. From this moment forward, you're mine."

My toes curled in my boots as his lips came down on mine with a kiss that nearly brought me to my knees. Everything I was, he took. And I gave willingly. Opening up to him, baring my very essence to him like I'd never shown anyone before. His kiss explored every facet of who I was and I relished in how he took his time, gently nipping and suckling against my lips. His tongue rolled against mine in languid movements.

He was right. I was irrevocably his. When we parted, our breaths becoming one, I looked into his eyes and knew that he was mine too.

Chapter 26

Ranger

The roar of the rushing river was no match against the thrumming of my pulse in my ears. It took every bit of my restraint to not lay Sarah in that field and claim her right then and there.

I'd heard what she said to Deacon over the phone a few weeks back about being a virgin. While I wanted nothing more than to bury myself inside of her right this fucking second, I also didn't want to act like a wild man and scare her off. We'd have plenty of time for that later. Our first time, I wanted to savor.

"Have you ever gone skinny dipping?"

I groaned as my cock immediately hardened at her question. Looking over at her riding Honey Blossom next to me.

"Here I was trying to be a good boy and not let my thoughts stray to dangerous topics and then you wreck my plans with that question, sugar."

Her quiet laugh sent a jolt through me. It was the best

fucking sound I'd ever heard. I knew at that moment I wanted to make her laugh for the rest of our lives if she'd let me.

Fire shimmered in her gaze. "Well, have you?"

"Of all the wild things I've done in life, no. I haven't gone skinny dipping."

Honey Blossom stopped walking as Sarah pulled the reins back slightly. "What're you doing?" I asked, turning Hank around before cuing him to stop.

"The craziest thing I've ever done is wreck my parents' plan of having a perfect daughter who married a rich man. I'm thirty years old and I have very little to show for it, Ranger. I want to *live*."

The gleam in her eyes had my chest fluttering as I slipped off the saddle and followed her to the bank of the river. "Living is one thing, Sarah. But jumping into a cold river in the middle of fall will only give you hypothermia. Get your ass back here."

With a wink over her shoulder, I watched as she shed her jacket and hastily lifted her long-sleeved top over her head. Those long curls bounced with the movement, cascading over her bare back where only the strip of her lacey pink bra remained.

"Fuck me," I groaned under my breath, immediately feeling the strain of my cock against my jeans. She was beautiful. The feminine muscles of her back worked as she lifted her hands to unclasp her bra. The swell of the side of her breast made my palms ache to reach out and touch her, but I couldn't fucking move. She was a vision under the dim twinkle of stars and I didn't want to look away. I *couldn't* look away. Not as she bent over to take off her boots and socks before shimmying out of her jeans.

"Sarah," a guttural growl ripped from my chest when her thumbs hooked into her tiny thong and she pulled the fabric down, tossing it on top of her discarded jeans.

"Come on, cowboy." She looked at me over her shoulder again with a come-get-me swagger I didn't know she had. Then she dashed into the water.

I looked up at the stars for a brief moment, wondering how the hell I got so damn lucky to end up in this exact moment when I got to chase a very naked Sarah Williams into a river. Truth be told, I didn't care how I got here. I was just thankful that I did.

With lightning speed, I shed all my layers and walked to the edge of the river bank. Sarah's sultry gaze landed on me as she swirled her arms through the water. This part of the river was shallow, the current moving at a leisurely pace around her. Her eyes slid down my body and I was thankful for the pure masculine desire that kept the cold from shriveling my manhood.

Frigid water hit my skin and I hissed at the contact, but kept pushing forward to where Sarah was wading in the middle.

"You're the only thing that could get me in this cold ass water, you know that?"

She smirked. "Then I consider myself a very lucky lady."

"Come here," I coaxed. Her breath clouded in front of her face as she swam the rest of the gap between us. When I snaked my arms around her waist, pulling her naked body flush against me, she gasped.

"You didn't think you could taunt me with that beautiful body of yours and have me keep my hands off you, did you?"

Her breathy giggle had my cock nearly standing at attention despite the cold water. "The whole point of me getting in this cold water naked was to have you follow me in. I wanted to see what I was working with." She arched a brow.

"Hmm. Maybe you're not so sweet after all." She yipped as I nipped her bottom lip with my teeth.

Then she pouted at me. "But I like being your sugar."

I chuckled. "And did you like what you saw?"

Even in the impeding darkness, I could see the faint blush creeping along her neck and cheeks.

She nodded, eyes casting downward. Even though her legs were wrapped around my waist, she kept her middle from touching me, her breasts away from my chest. And that simply wouldn't do.

"Well, I can tell you one thing for sure. You're the most beautiful woman I've ever seen and I don't want you ever hiding your body from me." With my hand at the small of her back, I pressed her against me until I could feel the tender flesh of her clit and her hard nipples against my body.

It was so fucking divine, a shiver racked through my body.

"Are you cold?" she asked, finally leaning into my touch, draping her arms over my shoulders. I could already feel the heat of her arousal where her center was settled just below my belly button.

"Not even a little bit," I admitted, having completely forgotten about the cold water moving past us. My other hand trailed up her back until my palm settled at her neck. "Look up," I whispered.

Her lips parted with a sigh as she took in the sky above us. A blanket of darkness was dusted with emerging stars, a bright crescent moon slowly rose from the horizon.

"Is this living enough for you?" I asked.

A smile split her face and her arms pulled me closer. It felt so damn good to feel her against me with nothing between us.

"It's beautiful." She looked back at me, wonderment shining in her eyes. "I never get to see the stars like this at my place. There's too many lights in the neighborhood."

"Well, you're welcome to come here any time you like." I nuzzled my chin against the crook of her neck. She smelled so good, it was hard to keep myself in check.

"Ranger." My name on her lips had me squeezing her tighter against me. Close. She was so damn close and I could feel her body melding into mine like she was made for me.

"Yeah, sugar?"

That blush stained her cheeks again as she said, "I want to taste you."

Fuck. I ground my molars together.

"We have a slight problem with that."

"Oh?" She looked nervous like I was about to let her down.

"I consider myself a gentleman and there's no way in hell I'm letting you get a taste without me granting you pleasure first."

Before she could say anything, I lowered myself into the river and grabbed the back of her thighs, lifting her up until they were draped over my shoulders and her pussy was inches from my watering mouth. Holding her firm, I took a few steps back until the water was only to my hips.

"Ranger!" she squealed, but I dug my fingers into her ass, keeping her firm in place.

Her hands roamed through my hair. I looked up at her and asked, "Is this what you want, Sarah?"

Without a second thought, she nodded, biting her bottom lip. Then I buried my face in her pussy, feeling the warmth of her body against my tongue as I licked her in one long stroke.

Her fingers pulled at my hair and I fucking loved it, watching her head lean back, her eyes close. I kept my gaze fixed on her beautiful face amongst the starry night sky as I sucked on her clit, letting her breathy moans drive me near the edge of insanity.

My length hardened so much it fucking hurt, but I didn't care. All I wanted was to watch Sarah come undone before me, with my mouth drawing moans from her pink lips.

"Please." Her legs quivered against my shoulders. "Please, don't stop."

I hummed in pure male satisfaction at her words, the vibration of my throat hitting her center. She shivered, fingers pulling tighter on my hair. She tasted so damn good I knew I could die a happy man with my face between her legs.

"Oh fuck," she breathed into the night air, her breath gathering in front of her serene face.

I knew she was close, I could feel her thighs clamping down against the sides of my face. She started rolling her hips against my lips and I grasped her ass to make sure she wouldn't fall. Running my tongue along the entire length of her sent her reeling off the edge. She pulsed beneath my tongue and I loved every fucking second of her undoing. With a final gentle suck over her slit, she nearly collapsed forward from her climax.

Lifting my arms to her ribcage, I pulled her down from my shoulders and cradled her in my arms. Eyes heavy with lust, she slowly blinked up at me. "That was amazing," she whispered, voice hoarse from the pleasure I wrung from her.

"Next time, I'll take my time with you, sugar. That wasn't even a fraction of the pleasure I can make you feel." And it was true. The next time I tasted her, I was going to spend all fucking night making her body writh in bliss. But the temperature was dropping and the last thing I wanted was for our first intimate moment to be tarnished with her catching pneumonia.

I waded us out of the river and up to Hank where I had stowed away two blankets behind the saddle for when I thought we might sit in the field for a while. Setting Sarah on her feet, I wrapped one of the blankets around her shoulders.

"I think next time we should go skinny dipping in the summer." Her teeth chattered as she spoke. I cursed, rubbing my hands up and down her arms over the blanket. "You need a blanket too," she said between quivering lips.

"Don't worry about me. I've been in worse places than a cold fall night with a beautiful woman."

My words must have hit home because something like regret flashed in her eyes. I didn't comment on it though. I wasn't going to let my time in prison ruin this moment between us.

When her shivering slowed, I grabbed the other blanket and dried myself off with one side before flipping it over and covering my body.

Sarah stepped toward me, opening her blanket a little as she let her hands settle on my hips. "I didn't know it could feel like that." Her voice was soft.

Bursting into my awareness, I read between the lines of what she wasn't saying out loud. "You've never had a man pleasure you before? In any way?"

She bit her bottom lip again and I moved to hide my growing erection. I wanted to bite that lip while I slid into her, so fucking slow and deep.

"My mother…she always told me that my future husband would want me to be pure—*untarnished*—so I never let any of my school crushes go further than a peck on the lips. And when I moved out to pursue my own business…I don't know. I think I was so consumed by making it work that I didn't allow myself time for other things. I was so scared of my business failing and having to crawl back to my parents to beg for their help that I stopped living my life."

Anger burned in my chest for her. For how her parents

made her feel ashamed of the life she wanted for herself. That she felt so damn terrified of not making it on her own that she spent the last decade doing nothing but work.

"I think that was the other reason why I took the deal my mother made me about Jones. I'd never had her approval before." Her nervous laugh struck me hard in the chest. "I honestly didn't realize how badly I still wanted it until she was standing in my work kitchen and she looked at me like I wasn't a complete failure when I agreed to date him. I guess some part of me will always want her approval."

I tucked a lock of her hair behind her ear. "There's nothing wrong with wanting people to change, Sarah. I know what it feels like. I wanted my mom to come back to us after my dad died. To see her smile again. But looking back now, I think it was a good thing she left. If she hadn't, Callie Rose and I would probably still be locked in that moment of losing our father forever."

Sarah's eyes shone. "How do I let go, Ranger?"

I sighed. She looked so fragile and small that it nearly crushed me. I wanted to take away all her pain, but I knew—better than most—that no one else could do it for her.

"I think the best thing you can do for yourself is find something worth changing for. Anything that will take the ease of losing your parents' favor away. For me, it was taking care of Callie Rose. She was so young when our father died and our mother became depressed. I didn't want her to live a life of sadness. I loved my sister so much I decided I couldn't let the fear of being without our parents win."

Her eyes slid down to my chest like she was mulling over

what I'd said. "I haven't been living at all," she whispered. More to herself than me, I thought.

Seconds ticked by until she looked up at me, the high moon reflecting in her irises. "I want to live, Ranger."

I smiled. "Then let me give you the world."

Chapter 27

Sarah

Then let me give you the world.

It was all I could think about the entire ride back to his house. There was no doubt about my feelings anymore. Not after what we'd shared tonight. My sex was still throbbing with each gentle bounce I took in the saddle.

Vibrators be damned. I'd never had anything as good as Ranger's tongue licking my clit like I was a damn buffet of his favorite dessert.

The cold wind on my wet hair did nothing as my body still clung to the heat of my climax, even as the lights of his home came into view.

But it was more than that. Tonight, he'd shown me a sacred place he once shared with his mother. He'd told me that despite my fears, he wanted to give me the life I never let myself live.

I was falling hard and fast for him. The man who was born an outcast from my society. The one who protected all others, even if it cost him his freedom. Ranger was more than just my childhood crush now. He was the one I wanted to experience life with. The person I chose to share all parts of myself with.

"Thank you," I said to him as he steered Hank towards the barn on the left side of the house.

"For what?" His shoulder-length curls were still damp from the river water. I hoped he wasn't too cold.

"For sharing everything with me tonight. I feel…different. Like tonight helped me discover what I truly want for myself. I don't think that would have happened without you."

A smile parted his lips and crinkled his eyes. "I didn't lie when I said I wanted to give you the world. Tonight was just the start of that."

Something that had long been broken inside of me started to mend from hearing his words. I realized then that maybe I wouldn't have the perfect relationship with my parents. That they would never approve of who I am and what I wanted for myself. But I had a choice in who I allowed to impact my life. I could let my parents continue to meddle in my business and berate me for my choices. Or I could lean into what Ranger and my best friends provided me. A found family of sorts. Letting Willow, Johnny, Deacon, and Ranger fill the void my parents left.

As we rode the rest of the way to the barn, I felt everything in me shift.

I couldn't stop smiling.

"Why is your hair all wet?" Callie Rose asked her brother before he could say a word as we made the final step up to the back deck.

Ranger looked down at me, eyes blazing with the secret we shared of what transpired between us earlier. I felt my cheeks redden and my heartbeat kick up.

"We had a little adventure. Nothing for your nose to be in," he shot back at his sister.

Her dark brows rose toward her hairline, but she didn't pester him anymore. "Sarah, you know my sister." I nodded, giving her a warm smile. Her lips were tight as she looked me up and down, assessing me. I swallowed the lump in my throat. "And this is Miles." He gestured to the man sitting next to his sister. Miles was just as big as Ranger, taking over the entire Adirondack chair, legs stretched out long. His light brown hair flared out a little bit around his ears and the back of the baseball hat he wore backward. Stubble lined his sharp jaw and freckles dusted the bridge of his pert nose and cheeks.

He rose from his seat and stepped toward me, hand outstretched. I took it, thankful for the moment of warmth against the cold. "It's nice to finally meet you, Sarah." His accent was thick, like he was born in the backwoods of the Blue Mountains. I noticed Callie Rose eyeing our interaction.

Damn, she's intimidating. She'd always been really quiet

in school, but then again I wasn't dating her only brother back then.

"It's nice to meet you too, Miles."

With a quick glance at Ranger, he settled back into his seat. "Do you want something to drink?" Ranger asked me.

Before I could answer Callie Rose lifted a large canister. "I made fresh hot chocolate."

"Ooo. That sounds amazing. Thank you."

She grabbed two metal mugs from the side table to her right. One was red speckled with black and the other was cream speckled with blue. She poured the hot chocolate into both mugs and handed them to Ranger and me before we settled into the empty chairs around the firepit.

Raising the mug to my lips, I went to take a sip of the hot liquid and immediately stopped as Callie Rose asked, "So, what are your intentions with my brother, Sarah?"

Ranger choked on the gulp he'd just taken and I was thankful I hadn't drunk anything yet.

When I looked at Callie Rose, there was no humor in her eyes. She was dead serious. I had to give the girl props. If it was my brother, I'd be grilling the girl he was dating too.

"Come on Cal, you don't need to do that to her," Ranger said giving me deja vu from when Willow asked the same question to him.

I placed a hand on his knee. "No, it's okay. She has every right to ask that question." He gave me an apologetic look like he was desperately sorry that his sister was about to put me through the ringer.

Shifting my attention back to Callie Rose, I told her

exactly what my intentions were with her brother. "I've gone through most of my life feeling unsure about my decisions. I tend to question everything I do and I think that's because I never had parents in my corner cheering me on. What I feel for Ranger is one of the very few things I've been certain of. I can only speak for myself when I say that I've never cared for anyone the way I do for your brother. So, I intend to continue caring for him and showing him just how wonderful I think he is."

Reflections of the dancing flames from the fire pit burned in Callie Rose's eyes as she considered my words. Her face was unreadable for what felt like countless minutes ticking by. And then…a slight tilt of her lips shifted upward and I loosed the breath I'd been holding.

"Caring for him is all a sister could ask for." Her faint smile turned into a grin as she took in her brother next to me. A quiet exchange happened between them and I only hoped it was her approval.

"But if you hurt him, I can't promise I won't hurt you." My heart stopped at her words.

"Noted," I croaked out.

"Callie Rose!" Miles and Ranger said at once and she just sat back in her chair with a smug look on her face.

"What?" She shrugged nonchalantly like she didn't just threaten me with physical harm. "I have to look out for my big brother. It's not like you will." She shoved Miles's arm. "All you've done is get him in trouble."

"I don't know what you're talking about." Miles took a swig from his beer bottle, eyes darting away.

"Oh, like that time you sank dad's fishing boat?! And then blamed it on Ranger?" Callie Rose's eyes were wide with mischievous humor.

It was Ranger who replied, "She has you with that one Miles. Sorry to say."

Miles guffawed at his best friend. "*You* were the one who convinced me it was okay to take the boat out in the first place!"

"Yeah, but I wasn't the one who stood up in it trying to catch a fish and ended up toppling us over."

Miles opened his mouth to respond but instead of words, a throaty laugh flew past his lips. It only took a few seconds for his laughter to catch on, leaving Ranger and Callie Rose clutching their stomachs.

Tears of humor creased Ranger's eyes and I didn't think I'd ever seen him look so handsome.

"I will never forget the way your face looked as you tripped over the side." Ranger's words were choppy from his laughter. "Then the boat nearly swallowed me whole as it tilted over. I still don't think my lungs have recovered from all the water I took in."

Callie Rose pointed at Miles, tears streaking down her face. "And dad's face was beet red when you both came up to the house, sopping wet. He loved that little Jon boat more than he loved us."

Their laughter finally started to settle. Ranger wiped at his eyes before he settled a hand on my thigh. "Nah. He definitely loved us more."

"Just maybe not on that day," Miles chimed in.

"Yeah. Definitely not on that day," Ranger said.

A comfortable silence settled over everyone. Each of them was lost in distant memories that I'd never been a part of. But it didn't feel like I was an outsider looking in. Their banter and love for one another reminded me of my friends and everything we'd shared together.

I wondered what it might be like for all of us to hang out sometime. I could just imagine how Willow and Callie Rose would get along. Each one showing their protective nature. It might be explosive.

"I'll be right back," Callie Rose said as she rose from her seat.

When the door closed behind her I looked to Miles. "So, Miles is there anything I should know about Ranger? Like does he snore in his sleep? Or forget to put the toilet seat down?"

Miles chuckled and I could feel Ranger's eyes on me, but I ignored him. Miles's eyes slid to Ranger and for a moment I thought he might divulge the man's secrets. But then he replied, "Nah. Not this one. He's pretty much as solid as they come."

It was exactly the kind of response Willow would have given and I appreciated that Ranger had someone to back him up, instead of selling him out.

Ranger's hand squeezed my thigh. "Trying to find my weaknesses, sugar?"

I winked at him. "Just trying to make sure I know what I've gotten myself into." He patted my leg with a smile.

Then Callie Rose came back through the door with an

acoustic guitar in hand. Ranger shifted in his seat next to me, an uncomfortable look on his face.

She handed him the guitar. "I think it's been long enough," was all she said as he took it from her hands.

Curiosity bloomed within me at her words. Playing the guitar was never something we'd talked about, but it seemed like it had once been a big part of his life based on his sister's comment.

He sat still for a few moments, hands grasped around the neck of the guitar while Callie Rose sat in her chair. Ranger's eyes were glassy, my fingers itched to reach for him but I was nervous to intervene while he was lost in thought. Then, with a look towards his sister that showed his disapproval of being bombarded, he settled the body of the guitar on his lap.

Clearing his throat, he draped his right arm over the front of the guitar, his left fingers lining up on the neck. And then he played.

I was damn near awestruck watching his fingers move up and down the neck as a beautifully sad melody surrounded us. His dark curls slid along his shoulders with each strum of the strings and I wanted nothing more than to twine my fingers through them while I kissed him slowly. Those bright eyes had turned dark, like a thundering storm over the lake. They turned toward me and I was lost in them. He played that guitar like it was the strings of my heart, each chord hitting home. Pulling me closer and closer to the edge. The look he gave me told me he'd be there at the bottom. Arms wide open and waiting to catch me.

Our gazes were locked when the aching melody came to

a close and something in my chest cracked at the absence of the sound. I wanted him to play for me forever.

"I've missed that," his sister said, severing the connection between Ranger and me.

"Yeah, man," Miles's face was sad, yet serene. "It's been too long."

I realized at that moment that the two of them had missed out on so much while Ranger was away. Ten years of having to live in a world where their brother and best friend was trapped behind bars for the crime of defending a kid against some rich assholes. My heart squeezed thinking of how many memories they'd all missed out on together because someone else decided he should be punished for protecting the innocent.

Tears hit the back of my eyes and I blinked quickly. I had no right to cry. Not when they'd lost so much.

"I'm going to grab another beer," Miles said, voice soft. "Callie, want to join me?"

Her eyes were locked on her brother and I wondered if she'd heard what Miles asked her at all. Then she blinked several times, coming out of whatever stupor had pulled her down. "Yeah, sure." I didn't miss the way Miles offered her his hand and how her body shuttered when she took it, like his touch had electrified her.

When they disappeared through the back porch door, I shifted in my seat so I could see Ranger's face clearly. "That was beautiful."

His Adam's Apple bobbed as he swallowed.

“Thank you.” He leaned the guitar against the side table next to him. “It’s been a really long time since I played.”

“You haven’t played since you were released?” I asked, my voice quiet.

He shook his head, his lips turned down slightly. “I was different when I got out. Being locked in a cage for that long changed me in ways that I can’t describe. I tried to be my normal self…for Callie Rose and for Miles. But something inside of me changed in those ten years. When I was released and came home, it felt like nothing had changed at all and that the entire world had shifted at the same time.

“Miles was granted custody of Callie Rose when she was sixteen to eighteen years old while I was gone. He made sure the ranch stayed alive and that my sister was taken care of. I gave up that responsibility the night I fucked everything up. Even though I knew he would take care of her and our home, I couldn’t get rid of the guilt that I’d left her for so long. I thought I needed to be punished.”

My chest twisted. I reached for his cheek, luxuriating in how his warmth seeped into the palm of my hand. He closed his eyes, pushing the side of his face against my skin. “You didn’t do anything wrong, Ranger. You acted in defense of a young kid who was being ganged up on by three men. The only wrong thing about it was how those guys were able to cheat the system with their money.”

“It doesn’t take back all the years I lost though.”

I swallowed. “You’re right. It doesn’t. And I wish, more than anything, that I could make it all right for you. That I could snap my fingers so you could have all those amazing years with your sister and Miles. But you don't need to punish yourself anymore. It's okay to be happy."

"You've shown me that." His voice was husky with emotion. "Before you came along, I was still stuck in the past. Feeling like there was no way out for me. That I would be stuck in the fear of losing my freedom forever. Being with you has shown me something different. That there's still joy to experience in this life."

"There is," I whispered, not caring about the tears that started to spill down my face. "And I'm so glad we get to experience it together."

Chapter 28

Ranger

"I think she's good for you," Callie Rose said as she lifted a box filled with carrots and stacked it into the wagon. Before shutting the truck door, she lifted the final box of beets from the seat.

"Yeah?" I grabbed the handle on the wagon and we walked to where her farmer's market tent was waiting.

Last night had been incredible. Showing Sarah the field where my mother took me as a kid, seeing her become so free on the land that had been passed down through generations in my family. Watching her with awe as she came undone from the pleasure I brought her. Fuck, I could still taste her on my tongue. I wanted more of her. More of how she made me feel like my life was finally worth living again. She chased away my fears like a star shining in the depthless night.

There was no more falling for her. I'd fallen already. Straight off the side of the cliff, headfirst.

Callie Rose's coat rustled against the small crate of beets she carried as I guided us along the park sidewalk, toward her tent.

"I knew that things would be different when you got out. I can't even begin to imagine how prison changes a person, but I was hopeful that you would find your way back to us—to Miles and me."

"You felt like I wasn't here?" I shot her a sidelong glance. Her eyes were leaden with worry as she looked at me.

"Not really, no. I saw you trying. Every day I knew you were giving us your best shot of trying to keep things light and normal. When you told me about the nightmares for the first time, I knew things were different. I told Miles I wasn't confident that we'd ever get you back. Not fully anyway."

My stomach coiled in a knot as guilt washed over me. "I never wanted you to feel bad, Cal. That was the furthest thing I'd ever want you to feel. I just…" I took in a deep breath, trying to get my thoughts straight. "When I was inside, I had this whole plan of what I was going to do with my life when I was released. I wanted to make the ranch better. Get our family out of transgenerational poverty. Help you in whatever way I could so you had a chance to live a great life. I never wanted to leave you. But when I got out… *fuck*. I was so damn scared of going back in that all the plans I'd made were dust in the wind."

Callie Rose stopped walking. The wagon creaked as I slid it to a stop and turned to face her. "You don't have to go back there, Ranger. Not ever. And we were okay. Miles and me. We made it work. Of course we would have wanted you to be here with us, but you don't need to feel bad about it anymore."

I hugged her. "I don't know when things shifted. When you became the one to give your big brother advice. But I'm thankful for it." She leaned into the side hug, careful not to drop the crate of beets.

"I've always been pretty awesome." Her voice was lighter, laced with humor. I bopped her nose with my finger. She tried to swat my hand away with the crate of beets and failed.

We started walking again as she said, "I was serious though. About thinking Sarah is good for you. I was worried when you first told me you were dating a blue blood, but she's different from what I thought."

Her acceptance of Sarah meant more to me than I could express. It wouldn't matter how deeply I felt for someone. If they weren't a good fit for my family, it wouldn't work. "I have to admit that she's different from what I thought too. I guess that's our own prejudice at work. Making assumptions about people just at first glance without really getting to know them."

"Yeah," she responded.

"I'm really glad that you like her though. It certainly makes my life a lot easier."

She smirked. "That's me. The best sister in the world, making dreams come true."

I flicked her on the nose. "Hey!" she shrieked, wringing a laugh from me.

It didn't take us long to set up the booth. We worked in tandem, organizing all the vegetables for patrons to easily access them. She set up her iPad in the center of the foldable table so she could take payments. We settled into the chairs I'd brought from my truck as the townsfolk started filing into the park.

I'd planned to help my sister for most of the morning before heading to the opposite side of the park where Sarah's booth was set up. Just as I was about to text her to see how things were going at her booth, two men strolled up to my sister's tent.

Blood roiled through my veins at the sight of LeRoy Cummings. The fucking bastard who had sued me for assaulting him after he'd ganged up on a college freshman with two other douchebags. His dark eyes landed on me, recognition gleaming.

"Look who we have here." He smacked his friend's chest with the back of his hand to get his attention.

Callie Rose went still beside me. I didn't have to look at her to know that hatred thrummed in her veins as much as it did in mine. He'd stolen ten years from us. From my fucking family. From my *life*.

Now, he was right in front of me. Smirking just like he'd been that day in the courtroom when the judge announced my sentencing. Ten years of my life had been stolen away while this jackass had walked free because the kid he'd beaten to a bloody pulp didn't have the courage to press charges. Not that I blamed him. They'd beaten him so badly he probably just wanted to get as far away from them as possible.

There were times, when I was inside, that I regretted my actions. But seeing LeRoy's eyes pinned on me like he'd won…*no*. There was no more regret. He deserved every fucking punch to his ugly ass face. Something in me savored the view of his once perfect nose and how it was slightly bulging in the middle from my fist breaking the bone.

His friend shifted toward Callie Rose and me, watching us with a bored look on his face.

"This is the dirtbag who thought he could get away with punching me." LeRoy ran a hand through his jet-black hair. "Little did he know I let him get the hits in so I could send him away for ten years."

"Oh shit," his friend laughed. The sound was chalky, it grated my nerves making my anger rise higher. "I'm surprised they let him out. By the looks of him, they should have kept him in that cage."

I bristled at the word *cage*. Flashes of my nightmares brimming the surface. I shoved them down. There wasn't a chance in hell I was going to let these assholes affect me.

I went to step toward them, red lining my vision. It felt like I was in a damn tunnel and the only thing I could see was a flashback of my fist beating LeRoy's face that night.

He wasn't supposed to be here. Back in my hometown. He was supposed to be somewhere far far away where I'd never have to see his fucking face again. But that was the thing about small towns. Everyone usually made their way back home.

Something pulled at my arm before I could take another step forward. No. It wasn't something. It was *someone*. Looking over my shoulder at my little sister, I swore her face looked different. Younger. Just like she'd been when I went away. And like a flash, my vision cleared and I could see how age had shifted her into a woman.

No words left her mouth, but I noticed the subtle shake of her head. The plea in her eyes as her grip on my forearm tightened. The rage in my veins stuttered when I saw the worry shining in her irises. If I did this…if I let my anger over these two assholes win then I would lose everything.

Our surroundings came back into focus. There were so many people and there was no way in hell I'd get away with pummeling his face again. Just like I hadn't when they'd somehow managed to pull a video recording from the store that monitored their alleyway.

Darkness shrouded my vision as I closed my eyes. With a few deep breaths, I steadied myself. My thundering heartbeat slowed and the anger I felt toward LeRoy and everything he'd taken from me settled.

Maybe I'd get my revenge one day. But not now. Not in front of my sister. And certainly not when anyone could fucking see me.

When I opened my eyes, Callie Rose knew I was safe. I could see the light coming back into her face. At that moment I felt proud that I'd made the better decision.

Without another look at LeRoy or his friend, I went back to organizing the empty crates and boxes at the back of my sister's tent.

I heard one of them say, “Fucking hick” under their breath. The other one snickered before the sounds of their feet hitting the sidewalk told me they’d grown bored and walked away.

Callie Rose loosed a long exhale. Heat crawled over my skin. I might have made the right choice of not engaging with them, but fuck if it didn’t feel hard.

“He doesn’t deserve to walk around with that smug look on his face,” she whispered.

“He doesn’t deserve to walk around at all."

“Thank you, Ranger. For not letting them win. You have too much to lose now.” Sorrow blanketed her face and I knew she meant that I’d found something really special with Sarah.

“I had too much to lose the first time,” was my only response before I went back to organizing the boxes and she started taking orders from patrons who were strolling up.

What I didn’t tell my sister was that it took everything in me not to make LeRoy pay for what he’d done to our family. For the years he’d shaved off my life like I was nothing.

I wanted to do better. To let it all go. But I knew, deep down, that if I ever had the chance to make him suffer without anyone knowing. I’d fucking do it.

"Hi, beautiful." Sarah's chestnut hair was held up high on her head in a messy bun. Long tendrils framed her face. She looked so damn pretty, it made my chest hurt.

"Hi!" she breathed, looking up from cleaning the now empty glass case where she'd sold out of her bakery items.

The glass door snicked shut and she hopped around the table with a bright smile on her face before jumping straight into my arms.

Sugar and spices overwhelmed my sense of smell in the best way. It was wholly *Sarah* and I breathed in deeply, taking note of exactly what she smelled like so I would remember it when we had to be apart.

"I've missed you," she said and then her soft lips met mine in a crushing kiss that had me drawing her closer. A soft moan had her mouth vibrating against mine as she opened up for me and I met her tongue with mine in long fluid strokes.

Fuck, she tasted so damn good. The way she melted against my body had my cock hardening against my jeans. I'd gotten a taste of her last night and my mouth watered for more. I wanted every part of her to be mine.

"I missed you too, sugar," I said as we parted. I framed her face with my hands and kissed her forehead.

"Are you ready for tonight?"

Her cheeks hollowed out as her lips twisted to one side. She was supposed to see the guy her mother had set her up with to end things. Even though I knew nothing had happened between the two of them, it still rubbed me raw thinking of another man taking her on a date. Even if she was going to tell him she no longer wanted to see him.

"Mmhmm." She nodded, burying her hands under my coat. I loved when she did things like that.

I stroked the back of her hair, loving how soft the strands felt in my rough hands. "I have to admit, I'll be pretty damn happy when it's over." I knew what ending things with this guy would mean for Sarah. She would have to face the wrath of her mother and whatever bullshit she would try to pull. But wanting Sarah meant wanting every bit of her. Sharing even an hour of her attention with another man had my head swimming with what I could only describe as jealousy. I'd never felt the emotion in my entire life before her.

"Honestly, me too. I'm tired of letting my parents influence what I do in my life. I don't want to be afraid of their consequences anymore. This is the first step in healing from all of that."

"If there is anything I can do to help, you just say the word and I'll be there."

She bit her lower lip. "Actually, there might be something you can do if it wouldn't be too much trouble."

"Name it."

She took a moment to consider her words. "He hasn't given me any true reason to think that he might react poorly to me rejecting him, but…I just have this feeling. I can't really describe it and I might be completely overreacting. But I get the notion that he has it in him to be a real douchebag if he doesn't get what he wants. Would you mind picking me up just in case I can't get rid of him?"

That fierce protectiveness that I got from my father immediately sharpened my focus. Sarah hadn't told me these concerns before. Now, I was on high alert for her safety.

"If you have a feeling like that, then you're probably right, Sarah. Are you sure you want to do this in person?" I wasn't going to control what she wanted to do. It wasn't my place, even if I felt jealous or protective. But I wanted to ask to let her know she didn't have to do this if she didn't want to.

"Yeah, I'm sure. Ending things will burn enough bridges through my mother. I don't need him telling everyone in town that I'm a coward who couldn't end things with him in person. I think it'll be okay, I'd just feel more comfortable having you as my getaway driver." She winked at me and her cute smile did something strange to my stomach. It felt like a swarm of bees or dragonflies were buzzing inside of me.

"Just name the place and time and I'll be there."

"Thank you." She pressed a kiss to my cheek that had me grinning like a fool.

"Let me help you finish packing up your car."

With her hand in mine, she guided me under her tent. "It's nice to have some big strong muscles to help me with these things now."

"You can borrow them anytime you want, sugar."

Chapter 29

Sarah

I'd chosen a basic chain restaurant for the date with Jones tonight because the last thing I wanted was to make a scene in a nice establishment where fellow patrons with prying eyes would likely gossip about what they heard or saw between us. News had a way of spreading like wildfire in a small town and it spread even faster when the news involved Mary Lynne Williams's daughter.

I swore it was like my mother had eyes and ears all over the damn town.

Jones had offered to pick me up at my place. I'd told him I preferred to just meet at the restaurant. I wasn't too keen on showing the guy exactly where I lived right before I was going to break things off with him.

Right before we'd sat down at the table, I'd sent Ranger a text message letting him know which restaurant we'd be at and that I'd text him toward the end of our meal. He'd replied instantly and said he was already on his way and he didn't mind waiting in the parking lot for however long it took.

There was no doubt in my mind that I was making the right decision. That didn't stop me from sweating up a storm and nearly picking my nails to death under the tablecloth. I'd never ended things with a man before and everything was made worse by the fact that I wasn't only ending things with Jones. I was also ending the agreement I'd made with my mother.

She was going to come for me…I knew it. As much as I'd tried to prepare myself for the fallout, telling myself that I had every right to live my own life, I still feared my mother's wrath. Mostly because it made me sick to my stomach that my own mother disliked who I'd turned out to be so much that she was desperate enough to strike a bargain with me.

Attempting to calm my nerves and steer my thoughts away from my mother, I slid my sweaty palms along the top of my jeans and urged myself to just *breathe*. Inhale. Exhale. Inhale.

"I'm really glad you agreed to come out with me again tonight, Sarah. I've been enjoying our time together. I think we connect pretty well," Jones said over the top of his laminated menu. The smile he gave me should have crinkled the side of his eyes, but the skin around them remained perfect. I wondered if he was a Botox user. I wouldn't put it past the guy.

Heat crept up my neck at his compliment. Thoughts scattered in my mind like a ping pong ball. On one side I thought it would be better to end things right after we ordered our food, so I could get it over with. The more rational and less chaotic side suggested I wait until our food was already out since the guy deserved to at least eat his meal before I let him down.

Now, I was questioning why I decided to tell him in person. This wasn't exactly the best time for my Southern manners to shine through. Not when I was fairly certain my neck was breaking out in a stress rash.

"Mmhmm," was all I managed to get out through the thickness in my throat.

He tilted his head slightly, eyes honing in on me. "You wouldn't agree?"

Okay. I guess we're doing this now.

"I actually wanted to talk to you about this. About how I've been feeling about us moving forward."

His lips pursed slightly as I squared my shoulders. "I know that our mothers thought we could be a good match for one another and I think you're a wonderful man, but I'm not feeling the spark to take things any further than being friends."

Refraining from letting out an obscene sigh, I held my breath. Waiting for him to respond.

A smirk tugged at his lips as he snorted a breath. "You honestly think you can do better than me?"

My mouth popped open in shock. I immediately closed it. *Who the hell does this guy think he is?*

"Listen, Jones—"

"No, Sarah," he interrupted, leaning forward. "You listen to me. Your mother made it very clear that the future of your career is in a precarious place should you disappoint me. I think we both know what that means. I don't like being disappointed, especially by a stubborn brat like you. So, do us both a favor and plaster another fake smile on your face and go back to doing what your mother told you to do."

Thoughts emptied from my mind, and then a million came flooding in at once. My mother told him about the deal I made with her? He knew this entire time that we were dating to give my mother what she wanted? None of it was real? Not that I wanted any of it to be real, but at the very least I thought that maybe his desire to go on a date with me was genuine.

But no. His interest in me was feigned. He was only satisfying his own mother's twisted game of merging our two powerful families. For some reason that hurt even though I had no interest in Jones from the start.

The sound of scraping on plates and patron chatter was growing louder by the second as I took in the scowl on Jones's face. I needed to get out of here. *Fast.*

Water splashed over the rim of our glasses as I rose from the table, my thighs bumping into the edge.

Out. I needed to get out.

I'd been to this restaurant hundreds of times, but I was disoriented from the feeling of being trapped. It took me a moment to remember where the front door was. I dashed towards it, throwing it open with so much force it nearly swung back and hit me. Starting toward the parking lot next to the small restaurant, I rounded the side of the brick building.

"Where do you think you're going?" I heard behind me before a hand clamped over my wrist, dragging me backward.

Jones whipped me around until I was flush against him. He held onto my wrist and his other arm snaked around my waist. He felt…wrong. I hated being this close to him.

"Let me go," I grunted, trying to pull my wrist free, but he held firm.

He sneered. "I always get what I want, brat. And right now, it's you. Don't think I don't enjoy seeing you squirm." Bringing his face to my neck, he breathed in deeply. "I fucking love it."

Dread had my stomach sinking down to the pavement as alarm bells rang out in my mind. All the little moments when he made me feel uncomfortable on our dates had been my intuition telling me this guy was no good. He was rotten to the fucking core and now he had me pressed against him.

"Let me go!" I yelled, stumbling to break free from him, but he only laughed as he wrenched me close again.

A car door slammed from somewhere behind me. "Get your fucking hands off her."

Ranger.

With Jones's grip still firm, a sense of comfort came over me. Safe. I was safe with Ranger here. I knew he wouldn't let anything happen to me.

Craning my neck over my shoulder, I saw Ranger walking toward us with menace in every step. His fists were clenched at his sides. Disdain rippling off him.

"Who the fuck are you?" Jones asked, loosening his grip

on me only slightly. "Oh wait," he chuckled. "You're that dumb fuck who LeRoy sent to prison for ten years."

A snarl ripped from my throat. I didn't care if he still had his body pressed against mine, it pissed me off that he would demean Ranger.

The sound I made grabbed his attention. His ice-blue eyes landed on mine as realization swept over his face. "Ohhh. I see. You're the kind of little rich girl who likes sleeping around with the trash of society to get a fun thrill. I wonder what your mother would—" A gurgling sound emanated from his throat.

"I said, get your fucking hands off her." In a single moment that happened too quickly for me to register, Ranger went from standing a few feet behind me to squeezing Jones's throat until he couldn't speak. Clawing at Ranger's hand, he let me go.

As fast as I could, I darted behind Ranger. Every muscle in my body shook with the understanding of what would have happened if I hadn't asked him to pick me up. I would have been all alone with Jones. Completely at his mercy.

Ranger stepped closer toward Jones, keeping his hand tight around his neck. "I should fucking kill you for touching Sarah. For not letting her go when she told you to."

Jones's eyes grew wide as he tried to suck in air. He was panicking. Part of me relished the idea of seeing him struggle.

"I should fucking kill you," Ranger repeated and I could see the darkness sweeping over him. He would do it if it meant protecting me from harm. Maybe Jones did deserve for something terrible to happen to him. He touched me without my consent, forced me into his body, and wouldn't let me go. Would he do that to other women? *Has* he done that to other women? The thought made bile rise in my throat.

Flashes of Ranger's sorrowful face when he told me about his time in prison had me reaching out to touch his arm. Jones deserved to suffer. But at what cost to Ranger? The last thing he needed was for someone to round the corner and see him pinning Jones to the brick wall with his hand around the guy's throat. I wanted Jones to pay for how scared he'd made me feel. But not at the expense of Ranger's freedom. Not at the cost of having him disappear from my life to live behind bars.

"He's not worth it," I whispered, drawing closer to his back. I rubbed his bicep up and down, his hand shaking around Jones's throat. "Don't let his stupidity take you away from me. I need you, Ranger. I…I don't want to go through this life without you by my side." The words were raw in my throat as I spoke the truth.

Ranger kept his grip firm but slowly turned his face to look at me. His blue eyes blazed with fury. Jones was just like LeRoy and this was a chance for Ranger to get his revenge. To protect what was his.

"Please," I coaxed, running my hand down his arm until it settled over his wrist. "Just take me home."

Something flashed in his eyes at the word *home*. His nostrils flared as he closed his eyes for a moment. Opening them, he looked at Jones and pressed him further into the wall. "You're lucky she was here to stop me. If I see you anywhere near her ever again, I'll make good on my promise. You won't see the fucking light of day, I'll bury your body so fucking deep in the ground no one will be able to find it." With a final shove, Ranger dropped his hold on Jones who bent over clutching at his neck, gasping for air. Without a second look at us, Jones scrambled away into the parking lot.

Ranger was quiet as he looked down at me.

"Thank you," I told him before wrapping my arms around his waist, taking in his scent of leather and sweet grass.

His shaking palm found the back of my head, his lips kissed my hair.

"I hate what he did to you, Sarah. I couldn't stand the fear in your eyes as he held you against him. I shouldn't have let him go."

"Shhh," I crooned, squeezing him tighter to me. I held him close, letting the warmth of his arms draw away the remnants of my fear.

When I leaned back to look at Ranger's face, his eyebrows were drawn together in a pained expression. I reached up, smoothing his skin until the wrinkles were gone. "You being here with me means more than seeing Jones be punished." I swallowed the lump in my throat. "I can't lose you, Ranger. Not when we haven't had any time. Not when we've just begun."

Tears hit the back of my eyes as I pressed my cheek against his chest. His large hands splayed against my back.

"You won't lose me, sugar. I promise I won't let that happen."

The cotton of his flannel was soft against my face as I nodded against him. "Okay."

We stood there, holding one another for a long while. "Take me home?" I finally asked him, my lips grazing a button on his shirt. I wasn't quite ready to let go of him.

"I like the sound of that."

Chapter 30

Ranger

Sarah's Craftsman-style house was quaint and picturesque with a small front yard and perfectly manicured lawn. It made me think she had her mother in mind when picking it out, but I kept that thought to myself as she led me through the front door.

To my left, I noticed exactly why she must have chosen this place to be her home. A huge kitchen with white porcelain countertops took up the massive space across from the living room.

I could picture her waking up every morning cooking herself a batch of blueberry pancakes. With her long hair in a bun on the top of her head, white speckles of flour gracing her nose and cheeks. The thought brought me comfort since I'd spent most of our ride here trying to keep from turning my truck around to hunt down that fucking asshole.

While I was waiting for her to leave the restaurant, I had

looked to see if there were any cameras in the area next to the building. I couldn't tell why my mind immediately went there, drawing me back to that fateful night. But I had a feeling that if Sarah's mother had picked the guy out, he probably lacked the ability to be okay with being rejected. Turned out…I was right. The guy was an ass and needed to be taught a lesson. I could still feel the skin of his throat pressed against my palm, his pulse quickening every time I squeezed harder.

It would have been so easy to beat him down for not letting Sarah go when she told him to. So fucking easy.

When I felt the warmth of her touch against my arm and the plea in her voice, I knew there wasn't anything in this world I wouldn't do for her. She brought me back to life when I never thought I'd experience true joy again. And for that, I'd give her everything.

"So, this is my home," Sarah said, rubbing her hands together and blowing her warm breath into them. The temperature had dropped significantly once the sun went down and it felt like she didn't have the heater on yet. "Let me make us a fire."

She started darting around the living room nervously, grabbing pieces of wood from a small holder next to the mantel. I came up next to her and took the two pieces of wood from her arms. "Let me," I said.

Positioning the extra pieces around the starter log, I reached for the long lighter tucked in a basket in front of the hearth and set the paper on fire. Bright orange flames licked away at the starter log and small embers glowed on the oak wood. We'd have a roaring fire in a few minutes judging by how dry the wood was.

I turned to Sarah. Her arms were wrapped around her middle and I hated how small she looked in the space. My vibrant, beautiful girl looked fucking terrified in the safety of her own home and I hated it.

"Come here, sugar." Moisture glistened in her chocolate eyes as she melted into my embrace.

"He wouldn't let me go," she whispered so low I could barely hear her. Her words broke something in me. "I told him to stop and he wouldn't." When her voice cracked, my chest ached so badly I couldn't breathe.

My throat was raw as I spoke. "I promise you, Sarah, that no one else will ever touch you again. No one." I kissed the top of her head, small whisps of her hair tickling my lips. "I wish I could take away every second of that experience for you. I wish I would have moved faster."

Her head moved side to side against my chest. "No." Her eyes glistened as she tilted her head back to look up at me. "You didn't do anything wrong. The only person at fault here is Jones. He should have stopped when I told him to."

Wetness hit my hands as I palmed the sides of her face. Watching tears fall over her rosy cheeks was the worst thing I'd ever seen. I needed them to go away, replaced with her beautiful smile.

So, I leaned down and kissed the salty trails along her face. Pressing my lips just under each one of her eyes I trailed downward until I gently grazed her chin. A whimper escaped her lips as I carefully grasped the wrist Jones had grabbed her by and I kissed away that hurt too. Leaving only tender affection to replace the pain he'd caused her.

"Ranger," she breathed, my name was a prayer on her lips.

I let her wrist go and reached down to pick her up. My heartbeat pounded in my ears as she kissed me, opening up fully and dipping her tongue into my mouth. She was so warm and sweet. Her little moans vibrated against my tongue making me want her mouth on another part of me.

I settled us on the couch and watched as she leaned back, threading her fingers through my hair. "I love that you have long hair."

"Oh yeah?" I asked before bringing my thumb to her lower lip wondering what it might feel like to run the head of my cock over it.

Her tongue darted out between her lips and she took my thumb in her mouth, her cheeks hollowed as she sucked. "Mmhmm," she mused. "It'll make it easier to keep your head in place when it's between my legs."

My cock jolted. I yanked my thumb from her mouth and snagged her bottom lip between my teeth, suckling it with my tongue and lips before letting it go with a *pop*. When I smacked her ass, she ground her hips into me, another moan slipping out of her mouth. "You won't have to keep me anywhere, babe. I'll gladly feast on your sweetness for the rest of my fucking life."

Her lids fluttered, eyes dazed with lust. “But what if I want to be the one to taste you?”

Fuck. Me.

Grabbing the back of her neck, I brought her closer so I could whisper in her ear, “You wanna taste me?”

Tendrils of her hair tickled my cheek as she nodded.

“Then let me give my girl what she wants.” I lifted her off me and stood before her. The fear I’d seen in her eyes before was gone. Erased with the heady need we felt for one another and I was thankful for it. This I could do. Watching her eyes trace my body as I unbuckled my belt and undid my jeans. Seeing her in pain had been too much for me to bear. My chest had felt like it was caving in.

But this. Just the two of us together. This I could do all fucking night. Hell. All day *and* night.

Her breathing quickened as her eyes darted to where my fingers slid under the edge of my boxers. “You’re sure?” I asked.

Those molten eyes looked back up at me. “Yes, I’m sure.”

With her permission, I hooked my thumbs into the band of my boxers and pulled them down. My cock was heavy, pulsing upward as she took me in.

She swallowed. “I’ve never done this before, Ranger.” Those beautiful eyes I loved so much were wary like I might flee from her admission. What she didn’t know was that I didn’t give a shit about her being experienced. I only wanted her.

"We'll take it slow. Whatever you don't want to do, just tell me, okay?"

She nodded again as I grabbed her hand and sat back down on the couch.

"Kneel," I commanded and I watched as she lowered herself to her knees.

"Good girl." Seeing her kneel between my legs nearly had me seeing stars from how much my dick throbbed. Dark eyelashes fanned over her cheekbones when she looked down at my length.

"Wrap your hands around my cock and stroke me, beautiful." Her tongue darted between her lips. I sucked in air between my teeth when she wrapped both hands around my shaft and started pumping me slowly.

My head fell against the back cushion of the couch. Her hands were so fucking soft as they moved up and down, twisting back and forth in languid movements. When I looked back at her, those pretty lips were parted as she quietly panted.

"Run your lips over the head."

Excitement flashed in her eyes as she licked her lips and brought me to her. If her hands were soft, her lips were two perfect pillows with the head of my cock nestled right between them. She started pumping me faster, her chest rising and falling in quick succession. Seeing her eager to please me sent a shockwave down my spine, causing my balls to draw upward. It took all my control to focus on not coming as soon as I felt her lips against me.

Taking control, she started to swirl her tongue over the

tip. I reached down and took her long hair in my fist so it didn't get in her way.

"You look so fucking beautiful licking my cock. Fuck, Sarah."

She kept one hand low on the hilt as she suctioned her lips to the back of my shaft and ran her tongue along my entire length. "Holy—" The rest of my words were swallowed by a moan I couldn't keep in.

My breaths were ragged as I whispered, "Take all of me in that pretty fucking mouth."

Every part of my body was humming with pleasure as she finally took me fully, so deep my head hit the back of her throat.

I loved watching her mouth move up and down as I held her hair, slowly guiding her to keep going.

"You're so fucking good, baby. So good. Don't stop."

She hummed at my praise, the vibration at the back of her throat ran over me. It was too good. Too fucking sweet. I picked up the pace, lifting my hips to meet her mouth as she slid her tongue all around, licking every bit of my cock.

"Give me your tongue," I coaxed. Sarah opened her mouth and slipped her tongue out. I slapped my cock against her tongue, her lips widened into a sultry smile that would have had my knees buckling if I wasn't sitting down.

"Tell me you like it, baby."

"I fucking love the taste of your cock." She licked her lips.

"That's my girl." I pushed her head back down, the wet warmth feeling too good. I wasn't going to last much longer.

Not when she looked so damn beautiful taking me between her lips.

Her nails dug into the tops of my thighs as her head bobbed up and down. "I'm close, Sarah. I'm so fucking close." I let go of her hair in case she didn't want to swallow but fuck me if she didn't take me deeper until I could feel myself hitting the back of her throat again.

A tingling sensation crept over my thighs and lower stomach as my climax built. I was damn near off the edge and with one final flick of her tongue over my ridge, pleasure exploded within me. Sarah's throat worked, swallowing, as I came so fucking hard my vision hazed. I gripped the cushion of the couch in one hand and palmed the side of her face with the other as she slowed her movements, finally coming to a stop as she lifted herself off me and my cock hit my stomach.

Her cheeks were tinged with pink from the effort as I gathered her in my arms, pulling her into my lap. Her clothes were still on, but I didn't care. I just wanted her near me.

"How'd I do?" she whispered, eyes lowered like she was embarrassed.

Pinching her chin between my fingers, I raised her face to meet my gaze. "I'm not sure you need much help, sugar because that was the best blow job I've ever had."

She rolled her lips together and looked away. "Don't lie to me."

"Hey." I tilted her chin so she had to look at me again. "I wouldn't lie to you about this. If I needed you to do something different I would have told you. But you were fucking perfect, Sarah." I chuckled. "If being with you feels this good every time, I'm going to need to work on lasting longer. It's never been a problem until now."

That had a smile blooming on her face. "We definitely can't have that. I expect to be fully satisfied during my first time."

"Yes, ma'am," I said, my voice lowering an octave.

Another flash of hesitancy flickered across her face. "And you're sure it doesn't bother you? That I'm a virgin?"

I leaned back so she could see my entire face. "I don't think you understand just how tightly I'm wrapped around your dainty little finger. You being a virgin has no bearing over my feelings for you, Sarah. We go at your pace, when you're ready. I'd wait an entire lifetime to be with you if that's what you needed."

"Is this crazy?" She blushed, placing her hand on my chest, right above my heart. "How we can feel this wild about one another?"

I thought about it for a moment. "I think life is filled with twists and turns and if you spend too much time wondering if something is crazy by other people's standards then you lose out on the beauty right in front of you. I spent a lot of time letting my life waste away out of fear. You've made me forget about all that. So, no. I don't think it's crazy."

Her face brightened with a smile. "I love that I can just be with you. I've always had to pretend that I wanted other things for myself. That's how I ended up in the situation with Jones. But with you, I've never had to pretend. Not for a single moment."

"And you never will have to pretend again if you don't want to." I pressed my lips to hers in a gentle kiss, before scooting her down so she was nestled against my chest. I don't know how long we sat there with her in my arms, the only sound was a gentle crackle of the burning wood in the hearth.

I savored every precious moment like it was my last.

Chapter 31

Sarah

"Wait, what? He wouldn't let you go? I could strangle him!" Willow's neck was flushed with anger after I told her that Jones had grabbed me and tried to prevent me from leaving the restaurant.

We were on our way to the bridal salon for her final dress fitting when she begged me for an update on all things related to my love life. She said that since Johnny and she were doing so well, she didn't have any drama to gossip about in her life. I didn't know if I should have laughed or been insulted.

"Yup. I knew there was something off about him based on some of the questions he asked me and the comments he made. But I never would have thought he was the kind of man who would put his hands on a woman, especially when she told him to go away."

"Do you know where he lives? I wasn't kidding when I said I could strangle him," she scowled.

"I don't think we have to worry about him anymore. Ranger…well, he kind of took care of it."

"Um, are you going to elaborate?" she asked, giving me a sidelong glance.

"Let's just say he did the strangling and Jones barely walked away."

"Shit," she whispered.

"Yeah. I know."

She pulled her Mercedes into a parking spot in front of the bridal salon. After Willow shifted into park, she turned in her seat to face me. "Things must be getting pretty serious if he would put himself at risk like that again. It sounds like Jones comes from a family just like LeRoy's. He wasn't worried he would get into trouble?"

"He told me last night that there weren't any cameras surveilling the side of the building. I think he's started to look out for those kinds of things after what happened to him."

Willow's voice was quiet as she said, "Yeah. I guess so."

"What are you thinking?" I could tell she wasn't saying something by the way she kept being quiet and tentative with her thoughts. Willow wasn't a quiet kind of woman.

She grabbed my hand and gave me a reassuring smile. "I just hate that you were even put in the position to date someone you didn't like. Your mother never should have asked you to do something like that, Sarah. Does she know what he did to you?"

Anger made my throat feel tight. I swallowed, trying to ease the muscles but it was no use. Talking about my parents would always feel hard, I realized. "I haven't said anything to her."

"Why not?"

"Honestly? I don't think she will care. Image is the only thing she concerns herself with and as long as Jones kept things discreet, I doubt him doing anything to me would matter to her."

Willow's face twisted into a pained expression and I knew she was thinking about her mother and how societal influences had cost her so much. Silver lined her eyes as she patted my hand. "You deserve better than that."

Heat hit the back of my eyes. "I know." I forced a smile over my lips to keep them from quivering. "But I have you and Johnny and Deacon. And now Ranger. I think it'll be okay."

"It will." We both half-laughed through the tears we both refused to let fall.

"Speaking of Ranger," she said after we both wiped under our eyes. "How're things going?"

I felt the blush rise to my cheeks as images of him from last night came to my mind. Memories of tasting him had my mouth watering. I'd wanted to go further, to let him have every bit of me. But I wanted our first time to be just about us, not him having to chase away the fear that another man created for me.

"I'm really really happy, Willow." Tears started to well in my eyes again, but I didn't care to wipe them away this time. "I didn't know that falling for someone could feel like this. So…so…"

"Blissful?"

I laughed quietly. "Yeah."

"You deserve it, Sarah. Everything that love has to offer you, you deserve every bit of it. And I'm so glad you've found it with someone who is worthy of having you."

It meant the world to me that Willow understood what I was feeling. There was no judgment or concern at how fast I'd fallen for Ranger. Probably because she knew what it felt like to be head over heels for a man so much that she had waited twelve years for them to find one another again.

It made me understand that love, *true* love, had no bounds. There was no time limit or restraints on what love could do. It was the best thing this world has to offer and those of us lucky enough to find it…well, we better hold on tight to it.

"Thank you," I said to her. "But enough about me. Today is *your* day and I've already taken up enough of it."

"You could never take up too much, Sarah." She hugged me over the center console before we grabbed our purses and headed into the bridal salon.

"I don't know how, but it looks even more beautiful on you this time." Using the tissue the seamstress handed me, I dabbed at the corners of my eyes.

Willow bunched the white fabric in her hands and turned

away from the mirror so I could see the full front of the gown. She looked like a whimsical fairy in the best way possible. Hand-sewn silk petals graced the thin layer of chiffon. Her delicate frame was accentuated with a tight bodice and dainty straps that hung loosely off her shoulders.

"Do you think Johnny will like it?" she asked.

"Like it? He's going to devour you the moment he gets you alone." We both laughed.

I rose from the pink velvet sofa and grasped her hands. "You're a vision, Willow. And it's the perfect dress for a mountain wedding too."

"Did I show you the archway he and Deacon made for the ceremony?"

"Yes!" A few weeks ago, she'd texted me some pictures of a wooden archway the guys had made. It was going to be covered in cabbage roses in shades of ivory and light pink. "I honestly didn't realize how handy those two were."

"I know. I was pretty impressed with the finished product. We're going to put it right in front of the big oak tree behind the cabin. The one he carved our initials into."

Warmth blossomed in my chest. "It's going to be absolutely perfect, Willow. And this dress is going to be the icing on the cake. No pun intended."

There was no envy clawing into my mind as I was reminded of the incredible love story my best friends had. No more longing for something I felt would never happen for me. My heart and mind felt full of gratitude that I had found something special with Ranger and even though I didn't know where our journey would take us, being with him felt like I'd found my person. There was nothing else more that I wanted than to be near him.

Willow giggled at my joke before the seamstress started making final adjustments to her bodice and skirt. My phone pinged loudly through the store. "Oops! I forgot to turn the ringer off." Dishing my phone out of my purse, I glanced at the screen and my heart suddenly lurched into my throat.

Mom

> Sarah Grace Williams, I cannot believe you. After all I've done for you, helping you find a worthy life partner, you decide to throw it all away?

Dizziness swarmed my senses as I gulped down a lungful of air. My mother obviously knew I had ended things with Jones. I knew this moment would come, but I wasn't expecting to feel so upset by it. It felt like every time I worked through the pain of having my mother treat me with disdain, she would pop up and show me that there was still so much more to work through.

Another ping and I nearly dropped my phone trying to turn the silencer on. My hands were shaking.

> You have always been an ungrateful brat. Nothing has changed.

> But now you will be forced to face the consequences of your actions, Sarah.

I will not put up with your disobedience any longer. We made a deal and you broke it.

Message after message streamed in. Each one worse than the last.

"Is everything okay, Sarah?"

I looked over my shoulder at Willow. Her eyes were narrowed with concern.

I cleared my throat. "Yes. All good. Just texting Stephanie something about the bakery."

"Okay," her voice was wary.

More text messages had my phone vibrating in my hand, but I couldn't stomach looking at them anymore so I sealed my phone away in my purse and tried to focus on what the seamstress was telling Willow about adding a few additional silk flowers to the skirt.

But now you will be forced to face the consequences of your actions, Sarah. I couldn't get the image of my mother's words out of my mind. She'd always been vindictive. If things didn't go exactly the way she wanted them to, there were significant consequences. I knew this time would be no different.

Closing my eyes, I thought back to last night when Ranger and I fell asleep in front of the fireplace, bundled together in blankets. How good it felt to be wrapped in his arms with no one else around. A calmness settled over me, slowly easing the tension from reading the barrage of text messages from my mother.

She could taunt me and even punish me for living life the way I wanted to, but the one thing she couldn't take away from me was the love I was starting to feel for Ranger. Because love was the one thing that could transcend hate and cast out darkness.

Chapter 32

Sarah

I wasn't sure if it was divine intervention or some stroke of luck, but nothing had changed by way of my bakery being busier than ever after my mother sent those threatening text messages. And every night since then, Ranger and I had split time between our two places, exploring one another in the best way possible.

I'd never been a fitness babe, but I was finding that I might need to increase my cardio to keep up with the man's salacious appetite. We couldn't keep our hands off each other it seemed. Not that I was complaining. He was fucking hot as hell. If I could live with him between my legs, I would.

Lost in my debaucherous thoughts, I knocked over the tub of buttercream that I was using to fill the piping bags. "Shit!" Icing was everywhere and I was already behind on this order for a baby shower.

The door to my kitchen creaked open behind me as I grabbed the container from the floor. I looked over my shoulder to see Ranger assessing the damage all over the kitchen tiles.

He must have come straight from the ranch because his shoulder-length curls were peeking out from under his black cowboy hat. A shadow of stubble lined his lower cheeks and jaw. My center throbbed as I remembered what it felt like to have his stubble graze the inside of my thighs. How his lips felt pressed against my core as his tongue worked on me, drawing blissful pleasure with each stroke.

A clatter sounded from next to me and I jumped. I'd dropped the container of icing too far off the counter and it clanged against the metal, hitting the wooden spatula next to it.

"Need some help, sugar?"

Raising my frosting covered hand, I showed him the mess before I turned toward the sink.

A hand reached out and gently grabbed my arm, stopping me.

His voice was guttural as he said, "I think we can remedy that." He took two steps closer to me. I backed up, feeling overwhelmed by his presence and insecure with the amount of baking ingredients that were splattered all over me. I definitely wasn't looking my best and certainly wasn't worthy of this man's presence given my current state.

I watched as he tucked the long strands of my loose hair behind my ears and then he took my icing covered hand, raising it to his mouth.

My hand felt so small between both of his large ones as he gently massaged my open palm. A storm of desire turned his blue eyes molten like a flickering flame as he brought my index finger to his lips. I gasped in complete awe as he opened his mouth and placed my finger inside and sucked.

"Oh," I moaned, letting my eyes close as I felt the swirl of his tongue along the length of my finger. His mouth was warm and his tongue gentle as he worked every bit of icing off. I pressed my thighs together in search of any friction that might grant me release from the growing ache for him to put that tongue to work somewhere else.

When I opened my eyes, I found myself leaning into him. Needing something sturdy to keep me from toppling over.

Satisfied with the first finger, he moved on to my middle one. This time, a moan escaped him as I wrapped my other arm around his waist and slid my clean hand into the back pocket of his jeans. I'd lost all sense of reality as I watched his cheeks hollow slightly as he suckled the tip of my finger.

Heat soared through me. Squeezing my thighs together, I tried to create more friction with the inseam of my jeans. Anything that would ease the ache between my legs as he continued down the line of my fingers. Paying special attention to every single one until he finally released my pinky from his mouth and my hand fell slack to my side as his hands roamed my back and he pressed me flush against him.

"That's certainly one way to greet a lady." My voice came out sultry. I hardly recognized it.

"I've been missing you," he whispered against my neck, his breath tickling the rim of my ear.

"You just saw me this morning," I teased.

His eyes were bright as a fresh spring sky after the haze

of winter when he said, "No amount of time with you could ever be enough." Then his lips were on mine, tender at first with featherlight kisses against each corner.

I needed him closer, needed his body pressed against mine without anything between us. We'd had our fun tasting and exploring, but I wanted more. I wanted everything he was willing to give me.

Wrapping my arms around his neck, he grabbed my ass and lifted me onto the counter. His tongue moved against the seam of my mouth, a thrill shot up my spine wishing his tongue was lower. Wanting to feel his hot mouth against my clit. I couldn't get enough of him as I deepened the kiss, opening up for him, his fingers digging into my hips on the verge of pain that felt so fucking good, I dropped my hands and pressed his harder into my flesh.

Scooting to the edge of the counter, I ground my hips into the fly of his jeans. I was feral, wildly moving against him as he pressed against my back, his open palms sliding up and down.

We were practically panting when he broke the kiss, his forehead coming down to mine. "I have another surprise for you this weekend."

I groaned. "Can't we just spend all weekend in bed?"

His chuckle was throaty and warm. "My little vixen." He nipped my bottom lip with his teeth. "I think you'll like this one."

"Promise?" I pouted, blinking my eyelashes at him.

"Promise."

"Good, because—" The door to the kitchen swung open

so hard, that the metal slapped against the wall with a resounding thud. I looked past Ranger's shoulder to see my mother burst through the door.

A yip shot out of my mouth as I jolted off the counter and out of Ranger's hold. I stared at her wide-eyed, not knowing how or why she was standing in my kitchen again.

Then I saw Stephanie peek around the corner. "I'm sorry, Sarah. I tried to stop her, but she darted right past me."

My mother sneered. "No one can stop me from going where I want to go."

"It's okay, Steph," I said, voice shaky.

I felt Ranger step up behind me, his large frame was a comfort at my back. My mother didn't take her eyes off me. She ignored him completely and it pissed me off.

"When you didn't respond to my messages I knew I needed to address this in person. Your complete disregard for our family's legacy needs to come to an end."

"He wasn't right for me, mom." My voice was small when what I really wanted to do was yell. To scream that he put his hands on me and made me feel trapped. That he was awful and I hated her for putting me in the position to know him.

But I didn't say any of those things. Even with Ranger placing a reassuring hand on the small of my back, I couldn't stand up to my mother.

"You don't know what's right for you. You may be thirty years old, but you still act like an indolent child. Never willing to do what's necessary. The only person you think about is yourself."

"Indolent? I built a business from the ground up without your help. I work nearly seven days a week. How is that not enough for you?"

Just tell me I'm enough, the thought sank its teeth into my mind. The same thought I'd had most of my life. It was the only thing I wanted from my mother. The one thing I knew I would never get.

She scoffed like my accomplishments bore no weight in her eyes. "I don't understand, after all your father and I gave you, the life we provided you, how you could ruin it all by sullying yourself with the trash in this town." Her cold stare finally settled inches above my face where I knew she was looking at Ranger.

Something in me snapped. I'd taken so much of her emotional abuse over the years. Dealt with everything she threw my way and somehow buried it deep. Hoping that one day she would see the mistake she was making. The second she said Ranger was *trash*, the leash on my emotions broke.

"He's not trash," I seethed, my entire body feeling hot.

My mother took a step forward, her finger pointing at my face. "He's an ex-convict who spent ten years in prison, Sarah. He was born on a failing ranch with no penny to his—"

"Stop!" I screamed, the echo of my rage rang throughout the small space. She pursed her lips, eyes growing wide. I'd never yelled at my mother before. Never raised my voice. Not once.

"You can say whatever you want about me. Tell me how much of a disappointment I am to you. How I failed at being your perfect daughter. But I'm not going to let you talk about him that way.

"Ranger is the best thing that's ever happened to me. He's shown me love and kindness and support. Things I never received from you or dad. If you think I'm a failure, that's fine. But I hope one day you can look in the mirror and know that the truth is that *you* failed *me.* You were so wrapped up in conjuring a plot to get me to do what you wanted that you never stopped to assess whether or not Jones was a good man.

I stepped out of Ranger's space and towards my mother, feeling a sudden strength I didn't know I had. "Jones hurt me, mom. He grabbed onto me and wouldn't let me go even when I begged him to. That's the kind of man you sent your daughter to."

"Maybe he didn't mean to do that."

A menacing laugh ripped from my throat. "Even now, you would defend him. Why? Because his family has money?" I tossed my hands in the air and let them drop with a slap against my thighs. "You know what? I don't care anymore because I've finally realized that you and dad will never change and I'm not going to be a part of your world. I won't sacrifice my integrity just to save face with people who don't care about me. I won't do it.

"So, get the fuck out of my kitchen, and don't ever come back here again." I pointed toward the door, my finger surprisingly steady.

Her mouth popped open like she wanted to say something, but I didn't waver. I kept my arm outstretched, finger pointed toward the door until she finally spun on her stiletto heel and left.

When the door slid to a close, I exhaled loudly and my shoulders drooped. Strong arms wrapped around me from behind and I let myself melt into Ranger's embrace.

"I'm sorry you had to do that," he whispered against my hair.

"I'm not." I turned in his arms so I could look into his eyes. "It's been long overdue. She walked all over me for way too many years. I could have taken it. But not when she started talking about someone I—" Love? Did I love Ranger? Everything I felt for him certainly painted the picture of love. I hated that I couldn't say it out loud. I hated that I questioned whether or not he felt the same for me. Not because he didn't show me through his actions, but because I was terrified of letting someone be that close to me.

My gaze darted back and forth between his eyes, the word I wanted to say lodged in my throat. His low chuckle was a balm to my nerves. "You don't have to say it, sugar. But I feel it too."

My heart fluttered when his lips grazed mine in a sweet kiss. "We're definitely crazy," I murmured against his mouth.

His palms met the sides of my face. "If being crazy means that I get to be with you, then I don't fucking care."

I laughed as he pressed a kiss to each one of my cheeks. "Touché, cowboy. Touché." I reached up and covered his hands with mine. "I think I'm actually looking forward to your surprise this weekend after all that."

"Me too."

Chapter 33

Sarah

The next few days were a blur of emotions. On the one hand, it felt good to finally stand up to my mother in defense of Ranger. I wasn't going to allow her to demean him. He was too good, too amazing to be held under her wrath.

I thought that standing up to her might make me feel more empowered. I'd finally said what I was truly feeling about her and how she treated me. But all I felt was a giant weight lingering over me, supported by a tiny string that might break at any moment. I didn't want to be crushed, and at the same time, I felt like it almost needed to happen so I could walk away from my parents forever. They caused me too much pain and I was a glutton for punishment.

Ranger could tell something was up with my string of mopey text messages since then, so he opted to invite all my friends out for a night of fun before he and I shared the weekend and whatever surprise he had planned for me. We were going line dancing at *Cowboys* and I was ready for a night of distraction.

"Feeling any better?" he asked, driving his truck into the dirt parking lot. Holes in the lot had me jostling side-to-side in the passenger seat.

I looked over at him, feeling a lift in my chest as I took him in. His normal flannel was replaced with a long sleeve black shirt, tucked into dark wash jeans and his leather belt. His black cowboy hat didn't have a speck of dirt on it. I found myself wanting to climb into his lap and weave my fingers through his long hair. I just wanted it to be us, lost in the feeling of one another.

But my gaze flicked to his window where I saw Johnny and Willow getting out of Johnny's truck a few cars over.

Shifting my attention back to Ranger, I nodded. "Yeah, a little bit better I think."

Those stormy blue eyes assessed me. "If you get overwhelmed at all or just want to leave, say the word and we're out of here."

I leaned across the center console and kissed his cheek. "Thank you." Ranger knew I had problems with my parents, but this was the first time he saw my mother in action with her vile words and nasty attitude. It was embarrassing and I didn't understand how she couldn't see that. For all the effort she put into maintaining the perfect image, she didn't seem to care how mean she came across.

As Ranger got out of the truck and came to my side to open the door, I took in a few deep breaths, letting my shoulders fall from all the tension I was carrying. Tonight would be fun. I *wanted* it to be fun.

"Come on, sugar." Ranger lifted me from the seat of his truck and set me down. The smell of leather and fresh grass swirling around me at his closeness. Letting my eyes close for a moment, I held onto his forearms and allowed his presence to ground me.

"Okay, I'm ready." Hand-in-hand, we rounded the back of his truck and found Willow and Johnny walking toward us. Deacon was getting out of his truck at the end of the parking lot. I waved him over and he made his way.

Willow pulled me in for a hug and said against my neck, "Holding up okay?" I'd called her the night my mother stormed into my work kitchen and debriefed her on everything that had happened. She was furious, of course.

"Yeah," I breathed. "It feels hard right now, but I know it will be alright eventually."

If there was anyone in the world who understood complicated family dynamics, it was Willow. I was thankful to have her helping me navigate everything happening with my mother. But I was tired of talking about it. I wanted to forget about everything and enjoy the night.

"Let's go have some fun," I said, pulling back from her embrace.

She waggled her eyebrows at me. "Oh, I think we can manage that." Looping our arms together, we bounded for the entrance to the bar.

I was weightless in Ranger's arms as he spun me around the dance floor. The light in his eyes made my heart skip a beat. I loved seeing him like this. Carefree and wild, his heart racing beneath my palm where I settled it against his chest as we moved to the music. We were both slick with sweat as we danced the entire night away. The dance floor was looking slim compared to when we first arrived.

When the song came to a close, he led me to the small high-top table our group had grabbed. Willow was standing in front of Johnny, his arms draped over her shoulders, holding her close as they swayed to the building beat of the next song. Her eyes were a little glassy from the shots of tequila we did earlier.

"Where's Deacon," I asked. Johnny nodded his chin toward the bar and I found Deacon sipping on a beer next to a striking blonde woman. Long curls fell nearly to the small of her back hanging just above her Daisy Duke shorts. How she managed to not freeze her ass off on the way here was beyond me. Some women just had that superpower of being able to wear minimal clothing in cold temperatures.

"How long has she been trying for him?"

Willow hiccupped and giggled. "At least half an hour at this point."

Deacon had a problem. He was extremely good-looking but had a sour-puss attitude that kept anyone from getting too close to him. It wasn't that he was an asshole, you just had to work through his grumpy exterior to find the good parts of him.

"I think that might be a record," Johnny said, a grin pulling at his lips.

I snorted. "I think you're right, Johnny." I looked back over to Deacon and saw the blonde get off the stool and head toward the billiards tables where a few stragglers were playing. "Oh, looks like we spoke too soon. Another one bites the dust," I laughed as Johnny and Willow turned to see the blonde walk away.

"Maybe he just hasn't found the right one yet," Ranger offered, pulling me into him.

I smiled, all the heaviness from earlier in the night left me the moment we had stepped onto the dance floor and I felt his body move against mine. "Valid point, cowboy."

He brushed his lips against mine and my body hummed. I'd discovered that dancing with him was one long tease fest and all I wanted to do was devour him. Kiss every inch of his body until there was nothing left to claim.

"Ready to get out of here?" His breath tickled the cuff of my ear.

I bit my lower lip and nodded. His eyes flickered down to my lips. "Keep that up and I won't be able to wait until we're in the truck to make you mine."

I batted my lashes at him innocently. "But I'm already yours."

He growled before laying his arm over my shoulder.

"Alright, we're out of here," he announced to Willow and Johnny before he whisked us away to his truck.

I pressed the button to roll down the window and Ranger sped through the night. He gripped my thigh, eyes glancing at me every few seconds. It was so damn hot in the truck even though it was in the fifties outside. If we didn't get to my place soon, I was going to suffocate from the heat emanating from both of us.

When he slid his hand upward toward the crease in my thigh, I let out a whimper. His eyes shot to me, molten blue and gray swirling with the same desperate need I felt for him.

"Fuck it," he said, voice low as he turned the truck off the road and threw it into park.

"What're you doing?" I asked, but my words were lost in the silence as he hopped out of the truck and came around to my side.

My heartbeat quickened when he opened the door. "I need you, sugar. I've been waiting all damn night to taste you and I can't fucking take it anymore."

My throat was dry, my sex throbbing and I knew my panties were soaked. A bodily betrayal of the need for him that I was trying to hide all night. I didn't have a chance to respond before he reached his arm under my knees and back, lifting me out of the truck. He carried me to the hood and set me gently on the edge.

"Right here?" I gasped. "What if someone comes down the road?"

His fingers made quick work of my small leather belt and jeans. "It's two o'clock in the morning and we're in the middle of farm country. No one will be on this road. And if they are…" he smirked. "Oh well."

Giddiness filled my chest at his don't-give-a-fuck attitude. I loved that about him. He was wild and beautiful and he wanted *me*. I'd never felt more alive than when I was with him. The risks we took together had me wanting more. I felt like a wild horse running free in the wind. Nothing to stop me. Nothing in the world mattered except for him.

Lifting my hips, he hooked his fingers into my jeans and pulled them down to my ankles. Goosebumps rose along my thighs and calves as my hot skin hit the cold fall air.

"Aren't these fucking cute?" He toyed with the pale pink thong I wore, lifting the side straps up and letting them hit my hips with a snap. "Too bad they're in my way." He gripped where the triangle met the strap and ripped my panties apart. I didn't have a moment to protest before his mouth was on me, licking my clit in one long stroke of his tongue.

"Holy fuck." I nearly slipped on the hood as my arms failed at keeping me up. His eyes were dark, hooded by his lashes when he looked up at me. "Do that again," I commanded. His feral grin had my knees shaking as he looked right at me, his dark curls brushing the skin of my inner thighs as he flicked his tongue against my entrance, then licked my center from bottom to top. My head fell back and I swore I was floating amongst the stars above.

Grabbing my hips, he yanked me to the edge of the hood. "Tell me what you want."

Drawing my head forward, I said, "I want you to suck on my clit."

He nipped the inside of my right thigh with his teeth, sending a bolt of fire to my core. "That's it, sugar. I fucking love it when you tell me what you want."

His head lowered and his lips sealed over my sex, sucking and teasing my clit with his tongue. The wet warmth of his mouth was sinful as I reached down between my legs and grasped the back of his head, pushing him tighter against me. He growled at my neediness and the vibration of his tongue hit just the right spot, sending my vision into a spiraling haze.

Both his hands found the back of my thighs as he continued to work his mouth on my pussy. He pulled me further to the edge of the hood until there was nowhere else for me to go. I draped my legs over his shoulders, my ankles hitting his back. I was completely at his mercy and I loved every second of it.

Grinding my sex against his mouth, I felt him pull away just a little. Pressure hit my entrance as he slowly circled two fingers against my slick lips.

"Yes," I breathed, needing to be filled by him. "Please."

He pressed his fingers deeper, moving in slow motions. In and out. In and out. The same rhythm he used with the stroke of his tongue. It was a high no alcohol or drugs could buy. Being touched and licked by him was pure ecstasy.

"You're so fucking good, baby. God, I love the way you taste. So good." Even the feel of his breath against my hot clit was enough to send me spiraling towards release. When his mouth moved against me again, he pushed his fingers deep inside me, stroking easily against my spot.

"More," I cried out, grinding my pussy against his scruff. "I need more."

"That's it. Tell me what you want." His pace and pressure quickened, his lips and tongue suckling my clit while his fingers moved faster.

I writhed against the metal hood, stretching my arms out wide to grasp anything that would help me feel grounded, but it was no use. Off the cliff I tumbled, my orgasm shattering my mind, body, and soul. There was nothing left of me, it was all *his* and there was nothing I loved more than giving my entire being to him.

His movements slowed, riding the wave with me until he slowly withdrew his fingers and pressed a final kiss over my sex. I laid back on the hood of his truck, not quite ready to come back to reality as I gazed up at the stars. Ranger's hands moved over my legs as he slowly slid my jeans upward and zipped me back into them.

Finally, I propped myself on my elbows and looked at him. "I never want to stop doing that with you. Feeling you against me without anything between us."

Reaching behind my bottom, he slid me off the hood and into his arms. I hooked my legs around his waist as he held me at eye level. “We can do that for the rest of our lives if you want to.” A question flared in his blue eyes. A tentative step toward a path that had big meaning.

But I wasn’t scared. Not with him. Not ever.

“I think I’d like that very much.”

Chapter 34

Sarah

Gravel crunched under my feet as I looked up at the night sky where the moon was shining in all her glory. Mist clouded in front of my face from the cold fall air that was quickly shifting to winter. It wouldn't be long now before we had our first blanket of snow covering the ground. Likely a thin layer as we didn't often get heavy snowstorms, but I felt excited about the potential of the new season. To be bundled in blankets with hot cocoa in my hands and Ranger by my side.

Something in me had changed the day my mother stormed into my work kitchen and berated him. I'd finally discovered that it truly didn't matter what other people thought of me, as long as I was happy, I could let go of everything else. The pressure to succeed in my business or to appease my parents. Feeling like I was put in a box that was never meant to hold me. I could let go of all of it because I knew what waited for me.

Love.

I almost said it to him the other day, not fully realizing the words that were about to come out of my mouth. The way he'd looked at me called to my soul. An awakening that only he could draw from me. I knew I was one of the lucky ones who'd found their person. The other half of my heart. And I wasn't going to waste it on other people's thoughts about me.

Ranger came into view. His broad shoulders were working against the thin layers of his t-shirt and flannel as he finished saddling Hank. "Hi, cowboy," I called to Ranger.

His broad smile had me stopping in my tracks. He was so damn beautiful, I wondered how people couldn't see through his rough past to the man who stood before me. It truly was their loss and if it meant I got more of him to myself, I really couldn't complain.

Frigid air lined my lungs as I took a deep breath in.

"Hi, gorgeous," he responded, his Southern accent drawling with each word. Hank jostled his head up and down, bumping into Ranger's shoulder.

Standing on my tiptoes, I reached up and pressed my lips to the corner of Ranger's mouth. "I've missed you."

His smile tilted to the right. "We might need to remedy that one of these days."

My cheeks flushed, not from worry that his mention of us moving in together felt crazy. I was done with placing judgment on myself and the wants I had in this life. His words brought a twinge of excitement to my chest. Hope for a future I never knew was possible for me until he came into the picture.

"You know, I was just thinking about how I thought I had my whole life planned out. Make sweet treats. Open a bakery. Build my skills in cake design and take the industry by storm." Sliding my hands into the back pockets of his jeans, I pressed him against me. "I never accounted for a sexy rancher to steal my heart."

His fingers stroked the edge of my jaw. "And now that you're here, what do you think?"

I took a deep breath in, biting my bottom lip. "I think I like the view from here a lot more than anywhere else I've been."

His eyes softened, and his words came out rough. "I wish you could see the view from where I'm standing. It's the most beautiful sight in the world."

Time slowed as he pressed a tender kiss to my lips. I gripped the edges of his flannel shirt and leaned into him more.

When we pulled apart, he tucked a tendril of my hair behind my ear. "Ready?"

I nodded. "Should I go get Honey Blossom?"

"No, this ride is a bit treacherous and she hasn't been on the trail for a few years. We'll both be riding Hank tonight."

"Okay."

Ranger gave me a boost into the large saddle before settling in behind me. My legs were spread wide over Hank's back. Ranger took the reins and we started off into the night.

The air was colder in the mountains than it was in the valley of Ranger's ranch, but I hardly felt the frigid temperature with him at my back. Our ride was slow and feeling my ass rub against him for an hour was nearly torture when all I wanted to do was spin around in the saddle and kiss him like a mad woman.

But as Hank crested through the thick overhang of pine branches on the trail, my breath caught in my throat. Tears of wonderment hit the back of my eyes as I took in the space before me. We were on a carved ledge of the mountain that overlooked the valley below. A long stretch of the river Ranger and I swam in weeks ago threaded throughout the land. Above us was a mass of stars twinkling against the darkness. The full moon cast a silvery glow on everything below it.

"Oh my gosh," I whispered, bringing my fingertips to my open mouth. A gleeful laugh brushed past my lips. "It's so beautiful."

"And it's ours." Ranger's arms settled on the horn in front of me before I felt him move off the saddle. I could hardly tear my eyes away from the scene in front of me as he grasped under my arms and helped me down.

I walked toward the edge and looked around, feeling like I was floating above the world and nothing could touch me here. An owl hooted from somewhere behind me and there was a faint whisper of the roaring river below us where the smooth surface transitioned to a heavy path of rapids.

"What do you think?" Ranger said from behind me. I turned around, his tanned skin was illuminated from the shine of the moon.

"I'm thinking you've been keeping this incredible secret from me for a while and I don't know if I should be upset about that or not." I arched a brow at him and he chuckled.

Walking towards me, he slipped his arms around my waist, his palms settling where my back met the curve of my butt. "I couldn't give away all my secrets at once now could I?"

I bobbed my head back and forth. "We can debate that question another time." I rubbed my hands together to ward off the cold.

"Come on, let me get the fire started for you." I followed him a few paces back where there was a circular pit outlined with white stones, fresh logs of wood were already tepeed together. With all my attention on the beauty of the landscape, I didn't notice there was a thick pallet of blankets with a few pillows on the other side of the firepit.

Taking off my riding boots, I settled under the top blanket and watched Ranger blow against the glowing embers of the fire he'd started. It didn't take him long to get the kindling wood aflame before he took off his boots and settled next to me. Taking me under his arm, I leaned into his side, inhaling deeply my favorite smell of leather that always reminded me of him.

"I can't believe this place exists. Was this something else your mom showed you growing up?"

"No. I discovered this place myself. One day before I was sent to prison, Miles and I were working the cows below and I looked up at the mountainside and saw this cliff edge jutting out through the pine trees. I wondered what the world might look like from up here, so I took my time carving a path through the trees until I found it. No one else knows it exists besides me and you."

The heat of the flames started to reach the edge of the pallet, warming my feet. "Our own little hideaway," I mused, looking up at him.

He gripped my chin between his fingers and kissed me. "Ours," he repeated against my lips.

A hum vibrated in my throat as he slipped his tongue along the seam of my mouth. Heat soared through my body when his fingers threaded through my hair, his lips moving against mine with a need I felt in my core.

I moved to straddle him, my legs splaying wide across the length of his thighs. When he was gentle, I forgot how big he was, but then it didn't take much to remind me as I rolled my hips into him, feeling his length grow beneath me.

Our kisses turned desperate, nipping and sucking one another's lips and tongue. It felt so good to be with him, like I was so light I might float away and join the stars above us.

"I want you," I said, pausing our kiss, and gazing into the depthless blue of his eyes. "All of you."

I felt his heart rate kick up against where my palm lay over his chest. "Are you sure?"

"There have been a lot of things in my life that I've felt unsure of, but wanting you has never been one of them, cowboy."

His kiss was gentle against my cheek as he said, "Okay."

I rose from his lap and we both stood, facing one another. He didn't take his eyes off me as he stripped off his flannel and t-shirt, revealing his tanned chest and abs. I went to take off my jacket, but he reached for my wrist and said, "Let me."

"Okay," I swallowed the dryness in my throat. The flames from the fire danced in the reflection of his irises and I thought how fitting it felt to have a roaring fire right next to us when it resembled how I felt for this man. He burned away every bit of my insecurities and made me feel like I could withstand the heat of this world as long as I had him by my side. He made me feel alive. He made me burn bright.

With my jacket thrown to the side, he played with the hem of my long sleeve shirt, fingers grazing against the skin of my stomach. Every part of me he touched sent a thrill of electric energy to my core. I lifted my arms over my head and felt the scrape of his rough knuckles along my ribcage and arms before my head came through and I saw him toss my shirt onto my jacket.

Those blue eyes dipped to my breasts, nipples peeking through the sheer blue lace of my bra. Goosebumps rose along my skin as he reached behind me and unsnapped my bra with one hand. My breasts fell free as I slid the straps down my arms and dropped the dainty fabric on the ground.

He licked his lips, his Adam's Apple bobbing up and down as he took me in.

"My turn," my voice was hoarse. I stepped closer until we were toe-to-toe and reached between us. Cold metal bit at my skin as I unclasped his belt buckle, then worked my way to his button and zipper. The bulge of his cock and taut ass kept his jeans from falling, so I bunched the fabric in my hands and pulled down. His length tented his boxers, my mouth watering at the memory of how he tasted against my tongue.

Finishing it off, he glided his boxers down, freeing himself. My clit throbbed and I knew I was already soaking wet as I followed suit and stripped the rest of my clothes off. We stood there, staring at one another, a shiver running over my entire body as the low temperature finally started to settle over my skin.

"Cold?" he asked.

"Yes, but I'm okay."

Grabbing the top blanket from the pallet, he sat down in front of the pillows. "Come here," he urged.

I straddled his lap again, nearly hissing at the contact of his cock pressed against my clit. It felt so fucking good and he wasn't even inside of me yet. Then, he wrapped the blanket around my shoulders and leaned back on the pillows. A crinkling sound emanated between us as he reached into the pocket of his jeans next to him. He pulled out a condom and went to tear the packet, but I grabbed his wrist and stopped him.

"I've been on birth control since I was a teenager. I don't want anything between us."

His eyes were like raging storms as he nodded slowly. "You're in control. We go at your pace," he said, tossing the condom packet somewhere in the dirt.

"Okay," I whispered, my voice a little shaky. Nerves of excitement and anticipation had my body buzzing.

With the blanket draped over my shoulders and Ranger lying below me, I took a moment to settle my eyes on the details of him. How a crease formed along the corners of his lips with the tilt of his smile. The thickness of his brows framing his beautiful blue eyes with long lashes fanning around them. Down to his chest, where his skin was completely smooth, and out towards his arms where his corded forearms reminded me of just how hard he worked every day. And finally to his hands that held onto my hips, callouses scraping against my skin.

He was beautiful. So perfect.

And I got to share this pivotal moment with him. He was all mine and I was his.

My chest rose with an inhale as I reached between us, grabbing onto his length. He was hot and smooth against my hand. Guiding him to my entrance, I felt Ranger's grip on my hips tighten slightly. When I had him nestled against me, I rested both my hands on his chest and slowly worked my way down his cock, taking him in inch by inch.

"You're so beautiful," he whispered into the night around us, our eyes meeting. Words were lost to me. He filled me so fully the more I settled on top of him. I couldn't concentrate on anything other than where we connected, our bodies becoming one.

I'd broken my hymen years ago with a vibrator. There was no pain with Ranger. No resistance as I slid all the way to his hilt.

"Fuck it feels good," I hissed through my teeth. "You feel so good inside of me."

"Yes," he said through clenched teeth before he rose from his back and sat up with me. We were face-to-face, his cock hitting me deep in my core before he threaded his hands through my hair and kissed me.

I moaned into his mouth, sweeping my tongue against him. I started to move my hips forward and backward, working him slowly. Tingles spread over my entire body, my clit ground against him as I rode his cock. His mouth sealed over my right breast while he palmed the left. I let my head fall back as I moved up and down, stroking his cock with my pussy. I could feel his ridge and how every time I came down on him, his dick pulsed against me.

"Don't stop," I told him, his lips moving over to my left breast.

"Not a fucking chance." His tongue flicked over my nipple, then he took it between his teeth and pulled gently. The edge of pleasure and pain was like a lightning bolt to my clit. I couldn't get enough friction against him. My movements became frantic as my climax built deep within me.

Releasing my breast, he brought his forehead to mine, hand pressed against the back of my head. His eyes were piercing as he said, "Tell me what you want, baby. Tell me what your body needs."

"Rub my clit," I breathed.

He bit into my bottom lip in a searing kiss as his hand dipped between us, those rough fingers grazing over my clit. My pace quickened, riding him so fucking good as he rubbed my clit, back and forth. I looked down, watching my slick arousal coat his fingers, catching glimpses of his cock pushing in and out of me.

"Yes, baby. That's it. Please, don't stop. Just. Like. That." I closed my eyes, taking in the feel of him inside me. The way he moved against my clit, giving me exactly what I needed.

A moan escaped his lips as I slowed down, pulling myself up until his tip teased my entrance. Then I slid down so slow, I could feel every part of him filling me. This was what I'd waited for. Not some rushed chaos in the back of a car when I was a teenager. No. I wanted a fucking man to show me the true meaning of pleasure. Someone I loved who would take his time making sure I got what I needed. But as I opened my eyes, I knew it was even more than that. I was waiting for *him*. There was no one else in this world who could make me feel this way. And I wanted him to know that.

Grasping the back of his neck, I pressed my cheek to his. Our chests meeting with each breath. "I love you, Ranger," I whispered, a tear falling down my face. "I don't care if that makes me crazy. Because I love you and I never want to stop loving you."

His breath stopped for a moment as I pulled back to look at him, my hips still moving up and down because it felt too good to stop. His hands moved to frame my face, silver lining his eyes. “Loving you, Sarah has brought me back home. You’ve breathed life back into me. I love you.” He pressed a kiss to my lips. “I love you,” he whispered again.

A gleeful laugh burst through my lips, every fiber of my being was on fire for him. There was nothing I could do to hold back the rising sensation of my climax nearing. His words, his touch. It was all too much for me to contain.

He held me close, as I moved over him, our breaths growing quicker by the second. “I’m so close,” I told him, grasping at his back so I could feel every part of him.

“Keep going, baby. Keep going,” he pressed.

And I did, letting him fill me with each stroke. His cock slid over my spot over and over again as my clit ground over his pubic bone. Gripping my thighs, his fingers pressed hard against my flesh, he started moving with me, lifting himself up to meet where I came down on him. Heat flared in my core and I could feel him getting closer, his moans and short breaths driving me closer to the edge.

His lips crashed against mine, a mess of tongues and teeth as I felt his cock pulse inside of me just as I tumbled into my orgasm, the sensation near blinding.

Only the mountainside and stars above heard me scream his name, my body roaring from the crashing wave of bliss. I stilled, too sensitive to ride him any longer. My knees quaked next to his thighs, neither one of us willing to part as our kisses turned slower, less hungry, more tender.

He pulled back and looked at me. My chest swelled, nearly bursting from the emotion that took hold of me. "I love you, Sarah."

"I love you too, Ranger."

Sated and beyond happiness, I curled up beside him. He tucked me in close, his warmth warding against the cold air. With the sound of crackling wood and Ranger's steady breathing, it didn't take me long to drift into a peaceful sleep.

Chapter 35

Ranger

I woke to the smell of smoke and the bright rays of the morning sun streaming through the pine tree branches. Sarah moved in my arms, but her eyes remained closed, her breathing steady.

I didn't move, not wanting to disrupt her sleep. Fuck, she was beautiful. The sun caught strands of her hair, giving light to the subtle hues of amber and gold throughout her dark tresses. Dark eyelashes fanned out, making tiny shadows on her cheeks and I loved the way her nose was curved and came to a little ball at the end. And her lips. God, I hoped I got to kiss those lips for the rest of my life.

Last night had been the single best night of my life, connecting with her in that way. Sharing our newfound love for one another. I hadn't felt this happy since before I lost my dad to the war and my mother disappeared. Even then, those years of joy couldn't compare to what I was feeling for Sarah.

I knew she didn't set out to do it, but she'd mended my heart. Stitching over the years of sorrow, fear, and pain. Replacing all of it with a love so profound I could hardly breathe when I was near her.

Her eyelids fluttered open. "Morning, sugar." I nestled the side of her neck with my nose before I kissed her jaw.

"Mmm," she hummed, pressing her back further into my chest. "Good morning." Her lips parted with a smile as she took me in.

"How'd you sleep?"

"Like a log," she chuckled.

"Me too." I pressed a kiss to her temple. "Are you ready to head back for some breakfast?"

"Actually, that would be wonderful. I'm starving."

"Okay. Let's get packed up."

It didn't take us long to wrap up the blankets and pillows into the bag that I tied behind Hank's saddle. He'd eaten through all the pellet food I'd packed for him last night, even though it was a solid three meals worth. The big pig had a tendency to eat through anything extra I gave him, never willing to save it for later.

Sarah was near the edge of the cliff looking down at her phone as I tied the final strap together. "Everything okay?" I called out to her. She spiraled a strand of hair around her fingers, turning around to face me.

A solemn look from her had my stomach nearly plummeting to the ground. Something was wrong. I kept my breath steady when she started walking toward me.

“I got a text from my dad,” she said, her voice smaller than normal.

“Are you upset about that?” She’d only really talked about her mother or her parents as a pair. I wasn’t sure what her relationship was like with her father.

“Not upset,”—she looked up at me—“just confused. I don’t think my dad has ever sent me a text message since I’ve been on my own. We usually only talk when we see one another in person, which hasn’t been very often over the past few years.”

How a parent could go that long without initiating contact with their child was beyond me. Then again, my mother left Callie Rose and me. One day she was holed up in her room and the next, she was gone.

“What did he say?”

She slid her phone back into her coat pocket and sighed. “He asked me to come to Sunday dinner tonight. And to bring you.”

My brows rose. “That’s a surprise given how your mom reacted the other day.”

Sarah blew a raspberry. “Yeah, I know. He said that my mother is sorry for how she reacted and wants to make amends.”

I inhaled deeply. It seemed like our little retreat this

weekend was going to have an interesting close if Sarah chose for us to have dinner with her parents tonight. Part of me didn't want to leave this mountainside knowing what might await us. But I would follow her wherever she wanted to go.

"What are you thinking, sugar?"

Her lips drew into a straight line, eyes more serious than I'd ever seen them. "I don't know if I want to see her after what she said about you, Ranger. It's one thing for her to torment me, I'm used to it. But I won't accept them saying anything negative about you."

I took her into my arms, letting her sweet scent mixed with campfire fill my nostrils. "You don't need to protect me. I can handle anything they throw my way."

Her voice broke," But I can't. I won't stand for them coming after the man I love. They've already spent years telling me I wasn't good enough. That my choices would lead me down the wrong path. I don't think I can handle them saying anymore to me."

I stroked her hair in long soothing passes. It killed me to hear how much her parents had impacted her over the years. How much she suffered at their hands. I just wanted to make it all better for her.

"Is there any chance that they might be trying to form a truce? That they might apologize?"

She was quiet for a few moments. "I'm not sure. It is strange that my father was the one to text me."

I let her mull over her thoughts, holding her close. When she pulled away, the hard look in her eyes had softened. "If you had a chance to talk to your mother again, to hear her out, would you?"

Her question hit me. I'd never thought about it before. When my mother left, I felt nothing but anger and overwhelming dread. I put all my focus into supporting Callie Rose that I never gave myself the chance to wonder about our mother.

Thinking about it now… "If I had one last chance to talk to her I would take it. Even if she didn't tell me what I wanted to hear, I would know, without a doubt, that I could move forward. I wouldn't want to spend the rest of my life wondering if things could be different."

I studied the small yellow flecks amongst the dark brown in Sarah's eyes as they grew distant. She was thinking hard about what she wanted to do.

"Would you be okay to go with me?" she finally asked.

I cupped her cheek. "I'd go to the end of the world with you."

Her smile warmed my heart. "Okay, cowboy. Then I guess we're doing it."

Sarah

Ranger extended the bouquet of flowers toward my mother when she opened the front door to my childhood home. "It's nice to see you again, Mrs. Williams."

Her smile was tight as she took the flowers, the brown paper crinkled in her hands. "Thank you." Not much of a response, but it was better than her throwing a fit like she had in my work kitchen.

I looped my arm through his as we followed her into the house. I'd spent eighteen years of my life here, but I suddenly felt self-conscious with Ranger by my side. Everything in my parents' home was immaculate and bought from the most prestigious designers. Only the best of the best was bought for this house, but now that I'd had a taste of life beyond these walls, everything felt obscene. Cold. There were no shoes by the front door. Not a speck of dust on the furniture. It wasn't lived in. It was merely meant to show the status of who my parents were and just how much money they had.

"Hi, dad," I said as we rounded the corner to their formal dining room. He was sitting at the head of the table with an espresso cup in his hand. "This is Ranger Adams."

My father rose from his seat and buttoned his dinner jacket. Almost thirty years of my life and I'd never seen him at our dinner table without a suit on. I groaned internally. I could only imagine what Ranger might be thinking right now.

"Pleasure to meet you, sir." Ranger shook my father's extended hand.

"You as well." My father assessed Ranger, looking him up and down like he was trying to make sense of the black long sleeve shirt he wore tucked into blue jeans. But he didn't say anything as we took our seats.

The wait staff made their rounds, pouring everyone a glass of red wine to pair with the roast beef we were having. At least if everything went to shit, I knew we'd leave with full stomachs from a decadent meal that tasted like heaven. The food was the only good part about Sunday dinner with my parents.

"Where's Theo?" I asked. Now that he was back in town I assumed he would have made it to dinner. But I knew he was slammed with training for his big rodeo coming up in the new year. We'd hardly had a chance to talk since he started training.

"He's busy at the Carnelle's ranch," my mother responded, swirling the wine in her glass as she always did at dinner.

My father shook his head. "I still don't understand what possessed him to choose that ranch of all places. If he is going to change his career, I would have preferred for him to at least associate with good people."

I nearly laughed at his comment, but I choked it down. It wasn't that long ago when my parents were great friends with the Carnelles.

"They certainly had a hard fall from grace. But that's the price one must pay when engaging in unsavory behaviors." Her steely gaze landed on Ranger and I froze. I was giving them a chance, but I'd be damned if we stayed a second longer if she said one word to him about his time in prison.

Thankfully, the staff made their rounds with the pot roast, filling the center of our dishes with meat, potatoes, carrots, and a thin red wine sauce. My mouth watered. The savory aromas were a nice distraction from my reeling thoughts.

Glancing at Ranger, he didn't seem to mind my mother's eyes on him. He was already digging into the food. We all ate in silence for a short while and I hated that I didn't know what to talk to my parents about. Not having been around them for so long, I had no idea what was going on in their lives. I didn't even know where to start with asking them either.

"Ranger, do tell us about this ranch of yours. Has the land been in your family for long?"

He set his fork and knife down and wiped his mouth with the napkin before speaking. "It has, ma'am. Five generations. My father passed it on to me when he died in combat. I've been working hard to turn it into something great ever since."

My mother's delicately shaped brows rose slightly. I knew she was looking for a way in. A crack to seep through and garner information to embarrass him with.

"That's wonderful," my father said. "We certainly admire hard work in this family."

I stopped chewing my food. He had to be joking. Admire hard work? I'd spent over a decade working my butt off to build my company without their help. Endless nights in the kitchen baking until I was fairly certain flour had seeped through my pores and entered my bloodstream.

My parents didn't admire hard work. They admired people becoming rich from aspiring in a 'respectable' field of work.

Ranger must have sensed my growing tension because he slipped his hand over my lower thigh under the table. His touch soothed my fried nerves, reminding me that I wasn't here to fight.

My mother leaned back in her chair, food hardly touched, but the wine glass she held in her hand was already half empty.

"So, Sarah, why don't you tell us how long you two have been seeing one another?"

I stole a glance at Ranger, his expression was calm. "Um." I looked back at my mother. "We had our first date about two months ago now."

My mother's face turned serious. "Two months."

I swallowed. "Yes."

She leaned forward, wine glass still in hand. "So you were already seeing him when we made our little arrangement?"

The room seemed to be getting smaller, but I kept my focus on Ranger's hand over my thigh. I could do this. I could get through this dinner.

"Ranger already knows that I was seeing Jones at your request, mom. So, if you're trying to rattle us with that reveal, you're too late." The words seemed far away as I said them, but my voice was strong.

"Rattle you?" she scoffed. "Darling, you've already been rattled enough to decide it would be a wise idea to throw everything away and chase after a convict. You're a foolish child. Always have been."

I gaped at her. Ranger's soothing circles over my leg stopped. I looked at my father, but he was staring straight ahead of himself toward the other end of the table.

"You've got to be kidding me," I seethed. "I came here thinking that you might have seen the error in your ways. That you had a change of heart and would finally be willing to put your bullshit expectations and prejudices aside."

Fury burned in my mother's eyes. "You degraded yourself the moment you started talking to him!" She pointed right at Ranger's chest.

Enough. I'd had enough of her outrageous view of the world. I was sick and tired of being in the firing line for my choices and there was no way in hell I was going to make Ranger endure this any longer.

"Fuck you," I seethed, glaring at her before shifting my gaze toward my father. "Fuck both of you."

"You better watch your tone when you are under my roof." It seemed my father had finally joined the conversation. Not that it mattered at this point.

I rose from my seat, Ranger followed suit and just as I was about to open my mouth to give a retort, his large hand settled on my shoulder. A wordless demand. And then he spoke.

"Sarah loves you both, despite what you've put her through over the years. She came here tonight with hope in her heart that things might be different between you. I've been used to folks like you having an opinion about me my entire life. So, say what you want about me. But let me make myself clear." He took a moment to look both of them in their eyes. "I will not tolerate you speaking to my woman in the manner you've done tonight. As you know, I'm a dangerous man when provoked. So, I suggest you both keep quiet while we make our exit."

Tears of frustration started rolling down my face as Ranger stepped behind his chair and made room for me. I gave my parents one final glance before we rounded the dining room wall and left.

Chapter 36

Sarah

I woke up to the sound of rustling clothes. Blinking my eyes open, I looked around the dark space. The blinds in Ranger's room were open, but no sun was shining through.

"What time is it?" I croaked, my throat dry from sleep.

Ranger came to my bedside. The mattress dipped with his weight as he sat next to me, stroking my hair away from my face. "Way too early for you to be up, sugar." He pressed a kiss to my temple, his stubble scraped against my skin. "How're you feeling?"

Slowly, I rose to my elbows and sat up against the pillows and headboard. Last night…my parents…Ranger and I storming out. Right. I was so distraught last night, that Ranger brought me back to his place. We didn't say much, he just held me while I cried. I scrunched my face, feeling the remnants of dried tears from last night.

Where there was an ache in my chest last night, this

morning I felt only lightness. Almost like I cried all the tears I had left for my parents.

"I think last night was the last nail in the coffin for my parents and me. When I agreed for us to have dinner with them, I was hopeful that they might be trying to put their differences aside and get to know me for the woman I am now. But that was never their intention. All they wanted to do was trap me and you in their home so they could berate us.

"They're never going to change. Now, I have to find a way to move forward and live a life without them in it."

Shadows played across Ranger's face. His brows were bunched together as he contemplated my thoughts. "Last night definitely wasn't the outcome I wanted for you, but I think you're right. You gave them one last shot and now you have closure."

"Yeah," I smiled. I wasn't exactly sure if it was because I'd expelled most of my emotions last night, but I felt hopeful. Today was a brand new day. One I didn't have to live feeling bogged down by the expectations of others. I could be myself, fully. I knew the pain of losing the relationship with my parents would come in waves, but right now I was empowered.

"I'm going to cook you breakfast."

His face lit up despite the darkness of the room. "Are you sure you don't want to go back to sleep?"

"Yup! I'm sure."

"Okay." He scooped me up in his arms and led me out of the bedroom and down the stairs.

I held the large mixing bowl against my hip as I ran the hand mixer through the blueberry muffin batter until all the flour lumps were gone. Ranger sat at the kitchen island, a steaming mug of coffee in his hands as he watched me work.

"I know this is probably a given, but would you like to be my plus one to Willow and Johnny's wedding?"

His grin was wide over the rim of his mug. "I was wondering if you were going to ask me or if you had some other guy in mind."

I sat the bowl on the counter and looked at him. "I mean yeah, there's this guy named Joey who I was thinking of asking."

Ranger snickered.

"But I decided to choose you instead."

"And why's that?" he teased.

"Because you have bigger biceps."

Porcelain hit the countertop when he put his mug down. Then he rose from the stool and started rounding the island. "Is that right?" he mused, eyes narrowing on me.

I bit my lower lip. "Mmhmm. Yours are way bigger." He slinked towards me, movements slow and feline. "It was the obvious choice." I shrugged, then he snatched me up into his arms sending me into a fit of giggles and squeals.

"Ranger!" I screeched, his hands digging into my sides after he plopped me on the kitchen counter. His tickle assaults kept coming, I could hardly breathe. And I loved every second of it because I knew we could joke about things. That no matter how protective he felt over me, he trusted that he was my person and there wasn't anyone else in this world I wanted more than him.

I tried slapping his hands away, but it was no use. He was much stronger than me and I couldn't say a word past the laughter that had my lungs burning.

Someone behind us cleared their throat. Ranger stopped moving his hands along my ribcage, his attention shifting to the person behind me. I looked over my shoulder to find Callie Rose and Miles standing in the kitchen entryway smirking at both of us. "Are we interrupting something?" Callie Rose asked.

I hopped off the counter and made sure my pajamas were covering everything.

"Nope!" My voice came out high-pitched. "I was just making everyone breakfast before you got started with your day."

Miles watched Callie Rose saunter into the kitchen and take one of the seats at the island. I was in *her* childhood home with her brother who I knew she was wildly protective over. There was no telling what she might be thinking of me right now.

"What're we having?" she asked. My shoulders slumped, releasing the tension. Maybe I'd passed the test and she approved.

"Blueberry muffins and bacon if that's okay with you."

Miles clapped his hands and rubbed them together. “Alright! That sounds like my kind of breakfast.”

I smiled and noticed that the edges of Callie Rose’s lips tilted upward too. “It’ll be nice to not have to cook for these two buffoons every day. I’m glad to pass that torch over to you, Sarah. When you’re here that is.”

Ranger poured his sister and Miles a cup of coffee, sliding them each across the island counter. “Buffoons is a little harsh, Cal.”

“Yeah,” Miles chimed in. “I like to think of us as charming men. Hard workers. Studly even. You know”—he nudged her with his elbow—“all the wonderful qualities that speak truth to who we really are.”

Callie Rose snorted and rolled her eyes. But that didn’t stop her from leaning towards Miles. It was almost like she couldn’t help that gravity pulled her toward him. *Interesting*, I thought. Not that I’d touch that with a ten-foot pole, but I wondered if Ranger saw that his little sister had feelings for his best friend. Or maybe he was too oblivious to notice.

She made some retort towards Miles and Ranger while I put the muffin mix into a pan and slid it into the oven before starting on the bacon.

Their banter filled the space for the remainder of breakfast until all the plates were cleaned and placed in the drying rack next to the sink. I loved it. All the noise in the house. The teasing and poking at one another. It felt like how a home should feel, I realized. It was never something my parents, Theo, and I did. Most of the time we hardly talked to one another when I lived in their house. Or when we did speak, it was usually them telling me I was doing something wrong.

Watching Ranger with his sister and Miles showed me that family was what you put into it. And they certainly had a lot of love to share.

I took the day off and had Stephanie bring in one of her friends to help run the front while she kept the kitchen running. I wasn't quite ready to risk going in public where my mother might bombard me again. So, I'd made myself a small picnic and packed a blanket to bring with me to watch Ranger and Miles work the cows. They were in the field today. I'd found the perfect spot to watch on top of one of the hills overlooking the valley.

Ranger looked hotter than ever on top of his workhorse, Phillip. His face was mostly hidden from the brim of his cowboy hat, but I loved watching him move in the saddle, his strong arms spilling out of his rolled-up sleeves. How the man still only wore a t-shirt and flannel in this weather was beyond my comprehension, but I didn't mind it too much it it meant I got to see his muscles more easily.

"Hey," Callie Rose greeted me, a basket of flowers hanging on her arm. There was an arrangement of violas, dahlias, marigolds and chrysanthemums.

"Hi," I replied, moving to the left of the blanket so she could sit down.

"They're working hard today." She paused, looking out at the field of cows Ranger and Miles were herding.

"Yeah, they are." Shielding my eyes from the midday sun, I looked up at her as she sat down. "What're the flowers for?"

She set the basket of flowers in front of us and started laying them out one by one in a row. "When I was little, my mother would gather a basket of flowers at the turning of every season. We'd sit together and make flower crowns. Afterward, we'd dress up really nice, put on our crowns, and dance. I thought it might be nice to bring that tradition back, now that I have another woman in the family to do it with."

My heart nearly burst when she handed me a dahlia and smiled at me. "I'd be honored to do that with you, Callie Rose." I didn't hide the tears that started to well in my eyes. I wondered if she had some idea of what had happened with my parents. If Ranger had made a comment to her. But I also knew that pain recognized pain. She'd lost both her parents too and even though our experiences were different, we'd both experienced the sorrow of losing them.

She showed me how to thread the long stems of the flowers together and before long I had the beginning workings of a flower crown.

Callie Rose was working a flower through the stem crown as she said, "I wasn't too sure about you at first. I thought you might be just like most of the other blue bloods in this town. Elitist. Snobby. Mean. But you brought my brother back to me, Sarah." She looked me in the eyes. "That's a debt I'll never be able to repay."

I placed my hand on her knee. "I wouldn't want you to. Loving your brother has been the most incredible thing to ever happen to me. He's shown me that there is so much more to life than I ever thought possible. He's shown me that I can be loved even when I don't think I deserve it."

Tears spilled down her cheeks. "I'm so happy we have you in our family now." Her lips quivered with each word.

I hugged her tight. She was stiff in my arms for only a moment before I felt her shoulders sag and her body loosen. Then her arms came to wrap around me. "Me too," I whispered, rubbing her back up and down.

When we pulled apart, she wiped the tears from her face and said, "They'll never let us live it down if they catch us crying together."

I laughed. "Oh, I know. They'd make fun of us for years."

She reached for my flower crown. Holding it close to her face, she looked around the edges of my handiwork. "This isn't half bad for your first time."

When she handed it back to me, I took it and started threading more flowers through. "Thank you."

When we finished the crowns and the boys wrapped up their work for the day, Callie Rose let me borrow one of her dresses. With our hair and makeup done up, we paraded around the house, cooking dinner side-by-side until dusk turned into night and Ranger brought out his guitar. This time he played a happy melody—one filled with joy and mirth while Callie Rose and I danced. I laughed until my belly hurt and my heart was near bursting.

Chapter 37

Ranger

The past few months passed by in a blissful blur. Sarah's bakery was taking off to new heights once everyone got wind that she was the cake designer for Willow's exclusive wedding. Not that Willow and Johnny were trying to be exclusive, they just wanted their closest people with them on their special day. Turned out that Sarah's mother didn't have quite as much power as she alluded to, which I was thankful for.

We would have found a way to pull her business from the rubble of her mother's destruction, but I was glad Sarah didn't end up having to deal with it at all. Life was damn good and the fear that the other shoe was about to drop seemed to disappear from my mind months ago.

"Looking good, big brother." Callie Rose closed the front door behind her. A long thick braid held her dark hair away from her face. She wore a floor length burgundy gown with a white fur wrap around her shoulders. Heels clacked over the hardwood floors as she made her way into the living room.

"Thanks. You don't look too bad yourself." I fussed with the bowtie around my neck.

"Here, let me help you." Setting her small purse on the sofa, she reached for the bowtie and started working the fabric so it was aligned properly.

"A lot has changed since this time last year," I commented. It was difficult to remember the man I was before Sarah. All I remembered was feeling alone and fearful that something bad was going to happen. That time would be sucked away from me again and I'd be left with no life to live. Now, my life was full. Sarah and I brought our friends and family together. The farmhouse was always bright with laughter and the sounds of our favorite people.

"And we're better for it," she replied, finishing her work with the bowtie. "I'm really proud of you. I know mom and dad would be too."

Bittersweetness had my chest feeling heavy. "Thank you. That means a lot coming for you."

She patted the side of my face and then gave me a quick hug. "Ready?"

"Yeah, I'm ready." She grabbed her purse from the sofa and headed for the front door.

Looking at the picture of our parents hanging on the wall between the kitchen and living room, I knew my sister was right. They'd be proud of me for bouncing back and choosing to live life.

"You're dropping sauce everywhere, Deacon!" Sarah chastised as she threw a napkin at his face. It was true, the man ate barbeque like a wild hog in a trough. Dribbles of it lined both sides of his mouth, and there were splatters all over the front of his white button-down shirt and the tablecloth next to his plate.

Deacon swallowed his bite of food and said, "Keep screeching at me and I'll share some with you."

Sarah's gaze turned serious, her brown eyes morphing into slits. "Try it and I'll take you outside by the ear and hose you down myself."

I sat quietly, my gaze bobbing back and forth between the two of them like I was watching a tennis match. Everyone at the table went silent, taking notice of the stare down between Sarah and Deacon, waiting to see who might break first. Then, they both burst into laughter, releasing the tension in the room. Everyone went back to eating their meals.

It was the perfect rehearsal dinner for the couple we celebrated. All their best friends surrounded the large dining table in their home. Everyone was dressed to the nines for Willow and her love of fashion while we all dug into the best barbeque in town for Johnny's most beloved meal. It made me wonder what a rehearsal dinner for Sarah and I might look like one day. We were starting on some renovations in the farmhouse next spring to make it more to our tastes. She hadn't agreed to move in with me until then. Not because she didn't want to, but because she told me that she wanted things to look forward to in our relationship. That we had an entire lifetime to spend together and that she didn't want to do everything all at once.

It made perfect sense to me, even though we spent every night together anyway. Either she stayed with me on the ranch or I made my way into town to be with her. She was mine and that was all I cared about.

I draped my arm over the back of her chair. "So, have you two love birds decided where you're going to honeymoon?" I asked.

Johnny and Willow looked at one another, nothing but love shining in their eyes. "We actually wanted to talk to you and Sarah about that later, but now seems like as good a time as any," Willow said.

I stole a glance at Sarah and she shrugged, unsure of what Willow was talking about. Then Johnny said, "We're going to take two months to travel around Europe." Everyone around the table *awed* and expressed their congratulations.

Then, Johnny and Willow both looked at Sarah and me. "As Asher's official godparents, we were hoping you two wouldn't mind keeping him for us while we're away?" Willow asked, blue eyes gleaming with hope.

I looked down at Sarah and she smiled wide. Leaning into me, she whispered, "Looks like we might be moving in together faster than we planned."

"Our love has always been on a crazy timeline, sugar. As long as I'm on the ride with you, it doesn't matter to me. So, what do you say?" Her hair tickled my chin when I pressed my lips to her temple.

"We'd be honored," she finally responded to Willow and Johnny who both sighed happily with relief.

"He's going to love the ranch life," Miles chimed in from down the table. "Hundreds of acres for him to run free on."

"He might be a little chunky when y'all get back from your honeymoon," Callie Rose said. "I can't help but feed him treats when he gives me those big puppy dog eyes." Asher chose that exact moment to pop his head up onto the table right next to Callie Rose. She scratched between his ears. "You're not supposed to be this obvious, boy. I told you I'd give you some scraps later." He whined at her and we all laughed.

The rest of the night we spent reminiscing on distant and recent memories and talking about what we wanted for our futures. It was amazing how I'd always felt on the outside for most of my life and all it took was falling in love with the girl from the opposite side of the tracks to change everything.

"I have to say that I'm not the biggest fan of this tradition," I held Sarah in my arms by the driver's side of my truck.

"It's only for a short while. You'll have fun with the boys tonight at the ranch while us girls watch rom-coms and slather our faces with mud masks." She pressed a kiss to my lips. "Tomorrow will come before you know it."

"I know," I groaned, letting my hands fall to the curve of her ass. The marigold satin dress she wore should have been illegal. I spent most of the night having to readjust my dick in my pants to make sure our friends didn't notice the raging hard-on I had.

"I'll see you tomorrow, cowboy." She winked at me before slipping out of my arms.

"Hey! What about my goodnight kiss?"

"You'll get one tomorrow." She smirked. "It'll make you miss me more."

"My wicked little vixen."

"Always." Sarah winked again before disappearing up the steps and through the door to Johnny and Willow's house.

She was right. For the rest of the night, even with the distraction of my boys and good whiskey, all I thought about was her.

Chapter 38

Sarah

Everything was perfect. A light sprinkle of snow came down last night and the pine trees around Johnny and Willow's cabin had a thin dusting of white while the beautiful deep green of the pine needles shone through. The bright sun kept the cold temperature bearable.

I'd helped Stephanie unload their wedding cake onto the display table earlier this morning before I was swept away to spend hours getting our nails, hair, and makeup done by a group of experts Willow had flown in from Nashville.

Bubbles from the champagne I drank were giving me an airy feeling in my mind, or maybe it was just the sensation of being surrounded by so much love.

"I'm almost ready!" Willow called through the door of their bathroom while I waited in their bedroom.

"Okay!" I took another sip of champagne, cherishing the moment we were in together. My two best friends were getting married today. They'd fought through countless obstacles and over a decade of separation to get here. Love always had a way of winning if we were willing to fight for it.

The door behind me creaked open. I turned around and tears immediately burned my eyes. "Oh my gosh. Willow!" I whispered, bringing a shaking hand to cover my trembling lips.

Her face fell in a heap of emotions. "No, no, no!" Setting my champagne flute on the bedside table, I made my way to her. The fabric of my gown swished across the hardwood floors.

"No, crying." I snagged a tissue from the box we'd been carrying around with us all day and handed it to her. "Your makeup is too perfect to ruin it this early."

She dabbed the corners of her eyes and sucked in a deep breath. "Okay. Yes, you're right." Blinking a few times to keep the tears at bay, she finally looked at me again. Taking her hands in mine, I gave them a squeeze.

"If there were any two people in the world who deserved to have a day like this, it's you and Johnny. Willow, you have shown me that despite your biggest fears, love is worth fighting for. Today, we all get to celebrate what you and Johnny fought for."

She sniffled. "You're going to make me cry again."

Carefully, I took the tissue from her and ran it gently under her eyes to gather the stray tears that built up. "Are you ready to go marry your man?"

She nodded, unable to form words. I could see she was

barely holding on and I needed to get her down the aisle before she totally lost it.

"Alright, let me make sure the coast is clear." I opened the door and found the rest of the cabin to be completely silent.

"We're good to go." I turned back to Willow and gave her a big hug. "It's time."

"Okay," she managed to say. I took her hand in mine and we walked out the door of their bedroom to the back door of the cabin.

With a final hug, I whispered, "I'll see you out there. I love you, Willow."

She held me tighter. "I love you too, Sarah."

I left Willow to stand with the door cracked so she could hear the music for her cue. When I stepped onto the back deck, my breath caught when my gaze landed on Ranger. His shoulder length black curls were shining under the brim of his black cowboy hat. A baby blue long sleeve shirt peeked through the deep brown of his sports coat, bringing out the hue of his eyes. Every curve of his muscular thighs were accentuated with the grip of his blue jeans.

He looked delicious and I wanted a bite.

But the music started. The cue for me to walk down the aisle. So, I wrapped my fingers around the small bouquet of flowers that were waiting for me on the deck's railing, I squared my shoulders and made my way down the aisle. The rose petals outlining the aisle glimmered in the sunlight. Mrs. Sheehan, their officiant, gave me a warm smile as I neared the end.

"You look so handsome, Johnny." I gave him a quick kiss on the cheek as he hugged me.

"Thank you."

"You're going to love her in white." I winked at him. His laughter was rich as tears lined his eyes.

I took my spot opposite of Johnny and Deacon and turned my attention toward the people in front of me. It was a small group, but that didn't matter. Every person here today was a champion for the love Johnny and Willow shared. They were members of our family. One we'd created from love and respect. It made my heart sing knowing that my best friends would receive nothing but joy and admiration on their day.

When the music transitioned, I stole a glance at Johnny. He was bouncing on the balls of his feet, barely able to contain himself. Then the door of the cabin opened and everyone gasped and awed at the sight of Willow. Her long veil trailed behind her as she started her walk down the aisle.

Johnny's face crumpled, tears flowing freely down his face. I couldn't help the tears that started to roll down mine.

Love was so damn beautiful.

There wasn't a dry eye in the house as Willow made her way to Johnny. When they were standing in front of one another holding hands, Mrs. Sheehan began, "We are gathered here today to celebrate the eternal love of Willow Baxley and Johnny Moore."

As she continued, I found myself staring at Ranger, unable to look away from him. His face was illuminated with a brilliant smile. I'd never seen him look so happy before.

The joy on his face as he looked back at me had my mind reeling to a future where it was the two of us standing before everyone we loved, sharing words of endearment and promises of forever.

Our love had been a crazy ride and I knew life probably had a million more wild moments in store for us. But he was mine and I was his. That was the only thing that mattered.

Everyone's cheers and claps tore me from my thoughts and I looked to Johnny and Willow just in time to see them seal their vows with a kiss. Giggles blossomed from my chest as Johnny dipped Willow in an elaborate bow and kissed her again. Asher barked his excitement and dashed towards Willow, licking her face before Johnny could swing her upright again.

Laughter roared around them. It was the perfect beginning to the rest of their lives together.

They made their way back down the aisle, Asher prancing right beside them. Deacon and I high-fived before following the happy couple.

Doing my best not to topple over in my heels, I lifted my gown and jogged towards Ranger. Catching me in his arms, he spun us around before pressing his lips to mine. Butterflies soared in my stomach as his lips made their way to my jaw, then the edge of my ear, and down to my neck.

"Get a room!" Deacon called to us.

"I second that!" Callie Rose said, passing by us and following Willow and Johnny down the winding path that led to the outdoor reception area.

He stopped spinning us but still held me in his arms so

my feet were off the ground. "What they don't realize is just how tempted I am to carry you away to a room and have my way with you."

I kissed the tip of his nose. "As badly as I want that too, I have a bouquet to catch, cowboy."

His dark brows rose. "Is that right, sugar?"

"Mmhmm." I nodded quickly, a smile pulling at my lips.

My feet touched the ground as his hand slipped over mine, our fingers intertwining. "Well then. We better get our asses moving."

Ranger's scent of warm leather hung around me as we swayed side-to-side on the dance floor. Willow and Johnny had chosen a clearing in the woods several yards in front of the lake to hold their small reception. But they'd thought of everything to keep the party going all night long. Heat lamps were placed every few feet around the dance floor and they lined the walking path to the tables, bar, and food area. Twinkle lights hung in all the trees, casting a beautiful glow over all of us.

When the song came to an end, Ranger whispered in my ear, "Go for a walk with me."

"Okay," I whispered back, letting him lead me off the dance floor. I'd discarded my heels hours ago and Ranger had brought me a pair of winter hiking boots to keep my feet warm. We strode arm in arm through the trees next to the lake until we found a little alcove. It was a clear winter night with the moon hanging high and the stars shining bright.

I rubbed my hands together to ward off the cold. Ranger cupped his hands around mine and brought them up to his lips. Hot air blew over my skin, warming my fingers and palms.

"Thank you."

He pressed a kiss to my knuckles before taking me into his side, wrapping an arm around me so we could both look out at the water.

It was so easy with him. Standing in silence while we both took in the scenery around us. My heart felt full and yet I knew there was still room for all the moments we'd have together like this.

"Willow and Johnny's vows got me thinking," he said, voice low.

"Oh yeah?" I glanced up at him sidelong.

He shifted so we were able to look at one another. "I don't say it nearly as often as I should. Mostly because I don't know how to communicate my feelings very well. When it comes to you, Sarah, I feel a hell of a lot."

A smile had my lips tilting upward.

"I need you to know that you saved my life. Before you came along, I was a shell of a man. Tired of waiting for something to change in me, but too scared to do anything about it. When you asked me out on a date, I felt excited for the first time since I went to prison. I stopped myself from giving in to it because I was ashamed. I felt like I deserved to be punished for what I'd done and how it stole time away from my family.

"Then I saw you on that Ferris wheel and I think some part of me knew I'd loved you even then. My soul called to yours and from that point on, there was no more resisting you or what I felt.

"And I know that choosing to be with me hasn't been the easiest path for you. It's caused a riff in your life that I wish I could mend more than anything. I just want you to know that I will spend the rest of my life making sure you feel like your choice was worth the sacrifice."

My heart fluttered at his proclamation and the way love shone in his eyes as he slipped his hand through my hair, letting it rest at the base of my neck. I realized I would always feel electric when his hands were on me. Our love ran too deep for me to not be affected by his touch.

"Well, there's one vital mistake you've made, cowboy." I grabbed the lapels of his coat and brought him closer to me. "It's thinking that there is anything in this world that I wouldn't happily sacrifice to be with you. And it's not just because I love you beyond measure. It's because you've been my strength when I had none. You supported me and showed me what family means when my own family was never capable of doing that.

"You've made me feel brave when I was scared. And you've taught me that there are so many moments to cherish if I'm just willing to let my heart be open to them. You let me love you and it's the best thing I've ever done."

He chuckled, a warm throaty laugh as silver lined his eyes.

"I love you," I said. "And I'd give up everything to keep doing that."

Warmth spread through my face when his lips met mine. He pulled me close, running his fingers down my spine as I opened up for him. His tongue rolled against mine in a slow tantalizing motion that had heat pooling in my center. A preview for what was surely to come later tonight.

"Sarah! Ranger!" Someone called for us, their voice echoing through the trees.

"Damnit," Ranger whispered against my mouth. He grabbed my ass and groaned. "I'm getting a piece of this later."

"I'm down for that, cowboy. But I still have a bouquet to catch."

"If that'll get you to marry me faster, then maybe I'm not as upset."

I waggled my eyebrows at him. "Maybe I could be convinced." We turned to head back to the reception area. We called out to whoever was yelling our names to let them know we were coming.

The only people in line for Willow's bouquet were Callie Rose and me. She had a look of tortured pain on her face as she tried to hide herself in the corner of the dance floor even though her brother kept urging her to move forward. She shot him a crude gesture and Ranger laughed.

Fine by me, I had one goal in mind and that was to catch the flying bundle of flowers.

"Ready?" Willow looked at us over her shoulder.

I rubbed my hands together, playfully.

"That's my girl!" Ranger called to me, his hands creating a cup around his mouth.

"One! Two! Three!" The flowers soared through the air, tree canopies, and the open night sky a perfect landscape above.

I was thankful I didn't have my heels on anymore because Willow threw long and I had to dart backwards to catch them. The stems landed in my hands, delicate petals flickering to the floor from the impact.

"Woohoo!" I hollered, raising my arms above my head. More petals flitted down around me.

Everyone clapped and Ranger dashed onto the dance floor, picked me up, and spun me around. I let my head tilt back as laughter bubbled from my chest.

When we stopped, I slid down his front and showed him the now-destroyed bundle of flower stems, with only a few petals remaining.

"I got it!"

"You know what that means now, sugar."

"What's that?"

He smiled at me. "We're next."

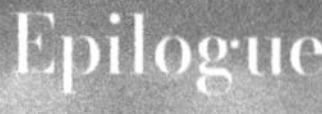

Epilogue

Ranger

Three Months Later

"Good morning, beautiful." I nudged Sarah's cheek with my nose and started planting kisses along the edge of her jaw.

Her lips were parted slightly, eyelashes fanning out over her cheeks. She was so cute when she slept, all bundled beneath the covers.

But I was starving for her and I needed her to wake up.

"Mmmm," she groaned. "What time is it?"

I glanced at the window. The shades were drawn, but rays of light were shining through. "The sun's up."

Batting her eyelashes a few times, she turned towards me and hooked her leg over my hip.

"You just want your way with me. That's why you're interrupting my beauty sleep, isn't it?" Her brown eyes squinted at me.

I tried to hide the smile creeping onto my lips and failed

epically. Trailing my hand down her side until I reached the curve of her hip, I palmed her naked ass. "You're too delicious. Just give me some of that sugar."

She blushed as I dug my fingers into her ass cheek and pressed my pelvis against hers. Sarah moaned at the contact. I fucking loved how her thick pink lips formed a circle. I imagined my cock sliding right into her mouth, feeling her wet tongue over my shaft.

"Okay," she crooned. "Only if you taste me first."

My dick hardened. "Yes ma'am."

Without a moment of hesitation, I threw the blanket and sheet over my head and settled myself between her legs. Nipping my teeth along the edge of her inner thighs, I felt her grasp the blanket beside me. I loved seeing her writhing from my touch. Giving her pleasure was more arousing than receiving my own.

Finally, I ran my tongue along her clit and moaned. She tasted so fucking good and the way she ground herself against my lips had my dick throbbing. I loved it when she took control and showed me what her body needed.

Flicking my tongue against her sweet lips, I heard a muffled sigh through the blanket, her thighs clamping against the sides of my head. I placed my hands on the inside of her legs and pressed them down so she was open for me.

The sweet and salty taste of her had my mouth watering as I nibbled and pulled on her sensitive bundle of nerves. Delicate fingers came under the sheets to grip the back of my head. A tingling sensation ran all along my back when she scratched her nails against my skull, in slow soothing circles while I kept my mouth around her pussy.

When I felt her legs starting to quiver, I knew her climax was already building. Her clit was so fucking sensitive, I barely got her to last more than a few minutes with my tongue hot against her.

Not wanting it to end too soon, I pulled myself over her body and popped my head out from under the blanket. Her hands moved to the sides of my face as she kissed me, her lips were cold from the lack of heat in the house.

I crowned her slick entrance. She opened her legs wider for me, already starting to roll her hips back to give me more access. Then I slid my way home, filling her completely.

"Ah, yes. Ranger," she whimpered my name like a prayer on her lips.

Rolling my hips back I pulled out of her completely. Then I slammed back into her, our bodies pressed together, the bed sinking beneath us.

"Fuck," I hissed, loving how her pussy squeezed around my cock. Sarah clawed at my back, wrapping her arms around me, she held on tight as I slipped back out and slammed into her again.

"Yes!" she cried out and I knew I hit her spot, so I did it again and again. Our bodies were slick with sweat as I palmed her breast, bringing my head down to suck on her nipple. Her back arched as I fucked her, grinding my pelvis over her clit to give her the friction I knew she needed.

"I love you," I said, feeling the inside of her squeeze around me. She was close.

"I love you too." Tears pricked the back of my eyes. I loved hearing her say that to me. I wanted to hear it for the rest of my life.

Grabbing onto my biceps, she started moving her hips to meet me, stroke for stroke. The sound of skin against skin permeated the air around us. Our breaths were haggard and wild.

Her orgasm barrelled around me. Her pussy tightened, but I pushed, burying myself deep in her as I reached my own climax, spilling everything I had into her.

Bowing my head to her chest, I lay there for a moment, listening to the air fill and leave her lungs. Her fingers threaded through my hair, chills spreading over my skin.

Finally, I rolled over and pulled her into my chest.

"I can't believe we get to do this forever," she said with a laugh.

"Forever sounds pretty damn good to me, sugar." I snuggled her closer to me, burying my face in her hair.

Bark!

I groaned. "It's like he knows exactly when we get comfortable."

"Don't worry, I'll get him this time." Sarah went to move off the bed.

"I'm already up. I'll make the coffee."

We got dressed in our long pajamas. As soon as I opened the door to our bedroom, Asher came running in like a tornado, weaving through my legs and bounding toward Sarah. She knelt down and rubbed all along his back. He gave her a few licks of appreciation.

When we made our way down the stairs, Sarah rubbed her hands up and down her arms. “Why is it so cold in here?”

“I’m not sure, I’ll check the thermostat in a minute.”

It had become our tradition to sit on the front porch and watch Asher prance through the snow before we had our morning coffee. I told Sarah we might have to get a puppy when Willow and Johnny came back from their extended honeymoon next week.

With Sarah beside me, I grabbed the handle for the front door and swung it open. “Holy shit.”

“Oh my God!”

Sarah and I stared at the mountain of snow that surrounded the wrap-around porch, mounds of it spilled onto the wooden deck. It had to have been at least four feet high.

“What the hell happened?” I whispered.

“I don’t think Georgia has ever seen snow this deep before.”

“Not in my lifetime.”

Sarah wrapped her arms around herself. “The weather-woman did say we were having a record year for snow. But I didn’t think it’d be like this. How’re we supposed to—”

She stopped talking because Asher darted between us, tongue lolling out of the side of his mouth.

“Asher, no!” We both yelled at once just as he leaped into the giant mountain of snow, disappearing completely. We both ran onto the deck. I reached my arms out to make sure Sarah didn’t fall on the icy mess.

Looking into the hole that Asher made, I couldn’t help but laugh. Snow clung to his yellow fur as he rolled around.

Sarah started to laugh too. "What're we supposed to do now?"

Her smile was so beautiful.

"I have an idea." Bending down, I grabbed her by the waist, threw her over my shoulder, and ran us back up the stairs and into our bedroom where I made our promise of *forever* count.

Don't miss out on the first book in the series,
If I Asked You to Stay. Available now!

Stay in the Know!

With the ever changing landscape of social media, the best way to stay in the know about my upcoming releases is to subscribe to my newsletter. Becoming part of the subscriber family also gets you exclusive access to bonus scenes from my books that will never be released anywhere else!

Subscribe at www.briannaremus.com

Also by Brianna Remus

Falling for You Trilogy

Dare to Fall

Dare to Need

Dare to Love

Pebble Brook Falls Series

If I Asked You to Stay

If You Loved Me

Acknowledgments

Wow, I cannot believe this book is out in the wild because it wasn't that long ago when I thought I would never write another book again. I'm so glad I pushed through those doubts because Sarah and Ranger's story pulled me into my author dreams.

There's certainly a lot of people I have to thank who kept me going during that tough time.

First, to my dear author friends who listened to my woes and kept pushing me to move forward: Anna Vera, Stephanie Stinski, and Vivian Mae. Our countless voice memos and FaceTime calls were what I needed and I love you for that!

I also want to thank Kaitlyn and Penelope for being the most incredible alpha readers. You ladies hyped me up throughout the gruelling drafting process and made *If You Loved Me* the best it could be. I'm so thankful for your time and incredible insights.

To my husband, who always believes in my dreams more than his own. You pushed me to come back to myself. I love you so much! And to our sweet fur babies, thank you for keeping me company in my office when I know you would have much rather been playing outside.

Finally, to my readers. I've never experienced this much excitement over a book before and seeing you fall in love with Ranger and Sarah has made this the most magical experience. I hope I get to meet you all one day!

About the Author

Brianna Remus is a Florida-based author who lives with her husband, three pups and terrorizing cat. A true romantic at heart, you can find her gazing at the stars, floating in the ocean, or reading a good HEA romance!

facebook.com/AuthorBriannaRemus

instagram.com/authorbriannaremus

bookbub.com/profile/brianna-remus

www.ingramcontent.com/pod-product-compliance
Ingram Content Group UK Ltd.
Pitfield, Milton Keynes, MK11 3LW, UK
UKHW021937190726
13853UKWH00004B/1502